"You're unbearable,"
she said in disbelief.

Kieran tossed the wood aside. It clattered against the side of the hut, startling her with the sudden movement. Unbearable, was he? She had no idea.

He captured her wrist, drawing her forward until she stood before him. "That's right, *a mhuirnín*. And you'd do well to stay away from me."

He gave in to his desires, tilting her head back to face him. And learned that her hair truly was as soft as he thought it would be.

Iseult stared at him with shock, her mouth drawing his full attention. A few inches farther, and he'd have a taste of her forbidden fruit.

He held her there, waiting for her to strike out at him. Cry out for help to the guard she'd brought. But she didn't say a word—just stood there watching him. Only the faint trembling in her hands revealed what she truly felt.

He released her, and Iseult stumbled away from him, shoving her way past the door.

Only after she'd gone did he realize he was also trembling.

* * *

Her Warrior Slave
Harlequin® Historical #922—November 2008

Author Note

When I was growing up, my father used to spend hour upon hour in his wood shop. The smell of wood shavings and sawdust were familiar, and they always evoked special memories. Upon a recent trip to Ireland, I saw a replica of a medieval lathe and a carved dower chest. I imagined a wood carver creating pieces of furniture and, at night, perhaps carving bits of oak. It was then that the character of Kieran was born. I imagined him as a fierce loner, falling in love with a woman he could never have, the bride of another man. I hope you enjoy Kieran and Iseult's story and their bittersweet journey toward happiness. For those of you who have read books in my MACEGAN BROTHERS series, look for a special connection between Kieran and these characters.

Please feel free to visit my Web site at www.michellewillingham.com to view "behind-the-scenes" photographs from the books. You can also sign up for my newsletter to be notified of future releases. I love to hear from readers; you may contact me by writing to me at P.O. Box 2242, Poquoson, Virginia, United States or via e-mail at michelle@michellewillingham.com.

HER Warrior Slave

MICHELLE WILLINGHAM

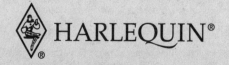

HARLEQUIN®

TORONTO • NEW YORK • LONDON
AMSTERDAM • PARIS • SYDNEY • HAMBURG
STOCKHOLM • ATHENS • TOKYO • MILAN • MADRID
PRAGUE • WARSAW • BUDAPEST • AUCKLAND

If you purchased this book without a cover you should be aware
that this book is stolen property. It was reported as "unsold and
destroyed" to the publisher, and neither the author nor the
publisher has received any payment for this "stripped book."

ISBN-13: 978-0-373-29522-7
ISBN-10:   0-373-29522-7

HER WARRIOR SLAVE

Copyright © 2008 by Michelle Willingham

All rights reserved. Except for use in any review, the reproduction or
utilization of this work in whole or in part in any form by any electronic,
mechanical or other means, now known or hereafter invented, including
xerography, photocopying and recording, or in any information storage
or retrieval system, is forbidden without the written permission of the
publisher, Harlequin Enterprises Limited, 225 Duncan Mill Road,
Don Mills, Ontario, Canada M3B 3K9.

This is a work of fiction. Names, characters, places and incidents are
either the product of the author's imagination or are used fictitiously,
and any resemblance to actual persons, living or dead, business
establishments, events or locales is entirely coincidental.

This edition published by arrangement with Harlequin Books S.A.

® and TM are trademarks of the publisher. Trademarks indicated with
® are registered in the United States Patent and Trademark Office, the
Canadian Trade Marks Office and in other countries.

www.eHarlequin.com

Printed in U.S.A.

Praise for
Michelle Willingham

HER WARRIOR KING

"Betrayal, mistrust and anger fire this medieval tale
about how love finds an aching heart when
that heart isn't looking."
—*Romantic Times BOOKreviews,* 4 stars

"The MacEgan tales just keep getting better. With
Her Warrior King, Michelle Willingham has set
a new standard of excellence. We will all be
impatiently awaiting the next novel."
—*CataRomance,* 4.5 stars

THE WARRIOR'S TOUCH

"[A] thought-provoking tale of love in the second
installment of the MacEgan Brothers."
—*Romantic Times BOOKreviews,* 4 stars

"I know we all wish we could have a MacEgan for our
very own, but since we cannot, be sure and pick up this
not-to-be-missed tale of the MacEgan Brothers,
The Warrior's Touch."
—*CataRomance,* 4.5 stars

HER IRISH WARRIOR

"Willingham not only delves into medieval culture,
she also tells the dark side of being a woman in that era….
The bright side is that in romantic fiction, a happy ending
is expected, and it's delivered in this excellent, plot-driven,
page-turner of a book."
—*Romantic Times BOOKreviews,* 4 stars

Available from Harlequin® Historical and
MICHELLE WILLINGHAM

Her Irish Warrior #850
The Warrior's Touch #866
Her Warrior King #882
Her Warrior Slave #922

Thank you so much to Dr. Aidan O'Sullivan,
Senior Archaeologist Lecturer at the University College of
Dublin for his help answering my questions on medieval
woodworking. I appreciate your suggestions and feedback
regarding tools and the care of wood carvings.

Also with thanks to my father, Frank Willingham,
for inspiring me.

**DON'T MISS THESE OTHER
NOVELS AVAILABLE NOW:**

#919 ONE CANDLELIT CHRISTMAS
Julia Justiss, Annie Burrows and Terri Brisbin
*Have yourself a Regency Christmas! Celebrate the season
with three heartwarming stories of reconciliation,
surprises and secret wishes fulfilled....*

#920 THE BORROWED BRIDE—Elizabeth Lane
Preparing to marry her childhood sweetheart, Hannah
Gustavson is torn by his sudden disappearance. Judd Seavers
cannot just watch his brother's woman struggle alone.
So begins their marriage of convenience....
Can he give up the woman he has come to love?

#921 UNTOUCHED MISTRESS—Margaret McPhee
Rakish Guy Tregellas, Viscount Varington, is more
than intrigued on discovering a beautiful woman washed up
on the beach. Helena McGregor seeks anonymity in London
from a dark past—but she needs the help of her disturbingly
handsome rescuer....
A Regency rake finds himself a mistress in name only!

Chapter One

Ireland—AD 1102

'He's going to die, isn't he?' Iseult MacFergus stared down at the bruised body of the slave. Lash marks creased the man's back, raw and unhealed. His skin was pale with hard ridges of bone protruding, as though he had not eaten well in several moons. Her mind rebelled at the thought of the torment he must have suffered.

Davin Ó Falvey handed her a basin of cool water. 'I don't know. Likely I wasted a good deal of silver.'

Iseult sponged at the blood, lowering her eyes. 'We don't need a slave for our household, Davin. You shouldn't have purchased him.' It was becoming less common among the tribes to own slaves. Her own family had never been able to afford them, and it made her uncomfortable, remembering her lower status.

'Someone else would have, if I hadn't.' He came up behind her and placed his hands on her shoulders. 'He was suffering, *a stór*. At the slave auction, they beat him until he could no longer stand.'

She covered Davin's hands with her own. Her betrothed was never one to let a man endure pain, not when he could intervene. It was one of the reasons he was her dearest friend and the man she had agreed to marry.

A hollow feeling settled in her stomach. Davin deserved a better woman than herself. She had done what she could to salvage her torn reputation, but the gossip had not died down, not in three years. She didn't know why he'd offered for her, but her family had seized the opportunity for the alliance. It wasn't every day that a blacksmith's daughter could marry a chieftain's son.

'Let the healer tend him,' Davin urged, his voice turning heated. She recognised the intent in his words, along with the hidden invitation. 'Walk with me, Iseult. I haven't seen you in a sennight, and I've missed you.'

She stiffened, but forced a smile. *Go with him*, her head urged. Though Davin had never once held her to blame for her sins, she felt unworthy of his love.

After summoning the healer, Davin took her hand and led her outside. The moon cast its shadow across his face. With fair hair and piercing blue eyes, Davin was the most handsome man she'd ever seen. He drew her hand to his bearded cheek. Apprehension sliced through her, for she knew he was about to kiss her. She accepted his embrace, wishing she could feel the same ardour that he felt for her.

Give it time, she urged. But even when she poured herself into the kiss, it was as if she stood outside her body, an observer instead of a participant.

He held her closely, whispering against her ear. 'I know you don't wish to become lovers before Bealtaine. But I'd be a fool if I didn't try to convince you.'

She pulled back, her gaze cast downwards. 'I can't.'

Her face brightened with shame, even now. The

thought of lying with a man, any man, only brought back grievous memories.

Tension knotted across Davin's face, but he did not press further. 'I would never ask you to do anything you don't want.'

And that was why she felt even guiltier. She didn't want to lie with him, but what kind of woman did that make her? She'd surrendered to a moment of passion years ago, and paid the price. But now that a man loved her and wanted to marry her, she couldn't seem to let go of the bad memories.

Davin dropped a hand across her shoulders, kissing her temple. 'I'll wait until you're ready.'

He walked her back to her dwelling within the ringfort, his hand holding hers. When they reached the hut, Iseult paused beside the wooden door frame, as though it were a shield.

'What will you do with the slave?'

'I don't know yet. Possibly he can help with the crops or tend the horses. I'll speak to him once he's awake.

'I will see you in the morning,' Davin said, regret edging his tone. He kissed her lips again. 'See what you can do to keep our slave alive.'

Iseult nodded, ducking inside the house. For a moment she stood at the entrance, gathering her thoughts. Why couldn't she feel the blaze of ardour that women spoke of? Davin's kisses and affection evoked nothing but emptiness.

What was wrong with her? He, of all men, deserved to be loved. He treated her like a cherished treasure, offering her anything she wanted. It made her feel unworthy of him.

Her heart heavy, she walked inside to join the others. Muirne and her family were busy setting out food for the evening meal. Though the Ó Falveys were not her kin, they'd willingly opened their doors to her, granting her hospitality. Because of them, she had a place to stay while growing accustomed to her new tribe.

And, bless them, it kept her from having to live with Davin's mother. The chieftain's wife didn't like her at all and made no secret of it.

'Who was the man Davin brought with him?' Muirne asked. A stout, raven-haired woman who had borne seven children, she fussed over Iseult as though she were one of her own. Without waiting for a reply, she continued, 'You haven't eaten this night. Come and sit with us.' She gestured towards the low table where her other foster-children sat, teasing one another as they devoured their food.

'He was a slave,' Iseult answered. 'Half-dead from what I understand.'

'Well, that's not much of a purchase.' Muirne rolled her eyes and handed Iseult a plate of salted mackerel and roasted carrots. 'But that's Davin for you.' She smiled as if speaking of a saint.

'Mother, may I have more fish?' one of the boys asked.

'And me!' the other chimed in. Glendon and Bartley charmed her, though the sight of them deepened the ache of loss in Iseult's heart. Her own son Aidan would have been two years of age now.

Iseult picked at her food, her appetite suddenly gone.

'Why haven't you wed Davin already?' Muirne asked, adding a slice of bread on to her plate. 'I don't understand why you'd want to wait until Bealtaine.'

'Davin asked me to wait. He wants a special blessing upon our marriage.' When Muirne was about to add even more food, Iseult covered her plate with a hand. 'I've had enough, thank you.'

'I'll eat it,' Glendon offered. Iseult slid the fish on to his plate, and the boy devoured it. Muirne muttered words beneath her breath about Iseult being too thin.

She tried to ignore the criticism. 'I think I'll take the rest of this with me and see if the slave is hungry.'

'You shouldn't be associating with the likes of him,' Muirne warned. 'He's a *fudir*, and people will talk.'

Iseult faltered. They would, yes. The wise thing to do was to remain here and not to think about the slave. Likely the man would die, a stranger to all of them.

'You're right.' When Muirne's back was turned, she tucked a slice of bread into a fold of her cloak. 'But I'm going to go for a walk. I won't be long.'

Her friend fastened a knowing gaze upon her. 'Don't do anything you'll regret, Iseult.'

She tried to muster a nonchalant smile, but it wouldn't come. 'I will be back soon.'

Outside, the moonlight illuminated a ring of twelve thatched stone cottages. The hide of a red deer was stretched across a wooden frame on one side, while outdoor cooking fires had died down to coals. The familiar scent of peat smoke lingered in the air, and the early spring wind bit through her overdress and *léine*. She raised her *brat* to cover her shoulders, seeking warmth from the shawl. Though she had only lived among the tribe since last winter, she was starting to consider the ringfort her home.

At last she stopped in front of the sick hut. Why had she come here? The healer Deena would already have fed the slave and tended him. Her presence would be nothing more than an interference. She almost turned away when the door opened.

'Oh,' Deena breathed, touching a hand to her heart. The healer had cared for members of Davin's tribe for almost a generation, but her hair still held its black lustre.

Fine lines edged her smiling mouth. 'You startled me, Iseult. I was just going to fetch some water.'

'How is the slave?' she asked.

Deena shook her head. 'Not well, I fear. He won't eat or drink anything. Stubborn, that one is. If he wants to die, that's his concern, but I'd rather it not be in my sick hut.'

'Shall I speak with him?'

'If it pleases you. Not that 'twill do any good.' Deena expelled a sigh of disgust. 'Go on, then.'

Iseult stepped across the threshold into the darkened room. The hearth glowed with coals, and she smelled the intense aroma of wintergreen and camomile. The slave lay upon a pallet, his eyes closed. Unkempt black hair fell across his neck, his cheeks rough and unshaven. He looked like a demon who'd crawled from the underworld, a dark god like Crom Dubh.

But as a slave, he might have travelled across Éireann. He might have seen her son Aidan or have news. She tried to shut down the wave of hope building inside.

Don't be foolish, her mind warned. With a countryside so vast, the chances of him knowing anything about a small boy were remote.

'Will you eat something?' she asked, kneeling beside the pallet.

He didn't open his eyes, didn't move. Iseult reached out to touch his shoulder.

His hand shot out, crushing her wrist. Dark brown eyes flashed a warning at her, and she cried out with pain.

'Get out,' he said. The razor edge of his voice shocked her. He had none of the penitent demeanour of a slave.

Mary, Mother of God, what sort of man had Davin bought? Iseult scrambled to her feet, wrenching her hand away from his grip. 'Who are you?'

'Kieran Ó Brannon. And I want to be left alone.' He rolled over, and Iseult shuddered at the sight of his raw back. The voice of reason demanded that she leave. Now, before he lashed out at her again.

'I am Iseult MacFergus,' she said calmly. 'And I've brought you food.'

'I don't want it.'

Steeling her voice, she added, 'If you don't eat, you'll die.'

'I'd rather die than live like this.'

Instead of grief, she sensed a seething rage within him. It terrified her, not knowing what he would do or say. Like a wild animal, he was ready to strike out at anyone offering compassion.

Iseult dropped the food on the ground beside him, not caring if the dirt mingled with the bread. 'If you're going to die, do it quickly. Or if you decide to live, know that you'll not be harmed here.'

Before he could reply, she fled outside. She would get no answers about her son, not from a man such as this. As far as she was concerned, the sooner Davin got rid of this slave, the better.

Kieran Ó Brannon wanted to laugh. It was fitting, wasn't it, for one of God's angels to appear before him. After the past season he'd spent in hell, the irony did not escape him.

Her hair was the colour of a sunset, gold and red intertwined. The blue *léine* and overdress she wore revealed a slim body and long legs. Once, he might have tried to charm a lady like Iseult MacFergus.

But women were not to be trusted, especially not beautiful women. He'd learned that the fairer they were, the more treacherous their hearts.

He stared at the fallen bread. Though his body cried out

for food, his mind refused it. He no longer cared what happened to him. If he could encourage death to come sooner, so be it.

The healer Deena returned a moment later. She sat across from him, a foul-smelling decoction in her mortar. Her black hair hung down in a long braid, covered by a length of linen.

'Why do you want to die, lad?' she asked.

She reminded him of his grandmother, a brook-no-foolishness woman who spoke whatever was on her mind. When he didn't answer, she prodded again. 'Now, then, I know you can speak, as you nearly frightened Iseult to death. You must know that it won't work with me. I can be quite a force to be reckoned with. Not to mention, I'll be preparing your food and drink for the next few weeks.'

His head ached from her chatter. She had kept up a stream of talking while she mixed up God only knew what in her mortar.

At last he answered, if for no other reason than to make her cease the noise. 'Why would I want to live?'

She shrugged, a faint smile tugging at her mouth. She'd won and knew it, too.

'You're an intelligent one, aren't you, lad? Somewhere, you've got a family. And you'll live because your kin would want it so.'

Had she read him that easily? Was she a soothsayer, as well as a healer? The unwanted memory of his younger brother sprang forth from his mind, Egan pleading for help. Like a cold blade, it sliced open his guilt, making him bleed from it.

His kin would rather see him dead.

But when she started to talk again, he shut off his emotions and picked up the fallen bread.

You don't deserve it. You deserve to starve, like the rest of your tribe.

He shut out the voice and ate. It tasted as dry as it looked, but the vicious hunger inside him begged for more.

Deena handed him a clay cup, and he took it with shaking hands. He was so thirsty, he didn't even remember the last time he'd eaten or drunk. When he tasted the bitter wine, he nearly choked at the vile taste.

Deena chuckled again. 'It's to make you sleep, lad. You'll need to be on your feet again soon.'

If it would bring about forgetfulness, he'd drink it all. Without argument, he drained the vessel.

The healer spread the herbal mixture on his back, and, as promised, the cooling effect of the medicine did ease the pain of his wounds. The lash marks weren't as deep as others he'd endured. He welcomed the pain, for it was a physical act of contrition.

'You'd best be on better behaviour with Iseult MacFergus,' Deena warned. 'She is promised to wed the man who owns you. Davin Ó Falvey won't look kindly upon anyone who mistreats his betrothed.'

'Then I won't speak to her at all.' Kieran gritted his teeth when she laid linen atop his lash marks. He knew why she was tending him. Not out of compassion. A weakened slave held no value.

The thought of servitude chafed at his pride. He'd never been any man's slave, and the instinct to fight back rose up, stronger than ever. Thoughts of escape tempted him, beckoning to his sense of pride. Healed or not, he could find a way out of this ringfort.

And then what?

He closed his eyes, wishing he knew. There was nothing for him to return to, nowhere to go. Perhaps his failures justified a life filled with suffering.

The healer handed him another slice of bread, which he

ate without thinking. His stomach craved more, cramping up at the unexpected food.

'That's enough for now,' she warned. 'As thin as you are, if you eat too much, it will only come back up again.'

She held out a cup of cold water instead of wine. It tasted sweet, like melted snow. Unlike any of the mud-ridden water he'd gulped down over the past few months. He savoured it, letting it assuage his thirst.

The healer eased him down to the pallet, to rest upon his stomach. The herbs had begun to steal away the pain, drawing him towards sleep. He closed his eyes, his spirit feeling as bruised and battered as his body. The dark temptation of death cried out to him, for the finality would silence the ghosts that haunted him.

He'd chosen this path, selling himself into slavery. He'd meant to rescue his brother and bring Egan home again. Instead, he had played into his enemy's hands. And lost.

His father would never forgive him for it. God willing, he'd never set eyes on his family again.

Chapter Two

~~~~~~~~~~~~~~~~~~~~~~~~~~~~~

Iseult draped a blanket across the black mare, vaulting atop the animal. She had packed a bag of provisions for the morning and early afternoon. Silently, she murmured a prayer. *Please, God, let me find him. Let today be different.*

She'd been searching for her son Aidan for nearly a year. And though she hadn't found him yet, she couldn't abandon the search.

'Iseult!' Davin called out. He strode towards her, gathering the reins of her horse. 'Where are you going?'

She flinched at the sharp inquisition. 'I think you know the answer to that.'

Davin hid his frustration, averting his gaze. Though he didn't speak a word, he believed her search was fruitless. The chances of finding a missing child after a year were small, at best. But she couldn't give up looking for Aidan. Not yet.

'I know you don't want to come,' she admitted. 'I won't ask it of you.'

'It isn't safe for a woman to travel alone.' Lines of worry creased his bearded face.

Iseult reached towards the dagger at her side. 'I am armed, Davin. And I'm only going to visit the nearby tribes.'

He took her hand. 'I'll come with you.'

'Really, you don't have to—'

'It's important to you.' He kept his face neutral, as though her quest were not an inconvenience. 'And perhaps one day you'll find the answers you seek.'

But Iseult heard the unspoken words: *Perhaps, one day, you'll give up.*

He might be right. But she didn't want to believe Aidan was dead. In her heart, a frail hope continued to beat.

Never could she forget the infant who had grasped her long hair in his tiny palm, pulling the strands towards his mouth. Nor the horrifying moment when she turned to him and found him gone.

Davin joined her, riding along in silence while she took the mare along the sands leading up to the Benoskee Mountain. Clouds skimmed high above the rocky surface of the peak, shadowing the face. The deep azure of the lake marked the location of the Sullivan tribe.

She rode to their lands often, asking if messengers had stopped with any news. In the past year, she'd been to every neighbouring tribe and clan. Her hands tightened on the horse's mane, as if she could somehow hold fast to her hope.

Perhaps today she'd find what she sought. Iseult steeled herself for the forthcoming pitying looks. They might think her foolish, but this was her child. She could never give up.

Davin stopped to let the horses drink, and she caught the impatience upon his face. She should have left before dawn. He could never understand this cross that she bore, for Aidan was not his.

Fate seemed to intervene at that moment, for a single rider approached at a rapid speed. The man didn't bother to dismount, but addressed Davin. 'You're needed back at Lismanagh. Your slave is causing trouble.'

'What sort of trouble?' Davin's face showed his displeasure at being interrupted.

'Fighting with the others. We've bound him, but since he belongs to you…' The messenger's voice trailed off.

'I'll come.' Davin urged the horse around, a determined look upon his face.

When he glanced at her, Iseult shook her head. 'Go with him. I'll be fine.'

'I want you to come back with me. I don't like leaving you here.' There was an edge to his voice, almost like an angry parent.

Iseult stared back at him. She hadn't wanted him to escort her, and now he treated her as though she were incapable of caring for herself. 'I make my own decisions. And I'd rather look for my son than bother with a disrespectful, arrogant slave.'

A strange flash took hold in Davin's eyes. 'What do you mean…"disrespectful"?'

Iseult bit her tongue, wishing she hadn't spoken. 'I went back to assist Deena. The slave awakened, but I didn't like him.'

'Did he threaten you?' The iron cast to Davin's voice made it clear that he was not at all pleased.

Iseult shrugged. 'He asked me to leave, that's all.' She waved her hand as though it were nothing. 'Go on. I'll join you this afternoon.'

When he hesitated again, she drew her horse alongside his and kissed Davin gently. 'Go.'

Her action had the intended effect, and he softened. 'Be careful. If I do not see you by the noon meal, I'm sending men after you.'

He leaned in and kissed her again, this time with more intensity. Iseult accepted it, but her mind was still on the Sullivan tribe. Within a few more moments, she'd know if her search had been for nothing.

'I'll see you later,' she promised.

Kieran strained against his ropes, hardly caring when the hemp bit into his flesh. They had bound him hand and foot, trussed like a fowl about to be roasted.

It was his own fault. He'd thought he could slip away without anyone noticing, forgetting that starvation had robbed him of his strength. When the men had sighted him, he'd fought them off as well as he could. Wounded a few of them, too, but in the end it hadn't mattered. His strength was diminished almost to a boy's. Blood matted his skin, his lips split from one of their punches. His back blazed with an unholy fire from the lash marks.

Would they kill him now? He steeled himself for it. Lowering his gaze, he stared at the damp earth. The scent of the smoke and straw were similar to his home in the south of Éireann. So far from here, almost a world apart. Away from those who would cast blame upon him.

He shouldered every pound of the guilt. It was his fault that Egan had died. If he could have put himself in his younger brother's place, he'd have died a thousand deaths. Only three and ten, his brother had never had the chance to grow to manhood.

Kieran saw the flash of a blade, but didn't move. A tall bearded man stood before him. He wore a dark green tunic, trimmed with gold thread. Wielding the knife in one hand, the man dismissed the others, authority evident in his voice. Their chieftain, perhaps, judging from his costly garments.

The man addressed him. 'I am Davin Ó Falvey.'

His owner. The possessive sound in the man's voice made Kieran want to snarl. He'd never been slave to any man, and bitter resentment filled him at his fate. 'You're the man who bought me.'

'I am. And from the stories they've told, I suspect you'd like me to slice this blade across your throat.'

Kieran lifted his chin in an invitation. 'Do it, then.'

Davin tilted the knife in the sunlight, the blade flashing. 'I could. But then you'd get what you want. And I'd have lost the silver I spent.' Davin reached down to help him rise to his feet, cutting the bonds around his ankles, but leaving his hands tied. 'What is your name?'

'Kieran, of the Ó Brannon tribe.'

'I've heard of your kin. They are a great distance from here, are they not?'

Kieran didn't answer. Didn't have to, for Ó Falvey already knew it. He studied his enemy. The *flaith* exuded a calm confidence, showing not a trace of unease. Davin watched him as if trying to make a decision.

'You want your freedom. I can understand that, and perhaps I'll grant it to you in return for your service.'

Kieran didn't answer, for nothing would make him endure servitude willingly. He'd rather die than live as another man's slave.

Davin reached into a fold of his cloak and held up a wooden figurine, the carved likeness of his brother Egan. 'Or perhaps you'd like to earn this back.'

The carving. He cursed, trying to strike out despite his bound hands, but Davin stepped sideways, using his foot to send him sprawling on to the ground. Kieran tasted blood and dirt, hardly caring as he tried to attack again.

Gods above, but the piece of wood was the only thing he had left of Egan. It was only a piece of yew, but he'd given it to his brother years ago. Seeing it in his master's hands ignited the same anger he'd felt towards the slave traders.

Davin caught him with a punch, and the air went crashing from his lungs. Kieran crouched down, trying to catch a breath. Blood trickled from the wounds on his back, and he bit back the pain.

'Did you carve this?' Davin asked softly, fingering the piece.

Kieran only stared at the man, rage seething inside him. He'd made a mistake, showing Davin that the carving was important to him. He forced a neutral expression on to his face as he got up from his knees.

'You have skill,' Davin remarked. 'I think I know a way you can earn your freedom. And this.' He tucked the figurine away in the fold of his cloak. 'Come.' Davin grasped the length of rope that held his wrists captive, and Kieran struggled to follow.

He didn't believe for a moment that Davin would set him free. His limbs ached, and the salty taste of blood lingered in his mouth. More than once, he stumbled, his knees shaking with weakness.

Davin led him inside a darkened hut, where Kieran smelled the stale odours of ale and old straw. Near the door stood a large oak chest, its height reaching the tops of his thighs and the length slightly larger than the spread of his arms.

The intricate carving was old, the wood hard and seasoned. Though his trained eyes saw a few deliberate flaws, nicks set against the grain, the chest was a masterpiece. And it was not yet finished.

'This is a chest commissioned by my bride's father. It was supposed to be completed last winter as part of her dowry.'

'Who carved it?'

'Seamus did.' Davin kept his voice low and pointed to the empty pallet. 'But he fell ill and died a sennight ago.' He lowered his head out of respect and made the sign of the cross.

Kieran ran his hands over the wood, like a familiar friend. Temptation beckoned, to sink back into the days when he could lose his hours, forgetting all else but the wood. He had missed this.

'A task such as this would be a simple matter and a worthy use of your time…' Davin paused '…unless you'd rather wait upon my father's table or work in the fields.'

Kieran had no intention of doing either, but didn't say so. 'Aren't you afraid of what I'd do if you gave me an adze or a knife?'

Davin stared at him for a long moment, as if considering whether the threat was genuine. 'I don't know who you are, or what lies in your past. But, perhaps once, you were a man of honour. And if that is true, you will not cause harm to others.'

A man of honour. His father had wanted him to become such a man. A future chieftain, someone to shoulder the burdens of the tribe. Perhaps once, he might have considered it. But that part of him was lost forever, from the moment he'd watched Egan die.

Despite his bound hands, Kieran ran his thumb over a thin ridge at the edge of the surface.

'If your carving is of fine quality, I will grant your freedom,' Davin said. 'I give you my word.' A dark warning flashed in his eyes. 'If you obey and adhere to my orders.'

Empty promises meant nothing. But the wood beckoned. He could envision the finished chest: patterns of grain for fertility; water and fire to symbolise the ancient gods; and the face of the Virgin Mary to offer comfort to a new bride. It would need tallow to prevent cracking. And sharper tools for carving, since the wood had lost its moisture.

It had been months since he'd held a knife. He wanted a means of forgetting, and this would grant him another chance. For a moment, he allowed himself to imagine it.

The ropes around his wrists chafed against the unhealed wounds. He closed his eyes, while the memory of his brother Egan rose forth.

Voices taunted him, the bleakness threatening to cut him apart. After all that had happened, he couldn't allow himself to find joy in the wood.

'What is your answer?' Davin asked.

Kieran raised his face to his master's. 'No.'

The slave's arrogance had to be broken. Davin had ordered him bound and left outside. A light spring rain had begun. Perhaps the discomfort would force the man to change his mind.

Never had he seen such skill. Any other man would welcome such a task, for it was far easier than the back-breaking work most slaves endured. He doubted not that it was Kieran who had created the carving of the young boy. From the expression upon the slave's face when he touched the oak, it was clear that this was a man of expertise.

Perhaps nobility.

Kieran endured pain the way most warriors did. And though it was cruel to expose him to the elements, it had to be done. His tribesmen expected the slave to be punished for attempting an escape.

A flicker of movement caught his attention, and he saw Iseult returning. Her hood was drawn over her face to protect it from the rain.

A lightness spread over him at the sight of her. After Bealtaine, she would belong to him as his wife. To know that he would be with such a woman, would see her beauty every moment of each day, filled him with satisfaction.

She stopped her horse near the mound of hostages and lowered her hood to get a better look at the slave. Davin's hand tightened upon the hide door, willing Iseult to turn away.

Iseult didn't speak to the slave. The rain had dampened the man's black hair, staining his cheeks with water and blood. He sat with his back to the wooden post, his wrists carelessly resting on his knees.

'Seen enough?' His low voice abraded her sense of security, making her uneasy. He was rigid with anger, tension filling him.

She wanted to ask what he'd done to deserve this, but he wouldn't give her the truth. A man like him was never meant to be confined. His eyes were watching the ringfort, as if seeking a way of escape.

She wanted to turn her back on him, to leave him without a second's thought. But she refused to behave like a coward.

'Why did he punish you?' she asked.

His jaw tightened. Rain slid over his face, outlining hollowed cheeks. 'Because I tried to escape.'

'You were not mistreated. Why would you want to leave?' Davin had saved his life. Was he not grateful for it?

'A woman like you could never understand.'

Iseult stiffened at the accusation. What did he mean, a woman like her? Did he think she knew nothing of suffering? 'You don't know me at all.'

He rose to his feet slowly, watching her. Within his face she saw pain, but he made no complaint. 'You shouldn't be here, talking to me,' he said. 'Your betrothed is watching us.'

'I've done nothing wrong.'

He took a step forwards, straining at his ropes. A fierceness tilted at his mouth. 'But I have.'

Her imagination conjured up thoughts of murder or other wickedness. Although Kieran was lean, there was a ruthless air about him. As though he would do anything to survive.

'Weren't you ever warned about men like me?' His rigid stare reached inside and took apart her nerves. The cool rain rolled down her skin, sliding beneath her bodice like a caress. She shivered, drawing her cloak around her. Not that it would protect her.

Kieran's face grew distant. Then his mouth tightened. 'Go back to your own master, Lady Iseult.'

Chapter Three

The second escape attempt failed. Kieran had made it beyond the gates this time, nearly to the forest before his body had collapsed. He didn't know how long he'd lain there. Hours or minutes, it was all the same.

The fecund scent of rain and grass had surrounded him, while he welcomed the promise of death. He'd awakened to an animal licking his face. A wolfhound, nearly the size of a newborn mare, had whimpered and crooned to alert the others.

It was the middle of the night when they dragged him back to Deena's hut. His skin was puckered from the rain, his body numb with cold.

Just as before, Deena treated the lash marks upon his back. She spread an oily salve upon the rope burns at his wrists. It stung, instead of soothing his irritated skin.

'You shouldn't bother,' he said. 'I'm not afraid to die.'

The healer studied him as she worked. Gently, she continued treating each of his wounds.

'I had a son once,' Deena said quietly, holding out a cup of bitter tea. Though he accepted it, he did not drink. Unless the brew would bring a final sleep, he had no interest in painkillers.

'A strong young man, about your age.' She smiled in memory, the fine lines crinkling around her eyes.

Kieran kept his gaze upon the simple wooden cup, as though he hadn't heard her. But he was well aware of her words.

'He was struck down by the evil spirits that cause sickness. On a spring night, such as this.' She took the cup and lifted it to his mouth, touching his cheek as she did so.

But still he did not drink.

'I did everything in my power to save him. I used every herb, prayed to every god in heaven or known to my ancestors. But it wasn't enough.'

Her wrinkled hand pressed warmth into his skin, the touch of a mother. 'For a long time, I blamed myself. I wanted to die, just as you do.'

Her other hand moved to his shoulder. 'The pain doesn't go away. You must endure it, one day at a time.'

'I don't want to take away the pain,' he said. Violence rimmed his words. 'I want to remember. And I want every last one of them dead for what they did.'

'I don't know what you've suffered, lad. I won't ask. But whatever evil befell you, it takes a greater courage to live than to die.' She tilted the cup, easing the liquid into his mouth. At first, he nearly choked. She moved the cup away while he coughed.

'Perhaps this is your penance. To be left alive.' She pressed the cup to his mouth again.

This time he accepted the brew, drinking steadily. Deena took the cup away when it was empty and approached a small chest. From within it, she brought out a dagger and set it beside him.

'I'm going to leave this here. And I'll return to my own dwelling to finish my sleep, as most should do in the middle of the night.' Deena's voice hardened. 'But if you truly want to die, I've given you the means.'

She stopped in front of the door, about to leave. 'If you're alive when the sun rises, put all thoughts of escape out of your mind. This is your home now. This is the path you're meant to take. God has put you here, perhaps to teach you humility. And you must accept your fate.'

He slept, harder than ever before. It was as if his body could not heal itself until he'd made up for every hour he'd lost. The sunlight pierced his vision when the door opened. Kieran rubbed his eyes and saw the dagger still beside him.

His penance, she'd said. And though invisible ropes tightened around his throat at the knowledge of his slavery, he knew she was right. He had failed his brother. He deserved to lose his birthright and his family. To become a slave, to accept this punishment.

The door swung open and his master, Davin Ó Falvey, entered the hut. His expression was grim.

'You caused a grave inconvenience to my men last night. I don't know how you managed to free yourself from the ropes, but I won't let it happen again. I'll sell you back to the traders, and they can do what they will with you.' His gaze narrowed. 'Unless you've changed your mind about the carving.'

There was no doubt Davin meant what he said. Many slaves were traded by the Norsemen, sent across the sea to Byzantium or to faraway lands. And though his life would never again be the same, at least he could remain upon his homeland.

All he had to do was agree to complete the dower chest.

It wasn't as if he had a choice, was it? He had to endure this fate and complete whatever task was ordered of him.

He sat up slowly, pressing through the pain. 'I'll begin working on the chest this day.'

Davin's shoulders lowered slightly, a barely perceptible relaxation. 'Not yet. Before I let you touch the chest, you must first prove your skills.'

Prove his skills? He'd been carving wood since he could hold a knife. There wasn't anything he couldn't bring to life from a block of wood. *This is your penance*, he reminded himself, swallowing his frustration and resentment.

'I want you to carve a likeness of my bride Iseult. If I find it worthy of her beauty, I will allow you to finish the chest.'

He might have known. The woman loathed the sight of him, and he didn't have any desire to spend time with Iseult MacFergus. Yet he had no choice if he wanted to capture her spirit in the wood.

'If I carve her likeness, you won't have the dower chest in time for a bridal gift.' It was a last, fruitless attempt to change his master's mind.

'I would like the figure, nonetheless.' Davin opened the door wider and pointed towards one of the huts. The morning sun illuminated the interior of the ringfort, the glaring light burning his eyes.

'The smallest hut belonged to our woodcarver, Seamus,' Davin said. 'Inside, you will find the tools you need.'

'And the wood?'

'It is there.' Davin leaned down and picked up the knife Deena had left behind. 'You will begin the carving after your confinement.'

Confinement? His knuckles clenched as the full weight of his slavery pressed down upon his shoulders. He was to be punished for running away again. Of course.

'For three days, you'll remain guarded, in isolation. If you do as you are told, on the last day the guards will leave, and you'll be permitted to begin the carving.' Davin tossed the knife and caught it by the hilt. 'You should be grateful for Iseult's mercy. I would have confined you outside for the three days.'

'I don't need a woman's pity.' The words came forth, behind a backlash of anger. 'There is no punishment I am unable to endure.'

Davin leaned down, the knife glinting. 'I will not tolerate disrespect towards her. She asked me to grant you mercy. For her sake, I will.' He turned the blade close to Kieran's skin in an unspoken threat. 'I'll send the guards now. They'll take you to Seamus's hut.' Without another word, he strode outside into the sunlight.

Kieran rolled over and stared up at the ceiling of thatch and wood. He didn't want to waste his days carving a woman's likeness. It didn't matter that she was the most beautiful woman he'd ever seen. He hardly needed Iseult's presence to create the image. Already he could see the curve of her cheek, the sadness in her expression.

He closed his eyes, trying to shut out the vision of the last female likeness he'd created. He'd almost wed Branna, but her heart had belonged to another man in the end.

Treacherous work, indeed.

'I'll come with you,' Davin said.

His offer didn't make Iseult feel better. Just the thought of being watched by the slave, letting him carve her image, made her nervous.

'I'd rather not do this at all.' She moved to a basket of mending Muirne had set aside and picked up a bone needle. The sewing gave her something to occupy her hands. 'It makes me feel vain. What need do we have of a likeness?'

'I want it.' He came up behind her, resting his hands upon her shoulders. 'I want something of you, for when we are apart.'

'You'll see me every day.' She wanted to talk him out of this. No other man had ever shaken her up in this way. There was something about the slave, both terrifying and fascinating.

On the day she'd found him bound outside in the rain, despite the miserable conditions, he had refused to let it break him. He was a fighter to his core. Somehow he'd freed himself, half-dragging his body through the mud in a desperate attempt for freedom.

Would she have done the same?

A pang clutched at her heart. Not for herself. But if she ever received word of her son, then, yes, she would never stop searching, no matter what happened.

Davin had no choice but to punish the slave; she knew that. But she didn't want to face Kieran again. The idea of seeing him bound to the mound of hostages, exposed to the elements, would only make the man even more savage. Like a wild animal, prepared to strike out at those who harmed him.

She hadn't wanted to see him again. Not like that. It was why she'd asked Davin to confine Kieran elsewhere. As if hiding him would make him disappear. Childish thoughts. She had to face him sooner or later, but if she showed him her fear, Kieran would only exploit it.

'Did he harm you?' Davin asked.

He'd questioned her about it before. And the truth was, he hadn't.

'No. It was only words. He was in a great deal of pain.'

She shrugged it off as though it were nothing. Rising to her feet, she took Davin's hands in hers. His broad palms covered her own, making her feel safe. 'Is this truly important to you? The carving?'

'It is. But more than that, it's part of a gift I want to give you. He's going to finish your dower chest.'

She wanted to say that it was simply a wooden container, with no meaning. But he'd commissioned Seamus to make it into a work of art, into a treasure. Though Davin wouldn't say why, she could see that it meant more to him.

She let out a breath. 'Then I'll go.' Laying a hand upon his cheek, she added, 'And I'll take a guard with me. You needn't come. I know your responsibilities to your father are more important.' As the chieftain's son, Davin had his own leadership duties. Not only that, but she refused to let this slave believe she was afraid of him.

She would not let an insolent man dominate her. Squaring her shoulders, she prepared herself for what was to come.

Three days later, Iseult strode inside the woodcarver's hut, as though meeting with the slave were an inconvenience instead of something she dreaded. *Be confident*, she reminded herself. *Don't be afraid of him.*

'You.' She pointed at the slave. 'What sort of spell did you cast upon Davin?'

Kieran turned around, a whetstone and iron blade in his hands. 'No spell.' Though it was only a carver's knife, Iseult's heart beat a little faster. The way he held the blade intimidated her. He drew it across the whetstone, honing it to a razor's edge.

She grimaced and dropped the bag of supplies Davin had sent before sitting down upon a tree stump. Outside the hut, she had brought one of Davin's men. The guard was more than a little irritated, having to watch over her, but it made her feel better.

'I suppose you know why I am here. For the carving, I mean.' The words came out of her mouth before she could stop them. She sounded like a babbling young maiden instead of a calm woman. Of course he knew why she was here.

'You want an image of yourself out of wood.' He spoke the words with a casual air.

How could he think that? This wasn't her idea at all. It was the last thing she desired.

'It was Davin's wish,' she corrected. 'I had nothing to do with this.' She wanted so badly to turn around and run.

But then, from the gleam in his eye, she wondered if Kieran was provoking her on purpose. His black hair hung unkempt about his shoulders, his demon eyes as dark as his soul. His tunic hung upon him, still bloodstained from the marks upon his back.

'You won't have to stay long,' he said. There was a hint of resentment beneath his tone, as if he hated anyone commanding him. He set down the knife, wrapping it carefully in leather before picking up a gouge.

Iseult looked around at Seamus's hut. She'd visited a time or two, and although the space was by no means built for a family, it was large enough for two people. A pallet stood at one end, a work bench at the other. It was no wider than thirteen feet in diameter, made of wattle and daub. The roof often leaked, as she recalled. 'You're staying here?'

'For now. Until he commands otherwise.' Again, she sensed the rebellion within his voice.

Iseult studied the work bench. Kieran had spent the afternoon preparing the tools, it seemed. Rows of knives and gouges were spread out upon the table, along with wooden mallets and chisels. The air smelled of wood shavings, and he'd built a fire in the hearth.

She sniffed suspiciously, then turned to him. 'What did you eat this evening for your meal?'

Kieran said nothing, lifting a block of yew. He sat upon a wooden stump, opposite her. His hands moved over the wood, studying it. He was so intent upon it, he didn't answer her question.

She already knew the answer. He hadn't eaten at all. And from his pride, this was not a man who would ask for help. She didn't know what kind of food or drink he'd had during his confinement, but it couldn't have been much of anything.

It pricked her conscience, to see a man suffering. Even this one, as harsh as he was, did not deserve to starve. If she offered to prepare food, he'd never touch it.

No. Better to appear that she was angry with him. Then he would eat, if for no other reason than to defy her.

'For the love of Saint Brigid, how do you think you'll ever finish this carving if you don't eat?' Indignant, Iseult grasped one of the iron cauldrons from near the hearth and strode outside. She filled the pot with water and hauled it back in.

The slave blocked her path. His eyes studied hers a moment, and the intense darkness of them caught her attention. Bruises and cuts lined his cheeks, and his jaw held a dark swelling. Beneath the unkempt appearance was a startlingly handsome man. Not the noble looks of Davin, but features more brutal and arresting.

'I don't take things that do not belong to me.' His hands curled over the iron handle, brushing against her as he took the pot from her. Iseult nearly jerked backwards at the contact.

What in the name of heaven was the matter with her? Her cheeks warmed as he set the cauldron over the fire. She busied herself with peeling vegetables from the supplies she'd brought. It kept her from having to meet his gaze.

'I promised Davin I'd stay for an hour,' she said, 'but that doesn't mean I'm going to sit and stare. You'll have to start carving now. After I've finished cooking, I'm leaving.'

She found a cloth-wrapped package of mutton inside her bag and chopped the meat, adding it to the water. A lock of hair fell forwards, and she brushed it aside.

All of her frustration and fury seemed to pour out of her. It had been another wasted day, with no news of her son. She wanted to curl up on her pallet and indulge herself in a fit of weeping. Instead, she had to endure the company of this man.

'You aren't flattered that your betrothed wants this carving?' he asked.

A slight scratching noise sounded from behind her.

'No. I've better things to do.' She rather be with Muirne and the children, helping to tell the boys stories. Anything to occupy herself and keep her from thinking about Aidan.

When she'd finished setting the ingredients in the stew, she turned back. He hadn't touched the block of wood. Instead, he was using a piece of charcoal to sketch a drawing onto a flat board.

'What are you doing?'

'As you've said, you have better things to do. I'll capture your image on the board and carve it later.' His hands moved rapidly, and Iseult drew nearer to see what he'd done.

He lifted the board away, hiding it from her view. 'Not yet,' was all he said.

'You've probably drawn me with two noses and three chins,' she remarked.

A flicker of amusement tilted at his mouth. 'No. But I thought of drawing horns and a forked tongue.'

Iseult sobered, stirring the pot of stew. She wasn't at all that sort of woman. Sweet-natured, Davin had called her.

But around this man, she was transforming into a shrew.

Instead of trying to come up with a swift retort, she stared at the pot of stew and imagined adding henbane to it. Then she realised that she'd forgotten any seasonings. And she'd put the vegetables in too soon.

As time crept onward, the peas grew mushy, and the meat tougher. She bit her tongue, knowing she was a miserable cook. Part of her thought it served him right, while the other part was ashamed at her lack of skills. What kind of a wife would she make for Davin?

Finally, she ladled a wooden bowl full of the stew and found a spoon for him to use. Kieran eyed the pitiful mashed vegetables and the meat boiled to death.

'Eat,' she ordered. 'I won't have you dropping dead when I've gone to this trouble.'

It was growing more difficult to uphold her bravado. She'd done a terrible job of cooking, but he made no remark on its lack of flavour, eating it slowly.

'What will you do next?' she asked when he'd finished the meal and set the bowl aside.

'I'll draw your face onto the wood and do a stop cut with this knife.' He held up a short blade, and the way he held it struck Iseult like a man ready for battle. With the cuts and bruises upon his face, she could imagine him riding from the field, battle cries resounding from his lips.

After Kieran set down the blade, he picked up the charcoal and board again. His gaze travelled over her face and down her body. He drew more slowly, watching her as though he could see deep within her.

Her heart pulsed beneath her skin. She considered calling the guard inside. Being alone with the slave made her wary.

Abruptly, Kieran shifted the rhythm. His hands moved rapidly with smooth strokes, as though he were capturing her without even thinking. She noticed several scars along his hands, like blade marks from battle.

'You were not a slave before this, were you?' she predicted.

He shrugged, casting a brief glance at her before turning back to the drawing.

'You're too confident to be a slave,' she continued, 'and too arrogant for a woodcarver.' She doubted if he were a king, but possibly a warrior or a chieftain's son.

'It doesn't matter what I was before,' he said, setting the board aside. The formidable expression on his face warned her not to ask any more questions. 'Only what I am now.'

She reached out to take the bowl and spoon, and a glint of trouble sparked in his eyes. Without realising it, she found herself studying the lean angles of his face, the harsh jaw that cut lines down to a tight mouth.

He disconcerted her, and yet she could not stop staring at him. Her body shivered, growing cold as he answered the gaze with soulless eyes. Quickly, Iseult changed the subject. 'Do you miss your family?'

'I don't think of them any more.' The bitterness in his tone voiced another warning. 'They have their lives, and I have mine.'

She shivered at the utter bleakness of such a life. Without meaning to, her thoughts went back to Aidan. Ever since he had been stolen away, there was an emptiness inside her that could not be filled. She gripped her arms, as if to force the sadness away.

'How did you end up a slave?'

He stopped drawing and set the board aside. 'We've finished for tonight.'

He walked past her and lifted the hide flap in a wordless command to leave. Iseult paused before the door. In that fraction of a second, her gaze drew to his. He was staring at her, as though she had cut off the air to his lungs. Her skin warmed, and when she looked at him, it was as though she had become the slave and he the conqueror.

Without looking back, she stumbled into the night.

Chapter Four

'Kieran!' his brother pleaded. The men dragged Egan to the edge of the wooden palisade and pulled back his brother's neck. With a casual glance to Kieran, they drew the blade across Egan's throat.

His brother never made a sound. A cry tore from Kieran's lungs when the boy's body struck the ground. The raiders never looked back, but stepped over Egan as if he were nothing but an inconvenience.

Kieran sat up from the dream, his hands shaking. Sweat poured over his brow, and he buried his face in his hands. For a moment, he couldn't remember where he was. The early morning light filtered through the crevices below the hide door. He ran his hands through his hair, staggering to his feet.

He went outside, inhaling sharp bursts of air, as if it could expel the nightmare. He'd lived with the memory for several moons now, and he doubted if it would ever leave.

In the cool morning stillness, he saw other slaves and members of the *fudir* tending the fields. He should have been among them. Hard labour was what he deserved, not a chance to do something he loved.

With the wood, he could transform the fibres into something almost alive. Like a god, he shaped and moulded his creations. It wasn't right that he was interested in the work, even if it did involve a beautiful woman.

In the distance, a purple and rose-tinged sunrise emerged from the east. Kieran moved towards an animal trough, dipping his hands in the water and splashing it over his face. Though Davin had kept his word, removing the guards from his doorway, he sensed the others watching him.

One took a few steps forward. With a shaved head and a long red beard, the man had an arrogant swagger to him. 'You, there. Slave,' he called. 'Bring us some water.' The man smirked at his companion, and Kieran's knuckles curled over the trough.

In the past, no man would have dared to command him. But these tribesmen expected him to jump to their orders, like a dog. Slowly, he lifted his gaze to the men and sent them a warning look.

He wasn't in the habit of obedience.

This is your penance, his mind insisted. *Do as they command.*

No. These men weren't his master. They wanted to exert their power over him, demeaning him. Although he would accept whatever tasks Davin gave, he wouldn't let these men gain the upper hand.

Against his better judgement, Kieran turned his back and returned to his hut. No doubt they would run off to Davin and complain. There would be repercussions, but he didn't care. He might choose to endure the slavery for a time, but it didn't mean he would bow down before every man.

He sat down with the door open, allowing the natural light inside. The carving tools rested on the table wrapped in leather, just where he'd laid them. His sketches of Iseult, along with the yew, awaited his attention.

He uncovered the carving tools from the protective leather. His thumb brushed the edge of a knife, judging its sharpness.

The red-bearded man shadowed his doorway, fists clenched. 'I ordered you to bring me water, slave.'

'Did you?' Kieran anticipated the rush of a fight and his hand curved over the hilt of a blade. His own height rivalled the other man's, making him an equal opponent. 'I'm not your slave, am I?'

'Davin will hear of your disobedience,' the man asserted. 'And I've a mind to punish you for it.'

Just try it.

Kieran lifted his knife, his body poised in a defensive position. He might have lost his former strength, but he knew how to wield a blade. 'Will you, now?' Slicing the weapon through the air, he invited, 'Well, then, let's see it.'

A growl emitted from the man's throat, and he charged Kieran, aiming for his wrist. Kieran turned sideways, cutting a thin slash across the man's forearm. Nothing serious, but an insult nevertheless.

Energy pumped through him, and he revelled in the chance to use his former skills. Long ago, he'd been one of the best fighters in their tribe. His muscles remembered how to move, though his body cried out with the pain of it. His opponent picked up the iron cauldron, sloshing its contents at him.

Kieran dodged the splash of vegetables and meat, beginning to enjoy himself. 'Hungry, are you?' He kicked the slab of overcooked mutton towards the man. 'Take what you'd like and get out.'

'I'll make you eat the dirt, first.' Before Kieran could

move, the bearded man seized his wrist and struck the raw wounds on Kieran's back. Pain shot through him, and Kieran was forced to drop the knife. He aimed a kick at the man's groin, twisting to avoid a punch.

'Enough of this,' a man's voice interrupted. Davin strode into the hut, stepping between them. To the red-bearded man, he ordered, 'Cearul, release him.'

Sullen and grim, the man obeyed. Kieran rubbed his wrist, angry that Davin had interfered. He could have finished the fight.

'He refused our orders, Davin,' Cearul claimed. 'He was supposed to bring us water.'

'I have set Kieran a more important task,' Davin said. 'When he has finished with that, then perhaps he can attend to other needs. For now, I would suggest you return to your own duties. The planting is not yet finished, I believe.'

Cearul reddened, and though he glared at Kieran, he nodded. A moment later, he departed.

'I want to see the work you completed last night,' Davin said. All traces of amicability were gone.

'You didn't have to stop the fight.'

'I didn't want you killing any of my men. It might have been a fight to you, but not to them.' Davin crossed his arms, pinning him with a dark glance.

Kieran forced himself to let it go. 'My drawings are there.' He pointed to the board he'd left on the table. 'I'll begin working on the carving this evening.'

Davin lifted the board, revealing nothing of what he thought. 'I'll send her to you again tonight. And I want to see the completed carving within a sennight.'

Kieran supposed it could be done, if he worked every spare minute upon it. But the level of detail he wanted would require painstaking work. He needed more subtle tools than these, gouges with narrow ridges and steeper angles.

'A fortnight would be more reasonable,' he bargained. 'And these tools are not of the best quality.'

'A sennight,' Davin repeated. 'If you are a competent woodcarver, you'll manage even without the tools.' He returned to the doorway. 'I'll order the others to leave you alone, but I'd advise you not to leave the hut without an escort. And if I find that you insult or endanger Iseult in any way, you'll answer to me for it.' He departed, leaving the door open.

Davin's warning was not an idle threat. Kieran suspected the man would have no qualms about killing him, were Iseult threatened. He could respect a man for protecting his betrothed. He'd have done the same once, had anyone bothered Branna.

At the thought of her name, his gut soured. With auburn hair and laughing dark eyes, he well remembered the feel of holding her in his arms. And now Branna embraced her new husband, the way she had once welcomed him.

He forced the vision away and stared down at the drawing he'd done last night. He'd caught Iseult thinking of someone, her face wistful and filled with longing. He'd also drawn her with flashing anger, her eyes sparking hatred. She intrigued him, with her beauty and spirit.

He cleaned up the fallen meat and vegetables, wondering why Iseult had troubled to make a meal for him. No one had done anything like that in a long while. She didn't like him; he could see it in her eyes.

Kieran picked up the yew and began tracing the outline of her face upon the wood. Within moments, he lost himself in the work, cutting out the background with an iron gouge. The scent of freshly cut wood mingled with the morning air, and he took comfort from it. The tools cut into the creamy sapwood, etching out details.

When at last he looked up, it was mid-morning. He saw that someone had left a bag of supplies just outside the door. He found bread inside and tore off a piece, enjoying the taste of the fresh grain.

Near the ringfort entrance, he saw Iseult leading a mare inside. Her face was pale, and her cheeks were wet as though she'd been weeping. Unbidden came the urge to find out what had happened.

It's none of your affair, his conscience warned. But for a woman about to marry, he'd never seen anyone look so unhappy.

Iseult pounded a mass of clay, water spattering all over the brown *léine* she wore. She didn't care. She released tears, digging her fingers into the clay as though she could strangle the unknown men who had taken her son.

'I must speak with you.'

She lifted her gaze and saw Davin standing before her. His sober expression promised nothing but grim news. 'What is it?'

'More raids. Father sent men to scout out what was happening. It may be the Norsemen again.'

Iseult left the fallen mass of clay and reached for a cloth to dry her hands. She supposed she should be frightened, but the stories of the *Lochlannachs* she'd heard seemed more like exaggerated myths, stretched to make a good tale. 'How do you know it's them?'

'We know their ships,' he reminded her. 'And for that reason, I don't want you leaving the ringfort again. Not until we know what's happening.'

Stay here? Iseult dismissed the idea. After her failed

search today, she would have to journey further. 'I'm going to start searching inland,' she said. 'No one has seen Aidan on the peninsula, and it's time to try elsewhere.'

She saw no danger in travelling away from the coast. It might take a few days, but she could bring supplies and speak to the different tribes.

Davin shook his head. 'Only after we've determined it's safe. Wait a few weeks longer, and I'll go with you. After our wedding,' he promised.

Iseult shook her head in denial. 'It's been almost a year, Davin. If I wait too long, I won't know Aidan any more. Even now, I can hardly remember his face.' The familiar pain of loss was a constant ache, mingled with her own guilt for not protecting him well enough.

'I know you'll never forget him,' Davin said, stroking her hair. 'But perhaps it's time to let this go.'

'You're asking me to abandon my son.' The thought was like a blade to her wrists. How could he even think of it?

'It's hurting you, and I don't want to see your pain any more.' His arms moved around her waist, his hands caressing her spine.

She didn't answer him, and he sighed, releasing her. 'One of the ringforts was attacked, near the coast. We need to ensure that the raiders don't come near us.'

'As you say,' she murmured, her voice unable to conceal her frustration.

He touched her cheek. 'Just a few more weeks, Iseult. If you're not ready to give up, we'll continue your search.'

Behind his promise, she sensed his reluctance. Though he would never say it, this was another man's child.

'Until later, then.' The lie fell easily from her mouth, but inwardly she intended to keep searching. She'd wait until

Davin left and travel east, closer to Trá Li. Though she didn't like the idea of going alone, no one else would help her. They, like Davin, believed she should give up.

'Come and dine with my family tonight,' Davin urged.

Iseult dreaded the idea of sharing a meal at the chieftain's table. She avoided it whenever possible, but she could not insult them by refusing.

'You should go and see Kieran now,' Davin said, kissing her. 'Make sure he's begun the carving of you.'

'How do you know he has any skill at all? I've yet to see him lift a blade to wood.' She disliked being the subject of such scrutiny, especially from the slave. He was unpredictable, fierce, and not at all humble.

'You should see this.' Davin reached into a fold of his cloak and withdrew a carved wooden figure of a boy. Iseult held it in her palm, struck by the intricate facial expression. The carved boy held the innocent wonder of early adolescence, coupled with a trace of mischief. When she ran her thumb over the piece, she understood what Davin had seen in it. This was a carving created by a master. 'Was this his brother?' she asked.

'I suspect it might be. He wants it back, and I have promised it to him, in exchange for your likeness. If he completes the dower chest to my satisfaction, I will grant him his freedom.'

She handed the carving back to him. How could a man with such hatred in him create a work of beauty like this? Lost in thought, she was barely aware of Davin's departure.

An hour later, she stood before the woodcarver's hut.

Kieran sensed Iseult's presence before he looked up from his work. The light floral fragrance surrounded her, like a breath of spring. It made him edgy, being around this woman.

At least she was betrothed to his master and was completely beyond reach. He could ignore the unwelcome awareness because of it.

'Davin asked me to come and see that you've begun the carving,' she began, stepping across the threshold without waiting for an invitation.

Of course, she had that right. He was a slave, and she would become his mistress soon enough after she wed Davin. His skin prickled at the invasion of his privacy. He preferred working alone.

He set down the gouge and flicked a glance at her. By the Almighty, she was an exquisite creature. Her light golden hair held the faintest touch of fire. It hung down to her waist, pulled back from her face with a single comb. A smudge of clay clung to her cheek, while upon her wrists he saw the faint traces of mud that she'd tried to scrub away.

In his mind, he envisaged her slender fingers twining the clay into coiled ropes. The vision conjured up an unexpected flush of heat, as he imagined her fingers moving over a man's skin. He didn't know where the thought had come from, but his body reacted to her nearness.

'I've begun the work, yes.' He covered the carving with a cloth, stretching his hands. The initial outline was good, but he hadn't captured her spirit yet. 'Was that all you wanted?'

Maybe she would leave. But no. She sat down upon one of the tree stumps. Crossing her wrists over one knee, she added, 'I don't like being here. But I suppose you'll need to finish your drawings.'

The honesty did not bother him. He preferred a forthright conversation and a woman who spoke her mind. 'I can't say as I like being here either.'

She stared at him, as if questioning whether he was trying

to be funny. Then she dismissed it, asking, 'Did you remember to eat? Or was that too much of an inconvenience?'

'I have the supplies Davin sent.' They were of the lowest quality, the bread heavy and coarse. Nevertheless, he'd eaten the food in solitude.

Picking up the board he'd used the other day, he began sketching her eyes. A deep sea blue, they held such sadness. Haunted, they were. 'I saw you weeping this morn.'

'It's none of your affair.'

True enough. Though women cried often, it wasn't something he liked to see. His sisters often used it to their advantage, weeping whenever they wanted something. They'd known he would relent to their demands.

Seeing Iseult weep was another matter. He sensed that her grief went beyond anything Davin could fix. Or perhaps it was because of Davin.

'We all have our secrets,' he answered in turn. 'Keep yours, if you will.'

Changing to another piece of the board, he drew her mouth. It was symmetric, rather ordinary. Never had he seen it smile, not even around her betrothed.

She straightened, looking even more uncomfortable. 'Will this take very long?'

He set down the charcoal. 'You are free to leave, any time you wish.'

'Unlike you. I know.' She crossed her arms. 'Don't think I haven't considered leaving. But the sooner I get this over with, the less time I have to spend here.'

He kept his attention focused on her mouth, though he gripped the piece of charcoal harder. As he drew and time passed, her lips began to soften.

He'd been wrong. This was not an ordinary mouth. Full and sensual, when she let herself relax, this was a woman any man would want to kiss. Would she taste as good as she smelled?

The piece of charcoal slipped from his fingers. *Stop thinking about her.*

Iseult rested her chin in her palm, her attention upon the glowing hearth, pensive and quiet. He liked the way she felt no need to fill up the silence with chatter.

He sketched more angles of her face and eyes, continually switching the angle of the charcoal to gain a sharper corner. At last, she spoke again.

'Did you truly carve the figure of that boy? Or was that a lie?' Without waiting for a response, she continued, 'I suppose you'd say anything to Davin to get your freedom.'

'I don't lie.' He tossed the charcoal aside, reaching for a different piece. There was no need to argue his skill. The wood itself would offer the evidence.

He heard the sound of liquid pouring, and Iseult brought him a cup of mead, crossing the room to stand beside him. He didn't have time to hide the drawing.

She drank from her own wooden cup, tilting her head to look at it. 'You haven't drawn my face at all.'

He'd sketched four different expressions for her eyes. On another part of the board, he'd drawn her mouth. He wasn't satisfied with the drawing yet, for it had not captured her.

'No. It isn't necessary to draw a complete face.' He accepted the cup and set it down beside him.

'Why not?'

Because he had already memorised it. Because a woman with her beauty would not be easily forgotten.

He drank of the mead, savouring its sweetness. 'Because I'm good at what I do.' Setting the cup aside, he picked up the charcoal again. This time he focused on the curve of her cheek, the softness of her ear.

She leaned in, watching him, and her scent tantalised him again. Sweet with a hint of wildness.

'Show me what you've carved so far.' Her quiet request slid over him like a caress. He knew she meant nothing by it, but the nearness of her made him react.

Críost, he wasn't dead. She would make any man desire her. Her eyes looked upon him with doubts.

'No.' He rarely showed his work to anyone, not until it was finished. They wouldn't understand the patterns and gouges, nor the intricacy, until the end. 'It's only an outline with the background removed.'

'I don't believe you carved that figure.'

She was so close now. He could reach out and touch her, thread his hands through the silk of her hair. See if it looked as soft as he suspected.

'And I don't care what you believe.' He didn't temper his tone. She was trying to provoke him into revealing what he'd carved. He'd not fall into that snare.

'If you're so eager to admire yourself, you'll just have to wait a few days.'

Her lower lip dropped in disbelief. 'You're unbearable.'

He tossed the board aside. It clattered against the side of the hut, startling her with the sudden movement. Unbearable, was he? She had no idea.

He captured her wrist, drawing her forward until she stood before him. 'That's right, *a mhuirnín*. And you'd do well to stay away from me.'

He gave into his desires, tilting her head back to face him. And learned that her hair truly was as soft as he thought it would be.

She stared at him with shock, her mouth drawing his full attention. A few inches further, and he'd have a taste of her forbidden fruit.

He held her there, waiting for her to strike out at him. Cry out for help to the guard she'd brought. But she didn't say a word, just stood there watching him. Only the faint trembling in her hands revealed what she truly felt.

He released her, and Iseult stumbled away from him, pushing her way past the door.

Only after she'd gone, did he realise he was also trembling.

Chapter Five

Iseult hardly spoke during the evening meal. She was still shaken by the slave's sudden move. Her skin had blazed with unwanted heat when he'd cupped her cheek. It had been a warning, not an act of desire. So why had she found it difficult to breathe? Possibly it was just humiliation. She could have Kieran whipped for touching her, if she confessed it.

But she didn't want to be the cause of another's suffering. The slave hadn't truly done any harm, only embarrassed her.

She reached out to her cup, but found it empty. She knew better than to ask Davin's mother Neasa for more wine. Though Iseult was their guest at dinner, Neasa made no secret of her displeasure about the forthcoming marriage. A beautiful older woman, her shining black hair showed no signs of greying, and her figure was the size of a young girl's, despite the three children she'd borne. She smiled up at her son, nodding for a slave to refill his cup.

Davin poured half of his drink into her empty one. Iseult sent him a grateful look. Leaning in, he whispered, 'You look lovely this night.'

Her skin reddened, but she murmured, 'Thank you.'
With her eyes, she sent him a silent plea: *Let me leave. I
want to go home.*

But he didn't seem to see it.

'Will you hunt on the morrow, Davin?' Neasa inquired.

'I will, yes. I intend to take several of the men with me.
I'm wanting a fine feast for my future wife.' He sent Iseult
a proud smile, and she nodded in acknowledgement. The
thought of their wedding brought a wave of nervousness.
She supposed every bride felt that way.

'Much can happen before Bealtaine,' his mother argued.
'There is no need to be married so soon.'

Iseult drained her cup, her hand tightening over the
stem. If Neasa had her way, they'd not be married at all. It
hurt to think that nothing she did was good enough. Never
did the woman cease reminding Iseult that she was the
daughter of a blacksmith and therefore unworthy to wed
Davin.

'It has been longer than I'd like,' Davin replied. 'Perhaps
I'll wed her at sundown tomorrow.' He wrapped his hand
around Iseult's braid in a teasing gesture. Iseult answered
his smile, but inwardly, she was wary. The last time she'd
considered a marriage, it had ended in humiliation. It was
hard to let herself trust a man again.

Her skin chilled at the memory of waiting alone with
the priest, for a lover who never arrived. She'd been
pregnant with his child, and he'd known it. So had
everyone else.

Shame filled her, remembering the way her friends and
family had stared at her. Murtagh had joined a monastery,
rather than wed her. And didn't that offer plenty of gossip for
long winter nights, along with his babe swelling at her waist?

Neasa hadn't forgotten about it; that much was clear.

She believed Iseult was unworthy of wedding a nobleman. Yet Davin had offered for her, treating her as though she were a princess, instead of a commoner. The man loved her, though she did not understand why.

'Davin, you will be chieftain one day soon,' Neasa reminded him. 'There are many responsibilities. Iseult has much to learn before she can be a proper wife.'

'I will be leader only if I am chosen by the people,' he corrected. Though he kept his tone even, Iseult saw the longing upon his face. He wanted to lead the tribe, and all knew there was no other choice but him.

Davin's father Alastar interrupted at that moment. 'Neasa, there's no need to speak of me as if I'm dead. I am chieftain and will be for some time.' Alastar rose and stretched. 'Come, Davin. I would hear your plans for Bealtaine.'

Iseult eyed the doorway with longing, but she hadn't been invited to go with the men. Silently, she helped Neasa clear the plates away.

'Is there anything else I can help you with?' she asked, when she'd finished.

'Yes.' Neasa set down the clay jug of mead and regarded her. 'You could refuse to wed my son, but I know you won't do it. You're too eager to wed a man of his rank.'

Iseult's temper flared. The woman made her sound greedy, as though she were wedding Davin for his gold. 'Davin is a good man. I intend to give him my respect and care.' She bit her lip to keep from saying more.

'He deserves a woman who understands how to be chaste. You've borne a child.'

'A child who was stolen from me,' Iseult argued. 'You, at least, have your son standing before you. I know not whether mine lives or is dead.'

The wrenching pain strangled her heart, and tears

swam in her eyes. Davin's quiet presence had been a balm to her bleeding soul when she'd lost her son Aidan. He had comforted her in her grief, treating her with such tenderness, such love.

'You understand a mother's love for her child,' Neasa said, though her voice was a sharp blade. 'And you know that I want what is best for him.' She wiped her hands upon a drying cloth and added, 'You could not possibly understand what it means to lead our people.'

Neasa was wrong. Though she might not be one of them, never did she fear the responsibilities that would become hers. Her only thoughts were to take care of Davin and to build a home with him.

'I may not be a chieftain's daughter,' she acknowledged, 'but I will do what is necessary to make Davin happy.'

Neasa shook her head. 'It's not enough.'

Iseult had endured her fill of the woman's criticism. She walked quietly to the door and opened it. 'It will have to be.'

She stepped outside into the cool darkness. Neither Davin nor Alastar was nearby, and she suspected they'd gone for a walk. Though courtesy dictated that she say goodnight to her betrothed, she continued walking towards Muirne's hut.

What was she going to do when she was expected to live with Davin's family? They would have to build a hut of their own, else she'd go mad. His mother would do everything in her power to undermine their marriage.

Iseult walked faster, releasing her anger with each step. Sometimes she wished Davin were not the chieftain's son. She wanted a simple life, one where they could live in peace. Perhaps with children surrounding them. And Aidan, safely home again.

Above her, the moon hid behind clouds, and Iseult

walked past Muirne's hut, needing a quiet moment alone. She passed the gates of the ringfort, until she could no longer see the flicker of torches.

Sinking down into the damp spring grass, she calmed herself. The fertile scent of the land granted her peace.

'You shouldn't be out here alone,' a voice said. She turned towards the sound and saw Kieran. He drew nearer, his profile shadowed by the light behind him. His black hair fell against his face, and he crossed his arms. Rough and wild, the locks cut against his cheeks, badly in need of taming. Though he said nothing, he kept watching her.

Iseult pulled her knees against her chest, suddenly uneasy. Not a guard was in sight, and outside the ringfort, no one would see them.

'I wanted to be alone. And I'm fine, as you can see.'

Again, he remained silent. His arrogance reminded her that this man knew not the meaning of humility or servitude. Unlike Davin's other slaves, he did not hide back in the shadows, nor keep his face averted.

Uncomfortable, she rose to her feet. 'You aren't going to leave, are you?'

'No.'

'Are you planning to try another escape?' It wouldn't surprise her if he did. She wanted to see him go, to be rid of this anxious feeling that happened each time she was near him.

'Not yet.' He was biding his time, feigning obedience. Couldn't Davin see this man for who he truly was?

Kieran continued walking towards her, moving as though he owned this land. As if he owned her.

It made her anger rise higher. If she wanted to take a walk, then she'd do it. She needed no escort.

Rising to her feet, she walked further until she was near the forest. It was as far as she dared travel.

Kieran shadowed her, keeping a slight distance back. But she knew that no matter how far she went, he would follow. His head turned as if watching the surrounding areas for danger.

But the only danger she felt was from him.

'I don't need a guard.'

'Yes, you do.' His voice resonated in the stillness, deep and commanding.

'It's not your responsibility to watch over me.'

Against the backlight of the torches, his silhouette merged with the darkness. Though his skin still held the sharp lines of hunger, she could not deny the strength in him. And beyond his unreadable expression lay such emptiness, it almost mirrored her own.

'Perhaps not.' His gaze lingered upon her face, as though he were trying to forge it into his memory.

The need to move away from him was so strong, she circled around, walking back to the ringfort. The hair on the back of her neck rose up in full awareness of Kieran. Though she didn't turn to see him, she sensed his presence.

Once they were back inside the safety of the palisade, she glanced around. Before him, she felt exposed, as though he could look into her soul and see the vulnerability there.

'Goodnight.' Kieran turned abruptly to leave, and yet Iseult couldn't bring herself to open the door. Her heartbeat hammered within her chest, and her skin warmed. Though there was no reason to be afraid of him, she couldn't help but feel something. Slave or not, he intimidated her.

And Davin expected her to spend time alone with this man each day? She couldn't do it.

Only a few days more, logic reminded her. It would not take that long to finish the carving. And when it was done, she would not see him again.

Davin Ó Falvey woke at dawn, staring at the empty space beside him in the bed. His chamber within his father's house boasted of wealth. Only the softest fabrics covered his bed, and polished tortoiseshell shields decorated the walls. He had everything a man could want: gold, fine clothing, and the promise of becoming chieftain. And yet it was nothing without Iseult to share it.

He loved her deeply and could think of no greater joy than waking beside her. Never had he seen a more beautiful or perfect woman. Though his mother argued about her lack of social status, none of that mattered. In a few more weeks, Iseult would belong to him.

He pulled on clothes suitable for hunting and chose a bow and arrows. He wanted to provide for her, to show her how very much he cared. And perhaps one day she would return his love.

Oh, he knew she didn't feel the same way for him. Not yet. God help him, every time he thought of the man she'd lain with, he wanted to gut Murtagh Ó Neill for touching her. And for breaking her heart.

Outside, he ordered a horse brought to him. When a servant returned with his gelding Lir, Davin stopped to study the slave's face. Unlike Kieran, this slave kept to himself, his head lowered in subservience. He couldn't even remember the slave's name.

Not so with Kieran Ó Brannon. Fierce and self-confident, Kieran bore his wounds with the carelessness of a warrior.

What sort of man was he? Davin had lived among servants and slaves for so long, he hardly noticed them. But

Kieran Ó Brannon brought attention to himself in a manner that made him hardly fit to be a slave. It made Davin even more curious about the man's past.

Kieran's carving skills were startling, a master's work. He far surpassed Seamus's creations. How had a man with such talent come to be a slave? He couldn't understand it.

He stopped in front of Seamus's hut and peered inside. Kieran sat upon a bench, tapping a chisel with a wooden mallet. He remained fully focused upon the task, and it wasn't until Davin blocked the sunlight that he looked up.

'I haven't finished yet.'

'I realise that. I'd like to see what you've done.'

Kieran set aside his chisel with reluctance. Davin stepped closer and set his bow down, taking the carving in his hands. The face of his beloved had started to emerge from the wood. Iseult's haunted eyes, the long hair that caressed the curve of her cheek…all of it was there. Except her smile.

Davin handed the wood back. 'It's a fine piece of work.' Stepping to the side, he let the light back into the hut. 'My men are hunting this morning. I want you to join us.'

'I must finish this,' Kieran argued. He picked up a bowl of melted animal fat and a leather cloth. With experienced motions, he rubbed the fat into the wood, bringing out the natural grains. It would prevent the carving from cracking.

'It wasn't a request.' Davin picked up his bow. 'I'll supply you with weapons. Meet us at the gate in an hour.'

Davin didn't care whether his slave wanted to go or not. He had his suspicions about the man's origins, and he hoped to get those answers this day.

Iseult rode hard to the east, leaning into the wind. After a bit of coaxing, her friend Niamh had agreed to accompany her. The two had known each other only since the past winter, and Niamh had become a close confidant. Though Niamh bemoaned her brown hair and grey eyes, claiming that no man would ever find her beautiful, Iseult secretly thought her friend had a nice smile. She also had a sense of adventure and a tendency to get into trouble, rather like herself.

'Are we nearly there?' Niamh asked, slowing the pace to let her horse drink from the river. The silvery ribbon cut a path eastwards, glittering against the meadows. 'We've been gone for hours. If I have to sit on this horse for another hour, my bottom will fall off.'

Mine, too, Iseult thought, but she didn't say so. 'If Hagen was right, it should be at the end of the river's curve.'

'Or if he's wrong, we've come all this way for nothing.'

Iseult shrugged. 'One more hour. And if we don't find the *rath*, we'll try again another day.'

Niamh gritted her teeth. 'Give me a moment, won't you? I haven't any feeling left in my backside.' She winced and patted her posterior. 'I'm surprised you didn't bring Davin with you instead of me.' The young woman grimaced at the mention of his name. It didn't surprise Iseult, since she knew her friend couldn't stand Davin. Niamh made every effort to avoid him, claiming that he was far too arrogant for her tastes.

'He had other responsibilities,' Iseult responded.

'More important than your child?' Niamh scowled at the idea. 'I'd like to know how hunting deer would be more important.'

Iseult shielded her eyes against the sun, straining to see the ringfort. 'I didn't tell him where we went.'

Niamh looked appalled at her confession. 'Why not?'

Because Davin had already given up. He no longer believed in her quest. 'Because he didn't want me leaving

Lismanagh. He is worried about the *Lochlannachs*,' she added. That sounded convincing enough, didn't it?

'And so am I.' Niamh shivered, eyeing the horizon. With a grudging shrug, she offered, 'I think Davin was right. The Norsemen are fearsome, so I've heard.'

'I've never seen one, so I wouldn't know.' But the memory of Kieran flashed through her mind. Raw and wild, he unnerved her, stripping away her sense of security. She wanted nothing to do with him, particularly a man so unpredictable.

'Iseult?' Niamh eyed her as though she'd been speaking and had received no answer.

She shook off the disorientation. 'I'm fine.' Forcing a smile, she added, 'I'm glad not to travel alone. Thank you for coming with me.'

'My father would have my head if I'd told him what I was doing. We should have brought the men with us.'

'And who would have come?' Iseult couldn't think of a single man who might have acted as their protector. 'They think I've gone mad.'

Niamh shrugged. 'You're right, I suppose. But we must return before sundown. Else Davin will send out every able-bodied man in the tribe after you.' She opened a clay flask of mead and drank, handing it to Iseult.

'It won't be much further.' Iseult drank and shielded her eyes, studying the landscape. 'Look atop the hill. I think I can see the *rath*.'

'Have you ever visited the Flannigan tribe?' Niamh asked. 'I've heard that they have nearly a hundred men and women. Several clans joined together, from what I gather, which makes them quite powerful.'

She hadn't known. But it increased the possibility of learning more about Aidan. 'No. But I've tried everywhere else. I have to go inland.' Thus far, today's journey was the longest she'd ever taken.

Though it was dangerous, she kept the vision of Aidan's face within her memory. Her son's serious blue eyes had always absorbed his surroundings. On the rare occasion of his laughter, Iseult had smothered him with kisses. The last time she'd seen him, he had not yet begun to walk. His tiny fingers had clung to hers while he struggled to march his bare feet.

I'll find you, she promised. *Somehow.* If it meant travelling to the ends of the earth, she had no other choice. She only wished Davin shared in her determination. To him, Aidan was a lost babe. To her, the child was a missing piece of her heart. She could never be whole until she knew what had happened to him.

Niamh pressed a hand to Iseult's shoulder. 'And if you don't find him? What will you do?'

'I don't know. Travel further, I suppose.' She took another drink, not wanting to think about giving up.

They rode side by side, and with each mile, Iseult's skin chilled. Her doubts taunted her: *You won't find him. He's dead.*

When they reached the gates, Iseult's hands began shaking. Dread welled up inside her as she steeled herself for more disappointment. Two fierce-looking men stood at the entrance, spears in their hands. They regarded her with suspicion.

'We wish to speak with your chieftain,' she began, her voice revealing her fear. 'I am Iseult MacFergus, and this is my friend Niamh.'

'Brian Flannigan is our king, not a chieftain,' the shorter guard corrected. 'Is he expecting you?'

Iseult shook her head. 'No. But I've some questions to ask him about my son.'

The man shrugged. 'I'll see if he will grant you an audience.' Iseult waited beside Niamh, her nerves growing more ragged with each moment.

This was not a wise decision. She was grasping at sand, the granules of hope slipping from her fingertips. There was no means of visiting every tribe in Ireland, and even then she might not find Aidan. After today, she would have to alter her strategy. Never would she find her son this way, with desperate searches.

After endlessly long minutes, the guard returned. 'Come.' He beckoned, and they followed the guard to a large dwelling at the opposite end of the ringfort. Built of wood, and twice the size of Davin's home, she understood what Niamh had meant about the tribe's power.

Inside, several groups of men gathered. Iseult hung back beside Niamh, fully aware of the men watching them. Her skin rose up with goose flesh, and she wished she had not endangered her friend. Now she understood why Davin had not wanted her to travel alone. These men could harm her, and there was nothing she could do.

Too late to let her fears strangle her now. Iseult lifted her face, trying to look braver than she felt.

She waited for a time until at last the king ordered them to come forward. Iseult knelt before him and explained about Aidan's disappearance.

'I have been searching for him over the past year. I would know if anyone from your tribe has seen a young boy, about two years of age, who was not born to your people.'

The king considered her story. 'Why did your husband not come with you?'

'I have no husband. But I did not come alone,' she

added. When the king's gaze turned shrewd, she drew closer to Niamh as if to gain support.

King Brian conferred with some of his advisers, then shook his head. 'We have many foster-children, but their families are known to us. If your son was stolen, it is likely he was taken into slavery. If he is still alive, that is. You might wish to ask the traders.'

With a nod, he dismissed them.

Though Niamh took her hand, Iseult barely felt the contact as they walked out. She knew of many children sold into slavery, but most were born of the *fudir*.

Not once had she visited a slave auction. The idea of hearing the children separated from their mothers, people's lives given over into servitude, bothered her intensely. Though Davin had never treated his slaves with anything but kindness, she'd rather have no servants at all.

'Let's go home,' Niamh urged, leading her to their horses. Iseult mounted, though she was hardly aware of them leaving. Another failed chance. And now, the possibility of her son being a slave. He might be a world apart from her now, for she'd heard that the trade ships, particularly Norse longboats, often sold Irish slaves across the sea.

A light rain fell over them, but Iseult hardly noticed. Kieran had been to the slave markets. He'd travelled across Éireann. Would he have any answers for her?

Her mind flashed to the moment when his hand had touched her hair. Kieran had warned her to stay away from him, and not once had he spoken about his past.

Why would she ever think he would help her? He was a stranger, and she didn't want to confide in him or expose herself in that way. He was the sort of man to take advantage of weakness.

But there was nothing else to be done. He was the only man with possible answers.

She had no choice but to ask for Kieran's help.

Chapter Six

'You wouldn't have come if I hadn't ordered it, would you?' Davin asked.

Kieran strode behind Davin's gelding. 'I wouldn't, no.' He resented the time away from his work. In another two days he'd have the carving completed. He planned to smooth out the wood with sand until it was polished like the softness of a woman's cheek. Then he would rub the surface with butter until the natural beauty of the yew emerged, along with Iseult's face.

Remembrance tightened inside him like a curled fist. He should never have touched her. He'd meant to frighten Iseult away, but instead the encounter had shaken him. Something unexpected had flashed between them, and he didn't want to know what it was. She was hauntingly beautiful, a woman etched into his mind like a blade into yew.

Forbidden.

He forced his mind back onto the hunting party. Without a mount of his own, he had to run lightly to keep up with their horses. Miles passed, and his muscles burned from weakness. Nonetheless, he'd not give up, not even if he collapsed to the ground. There was a sense of rightness, pushing his body to the limit. Regaining his strength and endurance, past all boundaries.

He ran alongside the horses, pain rippling through him. The lash wounds burned upon his back, but he kept on until his mind overpowered the weakness of his body.

When he inhaled the crisp air, he felt it renewing him. Life. Rebirth. The wind rushed against his ears like the whisper of his brother's voice. As though Egan were with him still.

The loss inside numbed him. His younger brother had embraced each moment of every day. And he wouldn't have wanted Kieran to surrender to death. It was too easy— a coward's path.

No. He would live after enduring this penance. Thirteen weeks, he decided. One for each year of his brother's life. He cared naught about Davin's promises of freedom. When the time came, he would seize his own fate.

Kieran studied the landscape, noting the location of water and familiarising himself with the territory. By Lughnasa, he would have his strength back and could make an escape without being found. He would learn where the tribesmen kept their weapons and supplies.

They travelled through the valley towards another forest. The flat meadows stretched into a wooded glen. After a time, Davin slowed his horse's pace. 'Did the traders starve you before they brought you here?'

'I had little desire to eat.' He'd tried to refuse, but as punishment, they had threatened to beat a small girl in front of him. *'If you do not eat, she will pay the price,'* his master had claimed. Though his stubborn body rebelled against the food, Kieran had choked down stale bread and water. He'd understood, then, that he held value for these men. And he cursed himself, for he had no power to set the girl free.

'I've sent provisions to you,' Davin said. 'I expect you to use them. I've no use for a weakened slave.'

Kieran's knuckles clenched in response to the accusation of weakness. Words of denial formed, but he held them back. Davin spoke the truth. He was nothing but a weakened slave. Nothing but a broken-down shadow of the warrior he'd once been.

But that would all change. He let his anger wash over him, accepting the punishment.

'Have you nothing to say?' Davin prompted.

'I received the food.' He lifted his face to meet his master's discerning gaze. No promises did he make, nor words of gratitude.

Davin's hand moved to the sword hanging at his side. A silent threat, but one Kieran recognised.

'You were a fighter once,' his master predicted. 'No *fudir* would behave with such pride.'

When Kieran made no denial, Davin grunted. 'I suspected as much.' With a hand, he gestured for Kieran to join the others. 'You'll be with us for some time,' he said. 'You should get acquainted with the other men in our ringfort.'

'There is no need for them to know me, nor I them.' Kieran kept his gaze upon the forest ahead. 'I am a slave. Nothing more.'

And in thirteen weeks, he would be gone from this place.

Davin stopped his horse and dismounted. 'You may earn back your freedom, if you complete the dower chest to my satisfaction. We have need of a woodcarver.'

Kieran kept his face veiled of any reaction. He wanted no part of it. These men were not his tribesmen. He crossed his arms. 'What are your orders?'

Davin's hands moved to a knife at his waist. He un-sheathed it, and offered it to Kieran hilt first. A gesture of trust, granting a weapon to a slave.

'You're going to clean all of the game we hunt and bring it back to the ringfort,' he said.

Kieran tucked the knife away at his waist. He led Davin's gelding away, welcoming the chance to be alone while his master joined the others. The men continued onwards into the forest while he waited along the peri-meter.

After an hour, he wandered a short way into the woods and set up snares near a small stream. Then he returned to the horses and took a moment to inspect his surroundings.

The land on the peninsula was magnificent, with forests covering the hills. Mountains, yellow with wild gorse, cast a craggy backdrop to a fierce blue sea.

He wondered if Davin had brought Iseult to a place such as this. The wild beauty of the land brought him a sense of peace.

And she'd been seeking that last night, hadn't she? Wan-dering into the darkness, away from everyone else. The anguish on her face had startled him. What troubled her so?

He'd followed her, intending to keep his distance. He'd wanted to guard her, to protect her from whatever was bothering her.

She didn't like him, and he hadn't been kind to her. And the truth was, being around Iseult discomfited him. She was the sort of woman every man dreamed of being with. Exquisitely beautiful, in a natural way that took no effort.

He'd learned not to trust women like her. They never meant what they said. With a few words, they could twist a man's will-power into dust.

Tonight she would come to him again, while he carved her image into wood. He swore on Egan's life that he wouldn't touch her. Wouldn't let his body or mind dwell upon illicit desire. He still possessed honour, though he might have lost everything else.

When the sun rose higher, Kieran entered the forest to check his snares and found two trapped rabbits. With Davin's knife he cleaned them, leaving the skin on and tying up the carcasses. Kieran tucked them into a pouch at his waist before returning to the horses. He ran his hands across the gelding's back, speaking softly to the animal.

When the men came back empty-handed, although Davin remarked upon the rabbits Kieran had caught, he did not ask him to surrender them for the noon meal. Instead, the hunters partook of dried meat and bread, before moving further west.

In the late afternoon, they reached another dense forest, several miles from the ringfort. They kept the horses on the outskirts, tethering the reins to keep the animals safe. This time, Davin beckoned for Kieran to accompany them. Oak and pine trees grew closely together, while dark green moss and ferns carpeted the forest ground. Faded sunlight streamed through the canopy, and the earth smelled of the rain that afternoon. Kieran noted the different woods, birch and hazel, ash and poplar. There might come a time when he would need them.

'Mind yourself, slave.' Cearul moved in front of him, directly behind Davin, keeping his knife drawn. Sunlight gleamed upon his shaved head, and his eyes remained alert. Kieran didn't fool himself into thinking the weapon was meant for hunting. The red-bearded man intended to exert his dominance.

The others spoke to one another as if Kieran weren't there, looking to Davin for leadership. It was a strange feeling, though not entirely unwelcome. So many times within his own tribe, he had shouldered the responsibility for making the decisions. And there were so many choices he wished he could take back.

One of the men was younger than the others, a lad barely past eight and ten, if he'd guessed accurately. Kieran waited until the others had passed, then fell behind the young man. Orin, the others had called him. His dark gold hair was ragged against his neck, as if he'd cut it with a dagger instead of letting it grow. A thin beard covered his cheeks, and the lad had an eager stride, as though he'd only just been allowed to come with the men.

Orin's mannerisms reminded him of what his brother Egan might have done, if he'd lived to be a man. He lowered his head, offering a silent prayer for his brother's soul before forcing his mind back on the hunt.

Kieran knelt, studying the ground for signs of animal tracks. He sniffed the air and froze his movement.

There. A few yards away, he spied what they'd been looking for. He crept forward and tapped Orin on the back, gesturing for silence. He pointed through the clearing and a young buck raised its head. The reddish coat stood out against the greenery, and small knobby points rested upon a new growth of antlers.

Orin lifted his bow, and Kieran held his breath, waiting for him to make the shot. The bowstring grew taut, then a smooth twang sang out from the weapon. The arrow pierced the buck in the stomach, but it was not a fatal kill. Kieran cursed as the animal took off in the opposite direction. He ran after the deer, his legs burning as he tried to overtake the animal. Almost there…

He closed in, while the deer's wounds slowed it down. Dimly, he heard a shout behind him. As Kieran unsheathed his knife, preparing to strike, a low growl sounded from the brush. He ignored it and dove at the deer. He pulled the animal down and ended its life.

The snarling increased, and Kieran kept the blade ready. A lone female wolf hung back, her ribs visible through her grey fur. Seeing the animal's hunger, he stilled, understanding that she had been tracking the deer as well. He paused, not wanting to surrender venison to the predator. Instead, he tossed one of the rabbits to her. The wolf dove upon the rabbit, tearing at the meat.

Kieran stared at her wild hunger, recognising a part of himself in her desperation. He'd known that savagery before, of the instincts that barely separated man and beast. And, gods above, he knew what it was to be that hungry.

A hunter raised his bow to kill the wolf, but Davin stopped him. 'Let her eat.' To Kieran, he ordered, 'Take the deer and bring it back to the horses. We have what we came for.' He said nothing about the meat Kieran had fed the wolf, but each man kept his eye upon the beast. The female wolf backed away, until she disappeared in the thicket.

The men seemed to breathe easier when she'd gone. 'You should have killed her,' Cearul insisted.

'She's no threat to us.' Davin mounted his horse and added, 'She's alone, abandoned by her pack. I'd be surprised if she survives the spring.'

'If she's nursing pups, they could threaten our livestock.' Cearul glared at Kieran, as though he blamed him for Davin's mercy. 'And that was a waste of good meat.'

'It was his kill,' Orin argued. The young man's face coloured, as though he'd startled himself by speaking. 'And his right to give it as he pleased.'

'The meat belongs to his master. Slaves own nothing.' Cearul looked to Davin for confirmation.

At that, Kieran lifted the deer over his shoulders, the weight bearing into his wounds. He didn't care about their petty arguments, especially not from men trying to gain status. He held no regrets for what he'd done.

Gritting his teeth, he carried the deer back to the horses. A light rain began to fall, spattering his tunic and skin. When he reached the edge of the clearing, he finished gutting the animal. Though he had slaughtered his share of game over the years, the sight of blood sobered him. Dark memories of his brother invaded with each slice of the blade. He swallowed hard, steeling himself for the task. Afterwards, he tied the hind legs to the animal's neck to prevent dirt from filling up the inner cavity.

Orin offered to help, but he refused. This was his duty and he'd not let weakness overcome him. Twilight had begun to overtake the day, and he felt the weariness creeping in.

Blood covered his hands, and he returned to a stream he'd seen earlier inside the forest. He dipped his hands in the icy water, washing the red stains off his face and hands. Then he returned to hoist the deer carcass over his shoulders.

'I'm sorry I missed the shot,' a voice spoke from behind him. Kieran saw Orin standing, his bow slung over his shoulder.

'It happens. But you slowed him down for me.' Kieran tried to offer a note of encouragement.

Orin nodded, raking a hand through his gold hair. 'You—you did well today. We'd have had nothing if you hadn't come.'

Kieran realised that the young man was trying to extend friendship towards him. It wouldn't be wise, for his status would only bring Orin down. He didn't want the lad shunned for interacting with him. Instead of continuing the conversation, he gave a nod and turned away.

The other men rode beyond him, their spirits merry. Orin continued to lag behind on his own mount, as if hoping Kieran would speak to him. In time, the young man sensed his desire not to talk and let him be.

Kieran trudged across the meadow, letting his mind imagine the wood carving of Iseult. The drawings gave the accurate shape, but not the emotion. That was the true challenge to him, bringing a face alive by revealing personality instead of mere appearance. He'd captured her eyes, but not her mouth.

It might be that Davin would want her smiling, but Iseult looked as though she hadn't been happy in a long time.

Had Branna been like Iseult, promised to him but unhappy? He'd never know why she had turned against him, opening her arms to another man.

Bitterness filled him, for he knew just what it was to love someone who didn't love you back.

When they reached the ringfort, his feet ached along with his back. Kieran didn't relish the idea of skinning the game, nor cutting the deer and rabbit into strips of meat. The life of a slave, he reminded himself. He would have to perform the tasks that others did not wish to do.

He lifted the deer over his shoulders again and took it to the slaughtering pit. A wooden table was set out over a low stone trench, allowing any remaining blood to pass away from the work area.

He worked on the rabbit first, distancing himself from the task as best he could. Orin rejoined him, unsheathing his own knife. 'I'll cut the meat,' he offered.

'I can manage.' Kieran nodded his head towards the others. 'You should join the other men.'

Orin grimaced. 'They haven't much to say to me. I'd rather be of use here.' Without waiting for a reply, he took out a knife and quartered the meat. 'Go ahead and start on the deer. I'll help you balance it over the trench.'

Kieran hesitated, but lifted the deer into position. Orin helped him, and together they finished butchering it.

It was then that he saw Iseult returning, another woman at her side. Their horses' flanks glistened with sweat, and both women looked as though they'd been caught in the rain. They also appeared guilty, as though they weren't supposed to be out alone.

Iseult handed her horse to one of the younger boys and stopped when she saw them. For a moment, she looked torn, as if deciding whether to speak to him. She lowered her mantle, and strands of wet hair framed her delicate face. Her skin appeared soft, like a woman who had just emerged from a bath. The folds of her *léine* moulded to her legs, her slender body like a young sapling. She took another step forwards and his traitorous body responded.

Don't. He shot her a warning look, not to come any further. She should know better than to speak to a man like him. He didn't care what she wanted to say. Whatever it was, he couldn't help her. Wouldn't help her.

Deliberately he turned his attention back to the meat, though he was fully aware of her. She moved towards Davin's hut, and he breathed easier when she was gone. It was better this way.

He hoped she wouldn't return this night. He didn't need her to finish the carving. When he was around her, he seemed to become a different man. Guided by instinct instead of honour.

Stay far away from her, he warned himself.

He dipped his hands into an animal trough to rinse away the blood after they finished butchering the meat. Some would be salted and smoked to preserve it, while he expected Davin would want some of the fresh venison at his table this night.

'I think we've finished,' Orin said, setting his knife aside. 'Dine with us,' he offered. 'My foster-father will want to hear the story of the hunt.'

Kieran shook his head. 'I am a slave, not one of you. It isn't my place.'

'Davin won't mind,' Orin insisted. 'He asked me to invite you.'

'Asked or commanded?' Kieran cleaned his blade and sheathed it.

Orin gave a feeble smile. 'Is there a difference? Come. Davin will be expecting us.'

'I haven't finished preserving the meat.' It was his last argument. They could not leave it out, else it would spoil.

'Bring it down into the storage cairns. The ground is still frozen in places, and it will keep until the morning. I'll show you.' Orin picked up two of the baskets, while Kieran took the remaining two. The young man led him inside one of the small huts, and Kieran descended a ladder into the storage chamber. Orin passed him the baskets one by one, and then he descended the ladder to show him where to keep the meat.

The air temperature was brisk, and the stones lining the walls kept it even cooler. Kieran set down the baskets, and Orin brought a piece of leather to wrap up several pounds of venison. 'We'll bring this to my foster-mother.'

With no other choice, Kieran followed the young man.

He hadn't guessed the connection between Davin and Orin, and it meant that Orin was younger than he supposed. Most young men finished their fostering at the age of seventeen.

As they passed his tiny hut, Kieran wished he could avoid spending time in Davin's home. He preferred his privacy and had no wish to speak with anyone. Nor did he want anyone prying into his past.

He followed behind Orin, pretending that he didn't see the eyes of the villagers watching them with interest. Kieran's defences rose up, his hands curling into fists. It was as though an invisible chain jerked him by the neck, dragging him towards his unwanted master.

Soon enough, he and Orin stood at the entrance. The young lad opened the door, and gestured for him to go inside.

'I brought Kieran to share our meal, Neasa,' Orin explained, handing her the leather-wrapped venison. A tall woman with dark hair, Neasa Ó Falvey wore a costly cream-coloured *léine* and violet overdress. Distaste lined her eyes when she saw Kieran.

'Slaves do not share a meal with the *flaiths*,' Neasa corrected. 'But he may serve our table this night.' She nodded to Kieran and pointed him towards the other slaves. 'Prepare the meal with the others and see to the guests.'

Kieran let no trace of emotion show upon his face. He'd expected this. Why Orin had thought it would be any different, he didn't know. Status meant everything to a chieftain's wife.

He tensed, looking for a way to leave. All he needed was to follow another man who was working outside. His eyes scanned the interior for an opportunity.

'Kieran is my guest,' Orin argued. 'If it were not for him, we would have no meat at all.'

Neasa cast him a sympathetic look. 'The man knows his

place, even if you do not. Now go and help your foster-brother.' Her firm tone offered him no chance to resist.

Orin's face fell. 'I'm sorry, Kieran.'

He shook his head, as if it were no matter. While he joined the other slaves, he watched the entrance, waiting for the right moment. Some of the men lifted furnishings into the room while the female slaves worked to prepare the food.

A maiden struggled to open a sealed clay container, muttering beneath her breath, 'I ought to bash you open.'

Kieran slid into the shadows, hoping to escape her notice. His luck failed him, for her gaze snapped upon him.

'I know you. You're Davin's new slave.'

He gave a faint nod. He recognised her as the woman who had travelled with Iseult. With damp brown hair and a softly rounded figure, she was fair enough in appearance. He took the container from her, loosening the wax that sealed it.

'She doesn't like you.'

'I know it.' He handed back the container, prepared to continue his escape.

'Wait.' The woman blocked his way. 'I saw her weeping after she left the carver's hut the other night. What did you do to her?'

'I never—' *Touched her*, he almost said. But that was a lie. He stiffened, not wanting to defend himself to Iseult's companion. He held his silence, giving her his most intimidating stare.

She tilted her chin up. 'Mind yourself, slave. She is my friend, and I won't have you bothering her.' The woman kept her eyes firmly upon him, completely disrupting his plans to get away. No doubt she would alert the entire household, were he to try it.

Though he had resigned himself to his servitude, it was

harder than he'd expected. He was accustomed to giving commands, not receiving them.

'Fill this with water,' one of the older servants directed him, pushing an iron pot into his hands. Kieran nearly dropped it, but caught the chieftain's wife watching him. She, too, expected him to disobey.

Instead, he stared back at her, willing her to look away. Her mouth tightened, showing her discomfort. No man would truly command him; he had chosen this act of contrition. The other slaves seemed to sense it, for they moved away from him when he walked outside for the water. Conversations dimmed, drawing even more attention.

Kieran returned with a full pot, hanging it over the hearth. No one said anything more, though one of the female slaves offered him a timid smile. At his dark look, she scuttled away and tended to the food. The others avoided him.

From that moment, he took the more strenuous tasks as his own. He moved among them, lifting stacks of peat and wishing he'd never accompanied Orin. Else he could have been back in the carver's hut, finishing the image of Iseult.

After another hour, his shoulder ached from the continuous strain. Lifting the deer earlier, coupled with these tasks, made him aware that his wounds hadn't healed. He kept his discomfort to himself, not letting anyone see the weakness.

As time passed, the rich aroma of venison filled the small space, and his mouth watered. The slaves revealed other dishes: puddings seasoned with onions and salt, roasted pork and oatmeal cakes studded with fresh currants. He couldn't remember the last time he'd eaten foods like these. Though he knew he would not sit at their tables, at least he might have portions of the food. It gave him something to look forward to.

When at last more people began to arrive, Neasa called him over. 'Slave, you will bathe the feet of our guests.'

Kieran stopped short, taken aback. Though he knew it was a task often given over to the *fudir*, his mind rebelled against it. The chieftain's wife meant to demean him, to remind him of his place. He hadn't cared before, but of a sudden, his skin warmed with embarrassment. The idea of kneeling before the others, humbling himself in such a way, made him grind his teeth.

He should simply walk out. Let another slave complete the task. One of the other slaves tried to hand him a basin of water and a linen cloth. Kieran ignored the man, taking a step towards the door.

He didn't care about the punishment. But before he could leave, the door opened.

Davin entered the hut, holding hands with Iseult. She had changed her gown since he'd last seen her and had pulled part of her hair away from her face, leaving the rest to dry upon her shoulders. The reddish-gold mass offered a striking contrast to the emerald *léine* and matching overdress. Her cheeks glowed, as if she'd scrubbed them clean. But then her expression drew taut when she saw him. She believed he was nothing more than a slave, a man beneath her notice.

The two of them sat down upon a bench, and, before he realised it, he was holding the heavy wooden basin. For a moment he considered dropping it, letting the water spill over the earthen floor.

He found himself staring at Iseult. She didn't acknowledge him, giving her full attention to Davin. And yet he noticed the faint blush upon her cheeks.

Though he didn't know why, he was tempted to provoke her. He wanted to see those rich blue eyes widen when he touched her bare feet.

He washed Davin's feet without looking at the man, a perfunctory gesture. Davin took the linen cloth and dried his own feet, walking over to greet his parents.

Kieran waited a moment, looking into Iseult's face. She kept her gaze averted, though he knew she was aware of him. As angry as she'd been the last time they spoke, he imagined she wouldn't hesitate to kick water into his face.

'What are you doing here?' she whispered furiously, between her teeth.

He lifted her ankle into the basin. 'Obeying my commands.'

His hand curved around the bare skin, his thumb upon the most sensitive part of her ankle. Iseult pretended not to notice, but he saw the goose flesh rising upon her skin.

'Aren't you supposed to be working on the carving?' Not once would she look at him.

He took the sole of her foot and scooped warm water on to her bare skin. His callused palms felt rough against her softness, and he ran his thumb over the sensitive arch. She reddened, but said nothing. When his hands moved up to her calves, she inhaled sharply, as though he'd touched her intimately.

'The carving was only one of my duties.' He took his time with the other foot, bathing the dust from her bare feet, massaging them gently.

'Don't do this,' she murmured. He glanced up at her face, and she tried to hide a shiver. His own breath felt shaky. This had been a game to him, but right now the rules had changed. Her vulnerability cast a spell over him, until he wanted to drag her forwards, kissing her and stripping her bare.

Wasn't this what Branna had done to him, betraying him with another man? What was he doing, caressing Iseult's skin the way a lover might?

He'd never let himself fall into that trap, no matter how beautiful she was. Iseult was the sort of woman to take a man's breath away, and he knew better than to play with fire.

He handed her the linen towel, and she dried her own feet. Leaning close to him, she added, 'I need to speak with you later. After the meal is finished.'

Not a good idea at all. 'I have to work on the carving. And I don't need you there.'

'This isn't about the carving.'

He stared hard at her, willing her to understand that he would not let her make a fool of him. 'Don't come.'

With the warning issued, he rejoined the rest of the slaves where he belonged.

Chapter Seven

Iseult paused before the door to Kieran's hut, a basket of food in one hand. Though he'd warned her not to come, she needed answers about her son. The chances of him knowing anything at all were unlikely, but she was willing to try anything.

She wanted to simply open the door, ask her questions and leave. But the memory of his hands upon her feet, even now, made her skin burn. She had almost imagined leaning down and feeling his lips against hers. Kieran Ó Brannon would not be considerate, like Davin. She could almost sense what it would be like, a wild stolen kiss. His sudden move the other night had made her feel like a captive, completely subject to his whims. It terrified her that she'd wanted to know what it would feel like.

She lowered her head. What was wrong with her? Did she crave the forbidden so much that she could not accept the embrace of a man who truly loved her? Saint Brigid, she despised herself for even thinking such thoughts. And she didn't even like Kieran. He was rude and insufferably arrogant.

Why was her heart beating so fast? She swallowed hard and bolstered her courage. In a few moments, she'd have her answers about Aidan. Without asking, she opened the door.

Kieran's back was turned. His skin glistened from where he'd poured water down it. She shivered at the sight of his barely healed wounds and the water tracing the ridges of his skin. His lean body was formed almost entirely of muscle, not a trace of softness about him. The waist of his trews hung low, exposing the edges of his hips.

The sight of him captivated her. She imagined sliding her hands around his waist, raising her palms up to his firm shoulders. As if in answer to her vision, her body responded, aching to be touched. Her clothes weighed down upon her, the tips of her breasts hardening.

No. Don't weaken like this.

'You could have knocked,' he said.

Iseult jerked her attention away. 'You wouldn't have let me in.' She pulled the folds of her grey *brat* around her shoulders, shivering in the cool spring night. The interior of the hut was as frigid as the outside, for Kieran hadn't bothered to build a fire. Two small clay lamps sitting on the work bench offered his only light. 'Aren't you freezing?'

'I hadn't noticed.' He reached for a drying cloth and wiped the moisture away. Bare-chested, he didn't bother to don a new tunic. It heightened the intimacy of the hut, making her imagination run wild. The forbidden desire to touch Kieran came over her again. Iseult dropped her gaze to the ground, forcing her thrumming heart to calm down.

She spied his old garment sodden with water, resting upon a bench. It struck her to realise that these were the only clothes he possessed.

Iseult set her basket down upon the earthen floor. 'May I?' She gestured towards the peat stacked near the hearth.

The need to do something, to take her mind off the present moment, was foremost.

He shrugged, and she gathered tinder and flint, sparking a fire. In time, her shivering ceased when the warm flames licked the fuel. She dragged two wooden tree stumps near the fire and picked up his wet tunic without asking. Wringing the remaining water out, she spread it to dry before the fire. Occupying her hands made it easier to avoid the true reason for coming.

Kieran said nothing, but behaved as though she weren't there. He sat upon the bench, his blade moving upon the wood. Tiny shavings flew into the air, and the fresh scent of yew filled the hut.

'I won't stay long,' Iseult promised. She wasn't certain how to ask him about the slave markets without bringing up bad memories. Surely it had been a barbaric experience, completely demeaning.

'What is it you want?' In his voice she heard the undertones of displeasure at being interrupted.

In the faint golden light, she saw white scars across his fingers and knuckles. They were the hands of a working man, not a nobleman. Like her father's.

Her heart softened as she thought of her da and how she missed him. Rory was the sort of man who laughed often and would gather her in a bear hug. Sometimes he'd made rings for her out of bits of iron, while working at his forge. As a little girl, she'd pretended they were made of silver and precious stones.

'Iseult?' Kieran prompted again. Impatience lined his voice.

She bit her lip, fearing he would have no information to give her. 'I wanted…to ask you about the slave markets,' she admitted at last. Her heartbeat quickened, and she rubbed her shoulders to bring warmth back into her skin. 'Were there any children there?'

'Many.' His face transformed into anger, his brown eyes fierce with the injustice. 'Some only a few days old if their mothers happened to give birth in captivity.'

For the first time, he set down his knife and stared at her. 'Were you thinking to buy a child?'

'No!' The very idea horrified her. How could he think her that cold or unfeeling? Though she understood that families were sometimes driven to desperation, she couldn't imagine selling a child for profit.

Kieran didn't press, but waited for her to continue. He picked up his knife, and she watched the blade dig into the wood, shaving the layers away. It disconcerted her to see her face emerging from the wood. Not the carefree girl she'd been once, but instead the weary face of a woman.

'I wanted...to find a particular child,' she said at last. 'A boy about two years of age. With dark hair and deep blue eyes. His name is Aidan.'

'I saw at least a dozen boys with that description. From all over Éireann.' Though his voice was flat, Kieran's eyes rested upon her with speculation. She was afraid he'd ask more questions, but he kept any curiosity to himself.

Her hopes deflated, she bowed her head. 'Thank you anyway.' Iseult picked up the basket of food and hesitated a moment. He still wore no tunic, seemingly unconcerned about his bared skin. Though she wanted to give him the provisions she'd brought, her face flushed at the thought of nearing him.

Don't be foolish. He's not going to attack you, she chided herself. Even so, she set the basket on the table and stepped away as though it were on fire. 'I brought you some of the venison. I doubt if Neasa gave you much of anything.'

He stopped his work and eyed it with interest. 'She offered bread and a little mead.'

Iseult dared a smile. 'She must have liked you, then. Most of the slaves have water and vegetables.'

Why was she chattering like a young girl? Like a witless fool, she'd let her tongue run off with her.

Kieran's eyes grew appreciative of the repast she'd brought. He took a piece of venison and ate slowly, savouring the meat as though he had not eaten such in a long time. Iseult tried not to notice his mouth, nor the way his hands moved.

'Did you have to steal it from her?' he asked idly.

'I helped clean up after the meal,' she said. 'I asked her if I could bring some of the food home, and she allowed it.'

'You don't live with them?'

Iseult suppressed a shudder. 'Not yet.' In spite of herself, she couldn't help the dread that passed over her at the thought of dwelling with Neasa. 'I am staying with my friend Muirne.'

He passed her the basket in silent invitation to share the food. Iseult withdrew the flask of wine and found two cups near the back of the hut. After pouring for each of them, she added, 'Neasa probably wouldn't have given me this, had she known I was bringing it here.'

The sweet fermented wine warmed her, and she knew she should go. Instead, she watched him. His hand traced the rim of the cup before he drank deeply. In the shadowed firelight, his skin gleamed.

When he set the cup down, he rose from the bench. With him standing so near, she could almost feel the heat from his skin. She wondered what it would feel like to touch him, to run her hand over the hard breadth of his shoulders.

Her nape grew damp, and she took a step backwards in retreat. Saint Brigid, she was losing her mind.

'You shouldn't come back again, Iseult.' He crossed his arms, but in spite of it, his eyes devoured her. She gripped her hands together so tightly, her knuckles went white. He captivated her, this man who should have terrified her. Right now she was wanting to feel his skin against her own, to experience the thrill of his kiss.

Her mind protested how wrong it was, even to imagine such a thing. 'I only came to ask you about my—the boy,' she amended. Her skin flushed even more.

'And that's all?'

'Of course that's all.' Did he think she had come to see him? She wanted nothing to do with him. 'If you have no answers for me, I'll go.'

She picked up the empty basket, but he caught her wrist before she could go. 'He's your son, isn't he?'

Her throat closed up, and she managed a nod. *Don't cry.* The effort to hold her composure made it impossible to speak.

'Why isn't Davin helping you?' He softened his grip upon her wrist, but did not release her. Iseult fought to keep herself from pulling back. She wasn't afraid of him, only her body's reaction to his touch.

'Aidan isn't his son.' Though Davin claimed he would help her find the boy, he'd never initiated any searches. His only contribution was escorting her around the countryside. And he wouldn't even do that any more, not after the threat of the raiders.

Kieran's thumb brushed against her pulse in a silent offer of sympathy. It cracked the frail edges of her control and the tears spilled over.

'Good eventide.' Iseult swiped at her eyes and left the hut. She ran to the far side of the palisade, ducking into the shadows. Sinking to the ground, she gathered her knees to her chest and wept bitterly.

Though she wanted to believe that somehow she'd find Aidan, she was beginning to fear the worst, that he was lost to her forever.

Kieran's eyes blurred from the sunlight. His muscles were locked and stiff. He'd stayed up the remainder of the night, finishing the carving. Iseult's revelation had been the final stroke he needed to complete it. Her sadness wasn't of a reluctant bride—instead, she was a grieving mother. It explained the sorrow upon her face, and her frustration.

He set the carving down and turned to the dying coals upon the fire. His tunic was dry, and he pulled it on, the wool still warm from the heat. She had set it there last night, as a wife might have done. The gesture rendered him puzzled. He'd seen through her feigned bravery, to the trembling she tried to hide from him. But she'd pressed on, asking questions for which there were no answers. She must be desperate if she thought he knew anything about her son.

What had happened to the boy's father? Though she might have been married before, it did not seem so. There was an air of innocence about her.

He'd wanted to lie with her last night. In the intimacy of the hut, he'd wanted to taste her lips and touch the silken skin that haunted him.

Kieran expelled a breath. As if she'd ever let a man like him touch her. He was a slave, not worthy of any woman. He had no right to be thinking of her, and he'd never deceive anyone in the same way Branna had betrayed him.

He remembered waking beside his beloved, stroking her bare skin. He ached for her, even knowing Branna did not love her. Now his perfidious bride slept in another man's bed. Escaping a marriage to her should have been a welcoming thought instead of a painful one.

Had he loved her? Or was it his pride that was wounded? When he tried to picture Branna in his mind, her features remained as clear as ever: soft auburn hair and eyes as dark as polished cherry wood. Her smile when he'd taken her into his arms.

His fingers dug into the carving, and Kieran forced his fingers to relax. She was gone now, wed to another man. Likely she never even thought of him. He wished he could drive her from his own thoughts so easily.

He drew his attention back to the carving and the shape of Iseult's mouth. Instead of carving the anguish in her features, he'd added his own touch: a note of hope. Though he did not give her a false smile, he'd carved her lips to hold a wistful dream.

It suited her. As he stretched his fingers to push away the numbness, he realised he'd enjoyed this challenge. Though he would have to give the carving to Davin, the piece had taken his mind off the past.

Twelve weeks of slavery remained. At the end of his self-imposed servitude, would he find absolution? Somehow he doubted if there would be any peace.

Last night, he hadn't been able to avoid being noticed, nor had he performed the tasks of a slave with adequate humility. He'd resented every moment of it. Which was, he supposed, the point of a sacrifice.

He opened a small cask of butter and used it to smooth the finish of the wood. As he forced the natural oils into the surface, he thought again of what he would do after he left Lismanagh.

He wanted to find a place where no one knew him, where he could abandon his heritage and rank. They would believe him, if he said he was nothing but a common woodcarver. No one had to know the truth.

He had no desire to see his father Marcas again. He'd sold himself into slavery, intending to rescue Egan. A part of him had believed Marcas would follow them, sending tribesmen to bring them both home.

But no one had come. Months had passed, and he hadn't seen a single man. And he understood, then, that there would be no going back. They didn't want him to return.

Kieran set the figure aside, wrapping it in linen. Then he opened the door fully, squinting at the brightness. It was not dawn, but rather mid-morning. He'd worked until the lamps burned out, but by then he'd had enough sunlight to continue. Perhaps he should feel exhausted, but he'd been so caught up in the work, it had renewed his energy.

Outside, he found another sack of supplies containing bread, venison and more wine. Apparently, Iseult had sent them, not Davin. Had she brought food to him over the past few days?

He didn't know why that bothered him. As Davin's intended wife, perhaps it was one of her duties to see to his slaves. Even so, while he broke his fast, he couldn't help but recall her plea for information last night. He doubted if he could help her. He'd seen as many children as adults in the slave markets. Finding a particular boy would be impossible.

Enough. He closed his mind off from Iseult. The time had come to give Davin the carving and to sever all contact with Iseult. He put the wooden figurine inside a fold of his tunic and walked towards Davin's home.

In the distance beyond the ringfort, he saw a small stone chapel. Beyond it, the rich soil had been tilled in preparation for planting. He could envision the green seedlings sprouting from the earth.

Around him, the familiar sounds of people reminded him of what he'd missed in the past few moons. Children laughing as they chased dogs around. The scent of peat fires and animals in their pens. Goats bleating while they were caught for milking. Sounds that reminded him of home. He ignored the slash of pain in his heart.

Neasa Ó Falvey caught sight of him, her long black hair caught up in a tight linen head covering. She wiped her hands upon her *brat* and raised her hand. 'You, there. Davin's slave. I need you to go and see to the sheep this morning.'

Kieran ignored her orders, searching for a sign of Davin.

'Didn't you hear what I said?' Neasa demanded, her hands upon her hips.

'I heard. But I am ordered to bring something to your son Davin.' He continued walking without listening to her.

'I know where he is,' a voice interrupted. Orin caught up to him, adding, 'I'll take you there.' He glanced back at his foster-mother and increased his pace to get away. Kieran imagined the young man was more than eager to end his fostering.

Neasa did not bother to hide her irritation, grumbling beneath her breath as the two of them left. Orin led him outside the ringfort and pointed to a group of men on horseback. 'There he is.'

Kieran raised a hand to shield his eyes and saw Davin mounted upon a dun gelding. 'Where are they going?'

'He's speaking to the scouts he sent out a few days ago. They went to the coast to track the *Lochlannachs*.'

Kieran tensed. He'd had his own dealings with the Norsemen and Danes. Harsh memories pierced his gut, as he remembered the hand that had drawn a blade across Egan's throat. He'd taken his vengeance upon the raiders, but none of it would bring his brother back. 'What do they want?'

Orin shrugged. 'Land. Wealth. Our women, I suppose.'

The prizes of conquest. Kieran's hands clenched into fists as he followed the young man down to the others. One of the messengers was reporting his findings.

'It's a small group, possibly thirty men,' the man said. 'Their ship was anchored near Baile na nGall. They've set up a temporary camp outside the ruins.'

'Any survivors?' Davin asked.

'If there were, they've left. We stayed away from the Norsemen and watched. It looks like they do intend to travel further inland. They were gathering more supplies when we returned.'

'How many horses did they have?' Kieran asked.

The men's faces swung towards him in surprise. Likely they weren't accustomed to slaves speaking. He didn't care. The number of horses would tell how many high-ranking soldiers were among them.

The messenger glanced at Davin, who nodded. 'There were five.'

Five men to lead a group of thirty sounded far too high. There must be more men waiting, possibly as many as seventy. Kieran held little optimism for this fight.

'We'll convene a council and decide what to do.' Davin dismissed the messengers, instructing them to get food and to rest from their journey. One by one, the others followed until only Kieran and Orin remained behind.

Davin's face held irritation at being interrupted. 'What did you want?'

'The likeness of my brother. Then the dower chest. I've finished my part of the bargain.' He passed Davin the cloth-wrapped figurine.

His master unwrapped the linen and studied the carving of Iseult. For a long moment, he said nothing. Kieran did not fear Davin's lack of reaction, for he knew he'd done his best work.

'It is her,' Davin agreed, finally lifting his gaze. 'By God, it's her. I wouldn't have believed it possible.' Carefully, he covered the wood and tucked it away. 'The figure of your brother is at my home. Come, and I'll return it to you now. We'll arrange for the chest to be brought later.'

They started to walk back to the ringfort, but Orin remained where he was, a hopeful smile playing on his face.

'What is it?' Davin asked.

'It's a fine day. The sea is calm and the skies are perfect.'

'I know what you're thinking.' Davin clapped a hand on his foster-brother's back. 'Gather your supplies, and I'll arrange for the boat.'

Kieran started to continue on without them. Though he wanted to begin work on the chest, Davin had other plans. Kieran was beginning to understand what it meant to be a slave, and it vexed him to be at the mercy of another man's whims.

'I think Kieran should come,' Orin added. 'Else we won't catch any fish. He brought us luck on the last hunting trip.'

'What say you, Kieran?'

He stopped in his tracks, acknowledging Davin's request. Or was it a command? The lack of control over his own decisions made him want to refuse. But then, the thought was tempting. He hadn't been out sailing in over a year. The taste of the salt, the feeling of absolute freedom, lured him beyond measure.

'We'll take the boat out and try our luck with the sea,' Davin continued. He mounted his horse, and glanced out at the grey ripples of foam.

Then there was no other choice. Kieran shrugged. 'If you have need of me.'

'A fitting reward, for such fine work,' Davin said, touching the figure of Iseult. 'This might be a last chance to go out sailing before the invasion. And…' his blue eyes sparked with teasing '…you may keep whatever fish you catch. My mother won't have anything except what Orin or I bring back.'

'As you like.' The unexpected invitation sent a lightness through him. It had been a long time since he'd had anything to look forward to. He followed the men back to the ringfort, grateful that he would receive the figure of Egan back again. Though his brother no longer lived, at least he had this reminder of him.

An hour later, Kieran walked down to the shore where he found Davin, Orin, and Iseult waiting. He'd tucked a few bits of metal into his mantle, after scouring the hut for fishing supplies. Davin and Orin were loading a net and long fishing poles into the vessel while Iseult carried two baskets of what he presumed was food and drink.

He hadn't expected to see her. But then, she was Davin's betrothed, so likely he had invited her to come. Davin's hands spanned her waist as he lifted her inside the boat. The dark grey overdress and lighter *léine* should have been unattractive, but it only highlighted her beauty. His touch lingered upon Iseult, and Kieran looked away, uncomfortable at the sight of them.

She was just another woman. It shouldn't matter if she joined them, should it? She belonged here, at the side of her betrothed husband. And yet her presence made him feel even more like an outsider.

She didn't look happy about joining them. Almost as if she were forced to come and didn't want to be here.

He felt the same way.

Kieran grasped the stern of the boat and helped the others shove it into the shallow waters. Iseult gripped the sides, keeping her back to them.

The icy chill of the sea soaked through him, and when they were far enough out, Kieran climbed aboard. He picked up an oar and they rowed out into Brandon Bay.

Iseult's long hair streamed behind her, wrapping around her throat as the wind increased. The waves rocked the vessel, and she held onto the wood to keep her balance.

Davin sat behind Iseult, and in every nuance of his body, Kieran could see how much the man cared for her. Her betrothed watched her as if fearing she would somehow disappear.

For a fleeting moment, Iseult glanced back at him. Misery dulled her eyes, and he had a sudden vision of her holding a child in her arms. Laughing with a young boy, teaching him to hold the pole. Sharing in his excitement when he caught his first fish.

And now the boy was gone.

How? When? The answers didn't matter, because she was still hurting. And Davin appeared completely blind to it. He was teasing, leaning forwards and whispering in her ear. Though Iseult forced her lips to curve upwards, it wasn't a true smile.

Kieran looked away, adjusting the ropes of the sail. This wasn't his business. She wasn't his betrothed, and it wasn't his task to help her.

But the urge to protect was not easily subdued.

In time, the sails filled with wind, increasing the vessel's speed. Kieran tasted brine and welcomed the brisk air lashing at his face.

He'd brought his sisters out in their father's boat time and again, though usually Cara tried to throw water upon him. An emptiness caught his conscience at the memory. Both Cara and Aisling had practised their feminine wiles, twisting him to do whatever they wanted. *Críost*, he missed them.

As he tied off the sail, he caught Iseult looking at him. 'Davin showed me the carving. You did well.'

He hadn't expected the compliment, nor the slight softening of her lips. Her clear blue eyes contrasted against the dark grey waters of the bay, while the wind nipped strands of gold hair against her cheeks.

Kieran inclined his head, acknowledging her before directing his attention back to the sea. His pride warmed to the words, though he didn't know why she'd spoken them. She didn't like him. Was afraid of him, even.

Or was she? Perhaps things had changed. He hadn't been able to answer her questions about her son. How would he have noticed a small boy, after the hundreds he'd seen?

When he risked a glance back at her, he found Davin watching him instead.

'It was fine work,' his master agreed. He laid his hand upon Iseult's shoulder, as if to claim her. Iseult touched her palm to Davin's in response.

Kieran's hands tightened upon the ropes. He felt like an intruder upon a private moment, and he turned away. The sun gleamed through fleecy clouds, and, at long last, they chose a spot to set down their anchor.

'Care to make a wager?' Davin asked.

Orin eyed his foster-brother with suspicion. 'What did you have in mind?'

'Whoever catches the fewest fish has to clean them.'

Orin winced. 'I'm not sure we should—'

'I'll take the wager,' Kieran interrupted. Cleaning fish

was never a task he enjoyed, and he felt fairly confident in his skills.

'And I,' Iseult responded. There was a competitive edge to her expression now, and he wondered what she knew that he didn't.

'I want to start with the net,' Orin said, still looking unconvinced that a fishing competition was a good idea.

'We'll take turns with the net,' Iseult assured him. 'You can begin. I'll use the pole.'

She opened the basket and withdrew chopped pieces of crab. Baiting her hook, she dropped the line over the side of the boat.

'Pass me some of those, won't you?' Davin asked.

Iseult raised an eyebrow. 'This is a wager. You'll have to get your own bait.' She tilted her head with feigned innocence. 'Or did you forget to bring any?'

Davin's eyes narrowed. 'Now that isn't fair, *a stór*.'

'Fair or not, it won't be me cleaning all the fish.' Her eyes gleamed with satisfaction.

Kieran adjusted his own line, unravelling a knot. He wouldn't deny that Iseult MacFergus was an intelligent woman.

But then, he wasn't above cheating.

Kieran waited until her attention was on the line. Then, he slipped his hand into her basket. With a quick gesture, he tossed a crab to Davin, keeping one for himself.

Iseult slapped his hand. 'Those aren't yours!' Her cheeks burned with colour, when she realised what she'd done.

'No, they aren't,' he agreed. Leaning forwards, he added, 'But you weren't paying attention.'

Her face reddened even more. This time, she set the basket between her knees. Lowering her skirt, she glared at both of the men. 'You won't be stealing my bait now.'

Were she any other woman, he would view this as a challenge. He imagined trapping her against the bow of the boat, moulding his hands against the base of her spine. He'd lower her against the wood until his body rested atop hers. Perhaps steal a kiss, if she were willing. Then the basket of bait would be all but forgotten.

Instead, he risked a glance towards Davin. 'I could distract her, if you'd like.'

'I don't know if I'm that brave.' Davin eyed Iseult with a light smile upon his face.

I am, Kieran thought. And from the way Iseult drew back, he supposed she knew it.

From that moment, she avoided looking at him. It was deliberate, and sensible. Whatever connection he'd sensed last night had been severed. They could never be friends, for they were not equals. She didn't know of his former rank. And even if she did, she belonged to Davin.

From inside a fold of his mantle, he pulled out several rusted pieces of chain. After tying the chain to the line to weight it down, he tossed it over the side. He'd have better luck catching larger fish in this way.

'I have something!' Orin exclaimed. Eagerly, he pulled the net up, and trapped within the woven fibres was a bass the size of his palm.

Davin hooted with laughter. 'You've caught your own bait, lad! Well done.'

'You never said what size the fish had to be,' Orin argued. 'I believe I'm winning the wager.'

'Not any more.' Iseult's arms strained, but her voice held a note of anticipation as she pulled against her pole. The water swirled, but she held steady, bringing the line in with her palms.

'Do you need my help?' Davin asked, reaching his arms around her waist.

'No. I've got it.' She tried to move away from his embrace, and abruptly, the line went slack. Iseult let out a moan of dismay. When she pulled up the remainder, she had nothing but a bent hook and no bait.

'Pass her the net, Orin,' Davin advised. 'Iseult needs another way to catch her fish.'

She cursed beneath her breath. 'I was doing well enough before you interfered.'

Davin grinned, but Kieran didn't share the jest. He kept his concentration upon finding the right location for his line. When a fish struck, he hauled it in, rapidly drawing in the line as it cut into his palms.

Orin let out a cheer when Kieran pulled in a flatfish the length of his forearm. 'Well done!'

'He cheated,' Davin said, shaking his head. 'You were supposed to distract him by putting your arms around him, Orin.'

A startled laugh escaped Iseult, and for the first time, Kieran saw her smile. A true smile, not one weighed down by her sorrows.

A woman as beautiful as Iseult should smile often, he thought. It had faded away, far too quickly.

Kieran caught Orin eyeing him, and he sent the lad a dark look. 'Try it, and I'll knock you overboard.'

With that, the cheating only got worse. When Kieran finally got a second fish to bite his line, Orin grabbed him, to prevent him from bringing in the catch. Davin tried to wrestle away the fish, but Kieran managed to grasp the trout before they could hurl it back into the water.

Iseult collapsed against the side of the boat, her sides shaking with laughter. Her gown was damp with seawater, while her reddish-gold hair had tangled into a mass down her back.

Stop looking at her, his mind warned him, even as Davin helped her sit up again.

When she gathered her composure at last, she passed Kieran the net. His hands touched hers, and abruptly her smile disappeared. The expression on her face was nothing like the teasing smile she'd given Davin.

No, this was more. It was a startled look of awareness, along with guilt. Were she not betrothed to another man, he'd have leaned over to kiss her. He'd have pressed her body against his, tasting the softness of her shoulder and neck.

Kieran tossed the net over the side, angry with himself. It didn't matter that he desired her, nor that he'd seen the same feelings mirrored in her face. Never would he let himself fall into that kind of dishonour, not after it had been done to him.

He'd be leaving by summer's end, if he managed to gain his freedom. And in the meantime, he intended to stay far away from Iseult MacFergus.

Chapter Eight

For the remainder of the afternoon, Iseult tried to concentrate on fishing. She'd caught four respectable fish, Davin had five, and Orin had seven. Kieran had caught twelve, and he alternated between using the weighted fishing line and the net. He sat up in the boat, fully intent on the line and hadn't looked at her once. Not since that moment when she'd given him the net.

From the second she'd touched his hands, every sense went on alert. His intense brown eyes blazed a warning, and her hands were trembling after she pulled away. Kieran Ó Brannon was a slave, not an equal. Not a man who could become a friend. Though he had gone along with the fishing trip, it was obvious that he didn't want to be here.

Only a command from Davin had made him come. And from his silent manner, she guessed that he was not accustomed to taking orders.

Everything about him made her think of a warrior. His stealth and cunning, coupled with a ruthless demeanour, spoke of a man who had endured slavery but was not born to it.

And yet, last night, his anger had softened. He didn't mock her, nor was he cruel after she'd revealed what had happened to Aidan. Instead, he'd held her hand. He'd somehow understood her.

Iseult looked down at her hands, holding the wooden fishing pole. When she looked back at Kieran, he was staring out at the sea. He had known the same pain.

No. Don't think of him like that.

She moved closer to Davin, sitting so near that her skin touched his. He smiled in response, putting an arm around her.

'I'm glad you came, *a mhuirnín*. You haven't been yourself in a long time.'

'I know.' She forced herself to take his hand in hers. 'I still miss Aidan.'

Davin smiled, but it held empty promises. It hurt so badly to think of her child lost and alone. It was hard not letting the search consume her. With each day that went by, the madness grew a little stronger.

She squeezed his hand in silent apology.

'Now stop,' Davin chided, pulling his hand away. 'I won't be letting you distract me. You're going to lose this competition, *a stór*.'

She hadn't meant it that way, but shrugged. 'If you want me to wed you at Bealtaine, then perhaps you should allow me to win.'

Orin laughed, pointing his finger at Davin. 'She has you there, my brother.'

Kieran said nothing, but reached into the bay for his net, the tendons in his arms straining. He had tied one end to the boat for leverage.

Suddenly, the wind jerked the vessel leeward, and Iseult fell back against Kieran. The muscles of his body were like stone, without a trace of softness. He steadied her, his hands cool from the seawater. When she regained her balance, he reached into the bay to retrieve the fallen net.

'I'm sorry.' She gripped the side of the boat. 'I didn't mean to make you lose your fish.'

'I'm not so sure about that,' Davin interjected. He helped Iseult back to her seat. 'She doesn't like cleaning fish.'

'It was an accident,' Kieran said softly.

Iseult made no reply. His close proximity made her all too aware of him. He'd begun regaining his strength, his body losing its hollow appearance. Yet never had he appeared weak. Lean and wiry, with a touch of danger.

Davin, in contrast, was strong and dependable. Always there for her. She caught her betrothed watching her, before his gaze narrowed upon Kieran. Iseult moved back to her place beside Davin, to reassure him.

When the sun reached its zenith, she pulled out venison, dried apples from last season and cheese to share. Davin teased her because she continued to fish, only stopping momentarily for a bite to eat. If there was a chance of not having to clean the fish, she'd take it.

'I arranged for the dower chest to be brought to Seamus's hut,' Davin said to Kieran. 'You may begin working on it this night if you wish. And I brought this for you.' He passed over a wooden carving. It was the boy, Iseult realised.

Kieran accepted the carving and studied it a moment before placing it within a fold of his tunic. His face remained sombre, and she wondered if the boy was still alive.

Davin passed her a flask of mead, and she took a sip before offering it to Kieran. His hand closed over hers for a fleeting moment. She resisted the urge to pull away.

To distract herself, she baited her last hook, tossing the line over the side. Davin helped Orin draw the net back inside the boat. Thankfully, Orin had nothing but seaweed.

Her own luck wasn't holding. Not a single fish seemed interested in her bait. She glanced back at Kieran, who had cast his own line into the water. Intense concentration filled his eyes.

'Have you been fishing often?' she asked.

He nodded, still not looking at her. Clearly, he had no intention of speaking to her. Had she offended him? His rigid posture suggested that he had no desire to answer questions or reveal anything about his past. Least of all to her.

They set the course for Lismanagh, and the men worked to change the direction of the sails. Iseult gathered up the fish in her basket, and it seemed she'd lost the wager after counting them. Wonderful. The last way she wanted to spend her evening was cleaning fish. She wrinkled her nose in distaste.

All throughout the journey home, Kieran neither spoke nor looked at her. In the sky, clouds drifted in to obscure the sun. The temperature had shifted, and the chilled air made her reach for her *brat*. She pulled the woollen wrap around her shoulders and over her hair to keep warm.

When they reached the shore, Davin lifted her from the boat, heedless of the cold sea water. His strong arms enveloped her in warmth, while he waded through the waves. Orin headed back to the ringfort, while Kieran lifted the basket of fish and started to walk back alone.

Where was he going with the fish?

Davin caught her look. 'Don't worry about the wager, *a stór*. Kieran will take care of the fish.'

She should have been overjoyed. She should keep her

mouth shut and let him handle the task. But honour pricked her conscience. She *had* lost. It was her responsibility to clean the fish, despicable as it was.

'Put me down, Davin,' she insisted. He obeyed, though once again his touch lingered upon her skin.

With long strides, she caught up to Kieran. He hardly spared her a glance, keeping his attention upon the basket. If he was trying to behave in a humble manner, it wasn't working. Instead, he seemed annoyed.

'I lost the wager,' Iseult reminded him. 'Therefore, it is my task to clean the fish.'

Kieran shook his head. 'You are his lady. I am a slave. It's better for me to do it.'

He was behaving as though she were an arrogant noble-woman, who thought herself too good to perform menial work. She didn't consider herself above the task, not at all. True, she didn't like it, but the truth was, he'd won. Though Davin seemed content to abandon the wager, it rubbed her sense of honour the wrong way.

She moved in front of him so suddenly, Kieran was forced to stop walking. 'Give me the basket.'

'No.'

Before he could push past her, Iseult grasped the handle. 'I do keep my word. And I don't avoid my duties.'

He paused and glanced back at Davin, who had come up behind them.

'You'd best let her have her way,' Davin advised. 'My Iseult has a mind of her own.'

She raised her chin. Well, at least one man knew what he was talking about. She dragged the basket away from Kieran, but it was heavier than she'd thought. It was a struggle, simply to hold it upright.

'Do you need any help?' Kieran asked softly.

'Not from you.' Or anyone else, she thought, half-gasping as she trudged up the hillside.

Davin caught up and walked behind her. 'I'll bring the basket to Muirne's,' he offered. 'You can clean them there.'

Her pride stung, but her arm muscles ached even more, so she relented. 'Leave the basket outside her hut.'

When he lifted the weight free, Iseult rubbed her arms. Already she'd begun to tire. And Blessed Saint Brigid, she had to clean almost thirty fish.

It's your own fault, for being honest, she thought.

'Are you sure you want to do this?' Davin asked. 'Kieran would take care of it.'

'I agreed to the wager,' she repeated. The idea of giving up seemed the mark of weakness. And it felt good to see the look of surprise on Kieran's face.

They walked past the circle of huts until they reached Muirne's dwelling. A few of the torches had been lit against the shadow of twilight. Iseult dragged a stool outside and set up a workspace near the side of the hut. Better to start and get it over with.

'Oh, Davin and Iseult. You're back!' Muirne opened the door, a broad smile on her face. 'And I see you've come with a feast. Iseult, I've never seen so many. I'll bring the knives, and we'll all help you.'

The warmth in Muirne's voice helped lift her spirits a little. Iseult sighed as she sat down. She selected a wooden board to rest upon her lap, and Muirne returned in a moment with several blades.

'I can manage, but why don't you take four of the bass and cook them for the family this night?' Iseult offered. Since they were the only fish she'd caught, it was the best use for them.

'It might be I'll do just that.' Muirne dragged another stool beside her. 'Will you join us, Davin?'

'Not this night, I'm afraid. I am meeting with the men to decide what's to be done about the Norse raiders.' He leaned down and kissed Iseult on the cheek. 'Good night, *a stór*.'

After he'd left, Muirne released a happy sigh. 'Many a woman would cut off her right hand to be wedded to such a man, Iseult. I imagine you'll be looking forward to Bealtaine.'

'I am, yes.' The words came from her mouth without thinking. She was nervous about the marriage ceremony, and later, lying with Davin.

Iseult picked up one of the blades and pulled over a wooden bucket to collect the fish scraps. Likely every cat in the ringfort would come searching for handouts. Reluctantly, she began cleaning one of the larger fish. Muirne chattered while cleaning the bass, and then she ducked inside her hut to begin cooking the fish.

Alone, Iseult worked her way through seven more fish. After a time she felt as though every inch of her smelled like the sea. She'd give anything for a bath right now.

Light footsteps trudged towards her, and she glanced up. Kieran stood in front of her, a knife in his hand.

'What do you want?' she demanded.

He shrugged and dragged one of the cut stumps nearby. He sat far away from her, and picked up a board and three fish.

'I told you not to do that. I lost the wager, and it's my responsibility.'

He shrugged again, slicing the first fish open and cleaning it.

'Don't.' She set her board and knife down. Did he think her incapable of doing the work? 'Just go back to your woodcarving. Or go and serve Davin. I don't care which.'

His presence made it even more difficult to concentrate. She waited for him to leave, but he continued until he'd cleaned three of the fish.

He stood and brought the fillets over to her. 'Where do you want these?'

She took the fish and put them in a clean wooden container near her feet. 'That will do. Go on, now, and leave me to my task.'

He was making her uncomfortable, watching her the way he did. 'Wager or not, it's a lot of fish. And I'd like to eat my evening meal within a reasonable hour.'

She huffed a strand of hair out of her face. 'Then take your twelve and leave.'

'Who's leaving?' Muirne stepped outside the hut, wiping her hands upon a cloth. When she saw Kieran, her eyes gleamed. 'Oh, you're the new slave, aren't you?'

'I am.' Though he lowered his head, Iseult saw not a trace of humility.

'It's good that Davin sent you to help with the fish. Our Iseult would have been here all night, otherwise.'

Iseult noticed that Kieran did not correct the assumption. She doubted if Davin had even thought of it, so concerned was he with the Norse raiders.

Muirne nodded to Iseult. 'Stop for a moment and dine with us. You can share a meal with us as well, slave. Bring a few more of those fillets, some of the smaller ones. It won't take long to add more food.'

'His name is Kieran,' Iseult said. 'And he was just leaving.'

'I wouldn't mind sharing a meal,' he said. 'It has been a while since I've had company.'

When Iseult glared at him, his expression held nothing but innocence.

'Come in, then.' Muirne opened the door and winked. 'Pity you're a slave. A handsome one you are, Kieran.'

He blinked at that, and Iseult nearly laughed. It served him right. With a flushed face, he entered Muirne's hut. The boys, Glendon and Bartley, were chasing one another around the small space. Muirne's husband Hagen calmly picked them up by their tunics and dropped them onto the ground beside the low table.

Muirne poured cold water into a basin and handed it to Kieran, along with a small cake of soap. 'Both of you wash yourselves. You've made my home smell enough like fish.'

Kieran gestured for Iseult to use the basin first. She washed her hands and face, emptying the soiled water outside before refilling the basin for Kieran. He stared at the water a moment before dipping his hands in, soaping them heavily.

'Is something wrong?' she asked.

He shook his head. 'I was just thinking that it's been a long time since I've had soap.'

'How did you bathe before?' He didn't smell bad, but she hadn't thought of it before now.

'Mostly in cold streams with sand. Sometimes the ocean.'

Iseult winced, thinking of his wounds. The salt must have been excruciating. 'Seamus has a basin somewhere among his belongings. I'll bring you some soap, if you'd wish it.'

'Thank you,' he said softly before taking the basin out to empty it.

Though Kieran said little throughout the meal, he ate well enough. Muirne kept his plate full, asking constant questions and chatting without stopping for air. Hagen held an amused air throughout the meal, though upon occasion he sent warning glances to the boys for interrupting.

'What happened that you became a slave?' Muirne

asked finally. 'It's obvious to me from your bearing that
you were a free man once before. Were you taken captive?'

He'd never answer that question. Iseult was certain of it.

'I wasn't a captive, no.' Kieran spoke quietly, giving his
attention to the remains of his meal.

Muirne's face fell. 'Oh, lad. I suspected as much, given
how strong you seem to be. No one should have to lose
their freedom in that way. I'm sorry to hear of your
family's decision.'

Iseult frowned. 'What decision?'

Muirne sighed and ladled another spoonful of stewed
cherries onto Kieran's plate. 'It's obvious, isn't it? His
family sold him into slavery.'

Kieran's face became strained. 'No. They didn't sell me.
I sold myself.' He stood, thanking Muirne for the meal.
'Forgive me, but I have work I must do.'

Seconds later, he'd gone. Iseult stared over at Muirne,
who looked as shocked as she felt.

'Sweet Mary.' Muirne reached over for Kieran's plate.
'I can't believe it.'

Neither could Iseult. Why would any man willingly surrender his freedom? What gain could there possibly be?

'Now there is a true nobleman.' Muirne sighed again like
a lovelorn maid. 'He probably gave the profits to his family.'

Iseult helped her clear the table off, not entirely believing it. There was far more to Kieran's story than this.

Outside, she finished cleaning the remainder of the fish
until her eyes drooped and her fingers were sore. She'd
nicked her fingers on the blade more than a few times. But
it didn't take as long as she'd thought, since Kieran and
Muirne had both helped.

Iseult set aside three watertight baskets and divided
up each man's share, deducting the fish Kieran had eaten

at the meal. Last, she filled each basket with a brine solution to preserve the fish until they could be smoked tomorrow morning.

Wearily, she crossed to a trough of water and rinsed her hands.

Muirne's foster-sons were more than happy to bring Davin and Orin their baskets, and she planned to bring Kieran his own share.

The ringfort was quiet and dark, save for the torches flickering around its diameter. Even with only nine fish, the basket was heavy. Iseult strained under the weight, reminding herself that it wasn't much further. She'd give him the fish, and then the man could do whatever he liked.

Iseult set the basket down in front of his door and knocked sharply upon the door. After a few moments of silence, she decided he must have gone to speak with Davin. Opening the door, she hefted the basket of fish and staggered inside with it.

To her surprise, Kieran sat at the bench, two oil lamps providing the light while he sketched a design with charcoal.

'Why didn't you open the door?' she asked, dropping the basket in front of him.

'I didn't want visitors.' He continued working upon a pattern of intricate lines.

'I've brought your fish. They're in the basket.' She added, 'I packed them in brine, so they'll keep until tomorrow.'

Kieran nodded, still not looking up from his work. Once again, she felt as though she'd done something wrong.

'Why are you behaving this way?' she demanded. 'You won't even look at me, will you? I cleaned your fish, and you haven't the courtesy to offer thanks.'

He set the charcoal down and stared at her. 'You know exactly why I'm staying away from you, Iseult.' He stood, his body shadowed by the lamps. In the tiny space, she grew aware of him. The gruff tone of his voice and the way he moved, like a hunter, froze her in place.

'I don't, no.'

Liar.

She forced herself not to move as he closed the distance. Kieran stood only a palm's distance away, intimidating her with his nearness. His hands smelled of fresh wood, and his hair was damp.

'I think you do know. And that is why you should leave right now.' His voice was barely above a whisper, and his hand caught her chin.

Though her instincts warned her to flee, she remained where she was. Dark eyes mesmerised her, along with the lean planes of his face. Kieran was unlike any man she'd known, and her heartbeat raced beneath her skin.

Don't do this, her mind warned. Her impulses didn't listen.

She reached out and touched the warm skin of his neck. Her own flesh seemed to answer, and the interior of the hut blazed with heat. He made her feel everything she didn't feel with Davin. And the thought alarmed her.

'I'm not your enemy,' Iseult whispered.

'Yes, you are.' And then his mouth descended upon hers, hot and wicked. His hand threaded through her hair, dragging her face to meet his kiss.

He offered no mercy, no tenderness. Only wild, forbidden desire. Her body flooded with heat, her breasts tightening at the feel of his skin pressed against hers. This was what she'd been missing with Davin. Even the one lover she'd had, the father of her child, could not compare to this.

His kiss bruised her lips, but she didn't care. She lost herself in him, grasping his shoulders for balance. All the frustration she felt towards him, the anger and need, came crashing down.

His tongue slipped inside her mouth, carnal and sensuous. Between her legs, she ached to feel him, to know his touch. Her reasoning cried out to stop, but she didn't have the strength to push him away. Shame filled her, and, at last, she lowered her head to break the kiss.

She tried to steady her breathing, but it was like trying to stop a rising tide. Kieran stepped back, his eyes fierce with hunger.

'I didn't know it would be like this,' she managed, her hands shaking as she wrapped them around her waist.

'I did. And that is why I don't want you to come here again. Stay away from me, Iseult. Or the next time, I won't let you go.'

She nodded, her eyes burning. Right now she understood why he'd shunned her and knew that she must do the same. There could never be a future for them, not while she was betrothed.

Davin was the man meant to be her husband, not a slave. She had lost her head to desire once, and paid a terrible price. She wouldn't do it again.

After she'd gone, Kieran sank down on the bench. Gods, how could he have been so witless? He'd meant to scare her, to send her fleeing back to her betrothed. Instead, he'd nearly seduced her.

He picked up one of his blades and stabbed it into a block of yew. Even now his mouth burned with the taste of her. Closing his eyes, he tried not to think of Davin touching her in that way. Jealousy seared him, and he gripped the knife, jerking it from the wood. For a moment, he stared at the blade. The sooner he finished the dower chest and left Lismanagh, the better.

* * *

Later that night, Kieran awoke to hear battle cries. He jerked to his feet, and reached for a carving dagger. His heartbeat pulsed an erratic rhythm, while his mind evoked vicious images from the past.

The roar of the invaders mingled with his people begging for mercy. Torches seared thatched roofs, decimating homes in a fiery blaze. His sister Aisling screamed for help, while another raider seized Egan. Torn between them, he'd killed the raider who had tried to take Aisling. And he'd lost Egan.

Kieran shoved the door open, his gaze raking in the sight of the tribesmen. Almost a dozen Ó Falvey men entered the gate, laughing while driving a small flock of sheep within. At the entrance, he saw three men bound as hostages.

A midnight raid upon another tribe. Nothing more. And yet his lungs closed up with the assault of vivid memories. Men like these had stolen his brother away.

Kieran stared at one of the hostages, whose physical strength looked tough enough to snap through the ropes in a single motion. The man surveyed the scene with a cool eye. Dark gold hair was pulled back with a leather thong, and his fierce features appeared more Norse than Irish. He wore the colours of a tribesman, however.

His expression remained calm—not the look of a helpless man taken prisoner. This was a man who'd let himself become a hostage—and Kieran didn't trust him.

While the other two men struggled against their bonds and cursed, the third captive didn't move. He let them chain him to a wooden post in front of a large mound.

Kieran stopped one of the Ó Falvey tribesmen. 'Who is he?' He pointed towards the third captive.

The man stared at Kieran, as if wondering why a slave

dared to speak. At last, he shrugged. 'One of the Sullivans. Our men captured more sheep, and some hostages.'

Though raids were common between tribes, Kieran couldn't dismiss his instincts. He studied the prisoner, and the way the man's eyes moved over each of them. Almost as if he were memorising faces.

Kieran stepped into the light, his hand still clenched around the knife. He strode forwards until he caught the captive's glance. More than ever, he was convinced the men were not Irish, though they dressed as tribesmen.

'Who are you?' he asked softly, using a few words of the Norse tongue.

The captive's gaze snapped to his. Then he gave a slow smile, though he did not answer.

In the man's eyes, he sensed a threat.

Chapter Nine

Iseult awoke the next morning to a hand stroking her cheek. She opened her eyes and saw Davin smiling down at her. Her cheeks burned when he leaned down to kiss her lips. Anyone could see them, and she didn't want the prying eyes of Muirne's boys upon them.

'Good morn, *a stór*.'

Iseult hid her embarrassment in Davin's shoulder, embracing him. It was hard to meet his eyes, for she feared if she looked at him, he might see her guilt at kissing Kieran. She'd never expected nor wanted it to happen.

Why had she done it? She should have pushed him away as soon as it happened. Instead, she'd kissed him back. Fool. Idiot. Remorse smothered her, and she inwardly vowed that she'd not betray Davin. She would never sink to that form of dishonour. She wasn't that sort of woman.

'I came to show you something.' Davin helped her rise, while Muirne's foster-sons giggled from their own pallets. Iseult ignored the boys and donned an overdress atop her *léine*. She wasted no time in going outside with Davin. Streaks of fuchsia cut the dawn sky, a portent of afternoon rain.

She stifled a yawn. Late last night she'd heard the men returning from their raid. She'd glimpsed hostages, but paid them no mind. Likely it had been Cearul's doing. The hot-headed tribesman loved nothing better than to lead an attack.

Davin directed her to a small clearing near the edge of the ringfort. At first Iseult didn't understand what she was meant to see. Nothing stood before them, save grass and dirt.

'What is it?'

'It's where I'll be building our new home.' He stood behind her and wrapped his arms around her waist. 'What do you think?'

Her throat tightened, for he'd guessed what she wanted most. A place of their own. A place where she could begin her life over again and forget the mistakes she'd made in the past. Her fingers clenched in her skirts. 'It's wonderful, Davin.'

'I won't be able to start it until we've built up our defences against the Norsemen. But after they're gone…' His voice trailed off, and he turned to kiss her.

Iseult tried to pour herself into his embrace, wanting to prove to herself that she could feel the same longing for Davin. From the way he pulled her tightly against him, she knew she'd kindled his desire.

And still she felt nothing.

'Lie with me, Iseult,' he whispered fiercely. 'I want you.'

Her face revealed the misery she felt. When he saw it, his visage tensed. 'I don't know what Murtagh did to you, but by God, if he ever crosses my borders, I'll murder him where he stands.'

She said nothing, fighting back tears. It was easier to pretend that Murtagh had harmed her than to admit that the failing lay with her. She had surrendered her body, but

Murtagh hadn't wanted her as a wife. Not even when he knew about their unborn child.

Davin pulled her into his arms again, pressing a kiss against her hair. 'I don't know how much longer I can wait for you.' He looked into her eyes. 'But I'll never force you. You know that I love you, *a chroí*. I'll wait as long as I have to.'

Iseult nodded, her throat closing up with unshed tears. *He isn't the same man as Murtagh*, her mind urged. *He would never humiliate you*. She had to believe that.

Davin took her hand, and they walked through the centre of the ringfort towards the opposite side. Iseult paused in front of the hostages, asking, 'What will happen to them?'

'When the ransom arrives, I'll release them.' Davin shrugged, as though he hadn't given it much thought.

One of the men was watching her, and Iseult shivered. His fierce gaze studied her with interest. Something about these men did not bode well.

'There was no need for prisoners,' she told him. 'Not from a simple raid.'

'There's no real harm done. The Sullivans steal sheep from us all the time. We're just taking them back.'

'Men aren't sheep.' She couldn't help but think of Kieran. He'd been a prisoner, just like these hostages. It didn't feel right, though she knew the men would not be treated as slaves.

'Perhaps they'll think twice before they attack us again.' Davin walked onwards, not sparing the men another glance.

Iseult took no comfort from his words. The hostage who'd been staring at her gave a malicious smile. At his taunting expression, she moved closer to Davin. Her instincts warned her that this man was far more dangerous than they suspected.

* * *

Kieran spent the next few weeks isolated in the hut. He immersed himself with carving, barely stopping to eat or drink. The evocative images seemed to flow from his hands, and he struggled to finish the design upon the chest. His tools were barely sharp enough to penetrate the seasoned wood. Normally he worked the oak while it was still green and soft, adding butter or animal fats to keep it from cracking afterwards. But this wood challenged him, for it had been worked over the course of several years.

He'd wanted to carve an image of the Virgin Mary into the chest, holding a child. And yet each stroke of the blade was a trial of strength and control.

He planned to give the Madonna Iseult's face. Sacrilege, perhaps. But he could easily envision her holding a babe in her arms, smiling down in wonder at her son.

Every day, he was conscious of her. Though he hadn't spoken to her, he couldn't stop himself from catching glimpses. Now that the weather had turned warmer, he sometimes brought the heavy chest outside, using the natural sunlight as he worked beneath a triangular thatched shelter.

The right panel of the chest had split down the centre and would need to be replaced. If he could cut a fresh piece of oak and create a simple joint, he could fix the broken piece. Although he'd found a small underground storage chamber where Seamus kept the dry timber, none of the pieces were suitable, nor the right size. The supply of walnut was very low, as well as the yew. And the oak was gone.

He needed to find an oak tree in the forest and cut a plank to fit the chest. Until he'd found it, he could do nothing further. Setting his tools aside, he covered the chest with a piece of leather and moved it back inside the hut.

On the opposite side of the ringfort, he spotted Davin talking to a group of men. He knew they were preparing to approach the western coastline and discern what the Norsemen wanted. If he didn't speak to Davin now about gaining the wood, his chance would be gone.

He stood on the edge, visible to Davin, but not interrupting the conversation. Though the men saw him, they ignored his presence. Kieran kept his breathing even, though with each minute longer, his frustration grew. He wasn't accustomed to waiting on others for the things he needed.

Damn it all. He'd not wait any longer. Instead, he strode back to his hut, picking up a small axe he'd sharpened the other day. When he reached the gates of the ringfort, he glared at the guards.

'Where do you think you're going, slave?' one of the men demanded.

'I'm gathering more wood to repair the chest Davin ordered. And since you haven't any trees growing here, I'll have to go into the forest, won't I?'

'Not without Davin's permission. We can't have you trying to escape.'

The guard glanced at the mound of hostages, likely thinking of the Sullivan prisoners who had escaped weeks ago. Kieran held back his frustration. If he'd intended to leave, he could have done so long before now. He'd chosen to stay here as penance and had completed several weeks of the imposed time. His hands clenched into fists, curling around the handle of the axe.

'Davin granted him permission,' a female voice interceded. 'I will speak for him, as the slave's future mistress.'

Kieran didn't turn to look at Iseult, though his senses blazed with awareness. He could smell the flower scents Iseult used for bathing, a light fragrance that surrounded her.

'He can't leave the ringfort alone,' the man insisted.

'Then I will accompany him.' Iseult's tone reminded the guard of her status.

The guard didn't like it, not at all. Kieran didn't either, but he needed the wood. The thought of Iseult walking alone with him was akin to torture. Even now, his mind thought of dragging her into the trees and kissing her until he could rid himself of the craving. For that was all she was: temptation.

'Shall I tell Davin that you are holding me prisoner, as well?' Iseult challenged the guard. 'I believe the slave will offer me protection, should I need it.'

Eventually the guard relented. Kieran led the way, Iseult following behind. For nearly a mile, neither spoke. Even so, he sensed her presence and the way she moved. He wanted to touch her, to taste the fragrant skin and give in to his desires. With each step, his tension worsened.

At last, they reached the edge of the forest. Kieran glanced back to be sure she was there, and waited a moment for her to catch up.

Her hair was pulled back from her face in a long braid, two wisps framing her pale cheeks. She looked terrified, as though he were going to attack her.

'You can wait here if you like,' he offered. 'I'll get the wood I need and then we'll go back.'

She nodded, her face drawn in as though she wanted to say something, but couldn't find the words. It was his fault she was so nervous around him. Why had she offered to come along? After the way he'd kissed her, he imagined she would stay as far away from him as possible.

The words of apology came to him, but they would not form. He *should* be sorry he'd kissed her. And yet, he'd gloried in the taste of her, losing himself in the moment.

'Kieran?' Her voice held regret and a question. 'About what happened between us—'

'It's over. No one will ever know about it.' He met her gaze, letting her see the intensity of his oath. He wanted to unravel her braid, filling his hands with the softness of her hair. His mind envisioned kissing her until she had to cling to him for balance.

Iseult lifted her chin, but he saw her hands trembling. 'I would never tell Davin.' She rested her palm against a thin sapling to still the motion. 'It was a mistake to kiss you. I'm still going to marry him, and I will honour the betrothal.'

'You should. He'll take care of you.' His gut twisted at the thought of Davin making love to her. Jealous thoughts had no reason for being, not any more.

'I wish—'

'Don't.' He cut her off, not wanting to hear it. 'By the beginning of summer, I'll have won my freedom. I'll leave Lismanagh and you won't see me again.'

She expelled a breath and inclined her head. 'That would be for the best.'

With the agreement sealed, Kieran turned his attention back to the wood. A single tree trunk would give him what he needed, or perhaps even a stout branch.

He walked through the forest, studying trees for those with the straightest lines. An oak tree stood near the edge, two hands wide in diameter. It would do well for his needs. He would cut the length needed for the panel and then ask Davin's men for help in bringing the remainder of the wood back to the ringfort.

'Stay behind me,' he advised Iseult. He swung the axe, and the blade bit into the tree bark with a satisfying thunk. He eased into the rhythm of chopping, his muscles welcoming the strain. This was work he hadn't been allowed to do at home, for it was considered beneath him. Strange that being a slave could be both liberating and confining.

He switched to the opposite side in order to direct the fall of the tree. Wood chips flew, and with a slight push, the oak tree cracked to the ground. Squatting down, he inspected the tree, using the axe to trim off the branches.

'Is there aught I can do to help?' Iseult asked.

'Not unless you've another axe.' Kieran continued to clear off the brush until he had a straight section. With an unhurried pace, he selected a length near the top of the tree and chopped the wood until he had the segment needed.

The fresh scent of cut wood was a familiar friend. He hoisted the log over one arm and gestured for Iseult to join him.

Along the way back, he spied a yew tree. He hacked off one of the smaller branches, for he had another carving in mind. He could bring nothing more without the help of an ox or cart.

When he glanced over at Iseult, she seemed preoccupied. He realised he hadn't seen her leave the ringfort in the past few weeks. 'Have you learned anything more about your son?'

She shook her head. 'I have to visit the slave markets. Perhaps they'll have a record—'

'No.' He set his axe down, appalled that she would even consider it. 'Don't go near a place like that. Not even with Davin.'

'It's the only place I haven't looked. If there's even a chance of finding him…'

She didn't seem to understand his meaning. 'Women like you don't belong there.'

'Like me?' Her mouth drew in a line. 'I'm not afraid of the markets.'

'You should be. They target beautiful woman like yourself. Sell them across the sea to be concubines.' He'd seen it happen, time and again. And the men at the slave markets wouldn't hesitate to defile or hurt her. The thought sickened him.

She paled, finally understanding him. 'Then what else am I to do?'

He lowered the axe. 'Ask Davin to go on your behalf. It is his responsibility.'

Her eyes misted with sadness. 'He doesn't want to find Aidan.'

'Why?' Kieran couldn't understand it. Clearly, this was important to her. What did it matter that she'd borne another man a child? It was her son.

She shook her head slowly. 'I know he loves me, and he'll be a good husband. But he wants to leave the past buried.'

'What about the child's father?' Kieran shifted the log to his other shoulder, adjusting the weight.

'Murtagh chose a different path. He's joined a monastery and is happy with his life there.'

Kieran detected a note of resentment beneath her voice. 'Does he know about the child?'

'Yes.' She turned away, staring off into the distance. 'And he made his choice to leave us.'

He didn't know what to say. No words would heal her hurt feelings. A man who would abandon his betrothed and unborn child didn't deserve a woman like Iseult MacFergus.

For a brief moment he paused and without looking at her, shrugged. 'You're better off without him.'

'I didn't think so at the time. But it was a couple of years ago.' She trudged beside him, pushing her way past the branches that blocked their path. A few strands of hair had worked their way free from the braid, and she tucked them behind one ear. The innocent gesture disquieted him, for he couldn't stop thinking about the kiss. He wanted to tangle his hands in that hair, feel the softness of her body against his.

She hadn't pushed him away, like she should have. Though he'd shocked her, she'd responded to him, sweet and wild.

So damned beautiful. And she belonged to Davin.

Frustration gouged at his sense of honour. It had been a grave mistake to come out here alone with her.

When they reached the opposite edge of the forest, Kieran shifted the wood again. Iseult walked alongside him, and she kept her gaze averted.

Her cheeks were flushed from the walk, her full lips tempting. He wanted to drag her against a tree and ravage that mouth until she moaned. For him.

Near the outskirts of the forest, she stopped and faced him. 'Did you find what you needed?'

No. 'Yes.' He needed far more than the oak and yew, but never would he reveal that to her. He had no right to even look upon her face, much less allow his imagination to dream of her.

'If you need to return, I can escort you again,' she offered.

He wanted to laugh. Was she truly that innocent? He lowered the oak log to the ground, stretching his shoulders. 'Don't come with me again, Iseult. We can't be friends, and well you know it.'

'I've done—'

'—Nothing wrong?' he finished.

Her eyes flashed with an anger he'd never seen. 'I'll admit that I shouldn't have kissed you back. You took me by surprise. But we've both agreed that it won't happen again.'

'Is that what we agreed?' He took a step forwards, waiting to see if she'd run from him.

'Yes.' She held her ground, facing him with no fear. 'You wouldn't dare touch me again.'

He wasn't going to let that challenge pass. She needed to understand that he wasn't like Davin. He'd been through the fires of hell, and he didn't live his life thinking about the future. There was only here and now.

He closed the distance and captured her nape. 'I'll dare anything, *a mhuirnín*.' The fragile pulse beat beneath his fingertips, her eyes shocked. 'And you should know better than to come out here alone with a man like me.' He slid his work-roughened hand across the smoothness of her cheek.

He'd meant to frighten her. But the second he touched her, his intentions fell apart. Dark needs ached, and he craved her body. Beneath him, wrapped around him.

'Let go of me.' Her order was firm, despite the shakiness in her tone.

Immediately, he released her. She quickened her pace, almost running to get away from him. Good. She needed to understand that he was not a man to be trusted.

He lifted the log upon his shoulders, welcoming the heavy load. The way he was feeling right now, he wished he had another log to weigh him down.

With his thoughts preoccupied, he barely heard the sound of horses. He glanced up and saw Iseult several paces ahead of him. A group of three riders came from the west, thundering towards her. They wore the Sullivan colours, and weapons were drawn. When Iseult saw them, she froze in place.

He dropped the log and raced towards her. 'Get back! To the trees!'

But his voice was drowned out by their battle cries. She ran towards the ringfort instead, too frightened to realise that the forest was a better haven.

The mounted riders chased her down, cutting him off. His lungs burned as he ran, the small axe his only weapon.

One of the raiders rode towards him, the horse bearing down. It was one of the hostages, the man he'd believed was a Norseman in disguise. Though Kieran didn't know how the men had escaped, if he couldn't save Iseult, both of them would become captives.

He spun away to avoid being trampled. Slashing against their blades, he fought his way towards Iseult. Another man had already dragged her atop his horse. She screamed, struggling against him, and the raider knocked his fist against her cheek until she fell prone.

Fury filled him at the thought of what they'd done to her. Though likely they only wanted Iseult as a hostage, the world became a sea of red. Kieran threw himself at the last rider, knocking the man off his horse with a slice of his axe.

The horse reared, and Kieran grabbed the reins. Blood rage poured through him, along with the pulsing fear that they might harm her.

He mounted and leaned forwards, urging the horse faster. What he wouldn't give for a sword right now, or a bow. A part of him knew he should go for help, but if he stopped, he feared he'd never find her again. His horse was tiring, but he forced the animal alongside the man who had taken Iseult.

She still had not risen from her position across the saddle, her body motionless. By God, if they'd killed her…

The man raised his sword, and Kieran blocked the blow with his axe. He couldn't risk unseating the horseman, or he might send Iseult down to the ground beneath crushing hooves. Instead, he ducked another blow and reached for her arm. Fighting one-handed, he unleashed his anger and struck at the enemy, his blade biting into skin.

He felt the slice of a sword against his upper arm, and

gritted his teeth. Tightening his grip on Iseult, he shoved the other man back with all his strength. The rider crashed to the ground, and Kieran fought to keep Iseult from falling. He grasped her about the waist and pulled her on to his own horse. A moan escaped when he held her steady.

The third raider retreated, urging his horse faster until he disappeared from view. Of all the men, Kieran wished he'd had the chance to fight that one.

He drew the horse to a stop, holding Iseult's body to his. Thankfully she was still breathing, though her face was swollen where the raider had struck her. His heartbeat still hadn't slowed down, and his lungs ached from exertion.

Kieran dismounted, cradling her gently. After a moment, her eyes opened. Gods, he wanted to crush her to him, to ensure that she was not harmed. Instead, he held himself back, laying her down upon the grass.

'Are you all right?' he murmured.

Iseult touched a hand to her cheek, wincing. 'I—I think so.' Gingerly she sat up. 'What happened to them?'

'One is dead. The other fell off his horse—I'm not sure how badly injured. The third got away.'

'Thank you for saving me,' she whispered. Her voice was like glass, almost about to shatter. Though she didn't weep, her hand reached up to his shoulder. He didn't breathe, not wanting to move away from her.

'Would you hold me?' she asked. 'I just need a moment.'

He closed his eyes, lowering his shoulders. She didn't know what she was asking of him. 'No. I'm sorry.'

The stricken expression on her face made him feel like a dog. He rose to his feet, walking back to where he'd dropped the wood. The axe handle was heavy in his hand, and he loathed himself for denying her comfort. But the truth was, if he held her in his arms again, he wouldn't stop there.

Chapter Ten

Iseult's nerves hung by a thread. She couldn't stop herself from shaking. Her cheek throbbed from where the raider had struck her, and Kieran walked so far ahead, it was as though he wanted to be rid of her. Her eyes welled up with unshed tears.

She shouldn't care that he'd refused to hold her. She should be grateful that he'd kept sight of his honour. And hers. But when she'd awoken, his expression was like a man she'd never seen. He'd been worried about her, and it had felt so good to rest in his arms. She had wanted to sink her face into his shoulder, to weep and feel his strength. Instead, he'd pushed her away.

Her mind twisted with confusion. She had never been so frightened in all her life. Though Kieran had defended her from the enemy tribesmen, she'd never been a victim before. If he hadn't been there, she truly would have been taken. The Blessed Virgin only knew what might have happened to her.

Davin's numerous warnings about never venturing forth alone suddenly crystallised. She didn't know what had come over her, following Kieran into the forest alone.

But when she'd seen him standing there at the gates, she'd spoken without thinking. Her mind and impulse had separated, for there had been no apparent reason. Only the deep sense that she needed to help him, no matter that it was wrong.

Had she wanted to be alone with him? Had she agreed to accompany him, with thoughts that it might lead to something else? She didn't know herself any more. Ever since the kiss between them, she'd felt her sensibilities coming apart. Kieran tempted her in ways she'd never known. And, God help her, she was afraid of the way he made her feel.

She couldn't let herself falter. Honour bound her to another man. She took a deep breath, clearing her mind. It didn't matter what her reckless heart wanted.

Kieran waited for her outside the gates of the ringfort. He balanced the heavy oak log upon one shoulder, the yew branch in the other hand. She didn't know why he needed it, but he treated the precious wood as though it were a prized possession.

Swallowing hard, she crossed through the gates. And ran straight into Davin.

'Where in the name of Lug have you been?' he demanded. Then he stared at the bruising on her cheek, and his face transformed into rage. When Kieran entered the ringfort, Davin smashed his fist into the side of Kieran's jaw. The wood clattered to the ground. Kieran straightened, his eyes cold.

'No!' Iseult protested, trying to put herself between them. This was her fault, not his.

Davin pushed her away. 'I'll kill the bastard for touching you.' His face sharpened with hatred, and he struck another blow at Kieran's ribs. Kieran grunted from the pain, but made no move to strike back. Instead, his expression remained empty. Almost as though he were accepting a punishment.

'He protected me from the Sullivan tribesmen,' Iseult said, grabbing Davin's wrist. 'If it weren't for Kieran, I'd have been their hostage.'

'You shouldn't have been out there to begin with,' Davin bit out, a vein pulsing in his neck. 'Neither of you had permission to leave.'

'And when did I become your prisoner?' Iseult demanded.

'You are under my protection. If that means keeping you confined, so be it.'

Her mouth dropped open in disbelief. Never had she seen Davin behave like this, with such anger. He wasn't going to see reason, so she turned her back on both of them and strode towards Muirne's hut. If she remained, she'd say things she'd later regret.

But then Davin's next words stopped her short.

'Bind him. He can spend the remainder of the day at the mound of hostages. No man leaves the ringfort henceforth without my permission.'

Scalding anger rose up inside her veins. How could he do this, when Kieran had been the one to rescue her?

Iseult turned back and approached Davin. 'I want a word with you.'

'Go and see Deena. Let her tend your face and we'll speak this evening.'

'What you're doing to Kieran isn't right. He protected me.'

Davin's mouth tightened, and he took her wrist, guiding her towards the palisade wall where they could speak alone. 'Why are you defending a slave who endangered you? You had no reason to leave the ringfort.'

'He needed wood. I saw no harm in—'

'But you did come to harm, didn't you?' He crossed his arms and let her see the full brunt of his fury. 'The *Lochlannachs* are only a day's ride from here. It isn't safe. If Kieran hadn't saved you from becoming a hostage, I'd have sentenced him to death.' His words were an icy threat.

'I offered to accompany him.' Iseult kept her voice even, despite her frustration. 'And so will you punish me as well, for defying your orders?'

'You were alone for several hours with a male slave.'

He was jealous. She saw that now, and her face flushed. It made her feel even lower than she already did. If Davin even suspected her attraction to Kieran, he would be merciless. He could never know about the kiss.

'Nothing happened,' she answered honestly. 'He found the wood he needed.'

Unexpectedly, he drew her into a possessive embrace. 'I don't want anything to happen to you, Iseult. We will be under attack in a few days. Promise me you won't leave the ringfort again.'

She managed to nod, but she couldn't bring herself to embrace him in return. He'd punished the man who had saved her.

The men dragged Kieran to the chains where the hostages had been kept, like he was a criminal. Stripped of his tunic, they locked his wrists in iron manacles. He didn't fight them off, his gaze staring off into the distance. Beneath the air of calm acceptance, she sensed a terrible anger. Not towards her, but against Davin.

She wanted to go to him, to set him free. Her stomach churned, for she felt responsible for his imprisonment. And yet if she approached him now to say anything, she feared what Davin would do. Instead, she looked to him with an apology in her eyes, hoping he would see it.

But as she'd feared, he wouldn't even look at her.

In the middle of the night, Kieran saw a cloaked figure approach him. Though most inhabitants of the ringfort slept, he knew who it was.

'You shouldn't be here.' If Davin saw her visiting him, he had no doubt it would mean his death.

'Eat.' Iseult fed him fresh bread and tender pieces of meat. The scent of food only heightened the gnawing pain in his stomach. He ate, trying not to pay any heed to her. But each time her fingertips pressed beneath his mouth, he wanted to taste them. Though she didn't mean anything, the act of feeding him became sensual.

He thanked God that chains were restraining him right now.

Kieran leaned forwards, inhaling the fresh scent of her. A lock of hair fell against his cheek, and his body responded almost violently when she laid her face against his.

Iseult broke away, offering him mead from a clay jug. 'I don't understand why he did this. If it weren't for you…' She shook her head and shivered.

'Leave me, Iseult.' He tried to still the need for her, to deny his body's reaction. He wanted her to stay far away from him. His willpower was stretched to the breaking point when it came to her. How it had happened, he didn't know. But right now, he wanted her more than anything else.

'You needed food,' she said softly. 'And I wanted to thank you.' In the darkness, she was shadowed from him. He couldn't make out her features, but his memory needed no reminders. His skin burned with dark needs, and he prayed he had the strength to keep her away.

He was no better than the man who'd stolen Branna from him. It had been over a year since he'd lain with a woman, and his body lacked all discipline when it came to Iseult.

She raised the mead to his mouth again. 'You were a warrior once, weren't you?'

'It was a long time ago.'

'I've never seen anyone fight like that before.'

He had no intention of revealing his heritage to her. 'My past will lie buried, Iseult. Don't ask me about it. Now go back to your home where you belong.'

She paled, but he offered nothing more. He didn't want her thinking there could ever be anything between them. If it meant being cruel, and forcing her to see the truth, he'd do it.

Davin wanted to punch his fist through the wooden palisade. Seeing Iseult's beautiful face and the red swelling at her cheek and jaw had enraged him. When he'd seen her with Kieran, something inside him had snapped.

She'd insisted that the raiders had been the ones to hurt her, but all he could think of was punishing the man responsible for taking her from the ringfort. At the moment he didn't know when he'd release Kieran.

Dawn rose across the ringfort, and Iseult had not spoken to him since the previous afternoon, nor had she dined with him that night. The movement of men near the gates caught his eye, and Cearul dragged a body inside. He recognised the Sullivan colours.

Why had Iseult defied him? Why had she gone alone into the forest with Kieran, a man she admitted she didn't like? His suspicions took root, and though he had the evidence to trust her, he wasn't ready to release the slave.

His men brought in the dead Sullivan hostage, waiting

for his orders. 'Wrap the body,' he told the men. 'We'll send it back to the Sullivans at dawn.'

They nodded, following his bidding without question. Davin walked towards the land he'd shown Iseult a few weeks ago. He imagined their home, and the sound of their children. He could visualise every detail.

For almost three years he'd been in love with her. She didn't know that he'd come to visit her tribe on the night of Bealtaine, so long ago. He'd participated in the rituals, never taking his eyes off her beauty. Though she was a blacksmith's daughter, he'd never seen a more breathtaking woman.

And when she'd taken a lover that night, he'd cursed himself for not speaking to her. It might have been him she'd chosen.

He rested his forehead in his hands. She blamed him for chaining Kieran, and he doubted she would forgive him, unless he set the slave free. He didn't want to, for his suspicions would not be allayed.

Yet she'd been right. The bruises she'd suffered were not from Kieran's hand.

With a heavy heart, he approached the mound of the hostages. Standing before Kieran, he unlocked the chains. 'I let my anger get the best of me.' He wasn't going to apologise to a slave, but he intended to make a point. 'You defended her, and for that I am grateful. But stay away from Iseult.'

'I intend to,' Kieran said. From the icy tone of his voice, Davin believed it. Still, he didn't want the slave near his bride. The thought of any man alone with her drove his jealousy beyond measure.

'Finish the chest,' he ordered. 'You have one fortnight.'

Kieran didn't touch the chest for three days. He'd used the axe, then an adze, to shape the oak log into the size and shape he needed. With careful measurements, he fitted the plank to the chest and took apart the older joints, discarding the cracked wood. He cut another box joint with an iron chisel, carefully adjusting the fit until he could hammer in the new piece to the existing chest.

The precision required a steady hand and pressure upon the wood. His arms ached, but he welcomed the pain. Once, work such as this would have required little endurance. He'd been able to work for hours with no effort at all.

It would take time to rebuild his lost abilities, he admitted. If he had possessed his full strength when Iseult was attacked, all three men would be dead. Now, he lacked the means to protect even one woman. It shamed him to think of it.

When he'd arrived here, he had planned to let himself fade into the background, a faceless, nameless slave. He was beginning to realise that it wasn't possible. He had led men into battle for so long, it was an extension of himself. His tribesmen had looked to him for guidance, to make the decisions no one else wanted to make.

His father had trained him to follow in his footsteps as chieftain. It had been an unwanted burden. He'd never wanted to be a leader of men.

When he was a captive, he'd held fast to the hope that his father and their tribesmen would come after them. He'd consoled Egan, telling him not to fear.

But no one had come.

He stiffened at the memory. It no longer mattered. They were as dead to him as he was to them.

He'd spent time thinking about where he would go next. The answer had come to him last night. He would live out his days as a mercenary, traveling across Éireann, defending those who lacked the means, killing those who harmed innocents.

He opened his palm, gathering his hand into a fist. With each remaining week of his penance, he would spend time rebuilding what was lost.

Yestereve, he'd heard the men talking about the *Lochlannachs*. Though Davin might wish to defend his tribe, he doubted if the ringfort was prepared for such an attack. Many segments of the palisade wall were vulnerable to an enemy breach. He'd studied every angle of the ringfort in preparation for his own escape. There was no part of Lismanagh he didn't know.

He didn't care if the raiders destroyed it. The Ó Falvey people meant nothing to him. Cearul and his tribesmen acted with their tempers, not their heads. They would be slaughtered within moments, the women taken prisoner.

He closed his eyes, thinking of Iseult. If he hadn't been with her, she'd have been taken. He had no doubt they would have hurt her, defiled her. It was like reliving Egan's capture. Only this time, he had saved her.

She'd wanted him to hold her, to reassure her that everything would be all right. He couldn't bring himself to do it. With every moment he stayed here, invisible bonds tied him to her.

Damn it all, she was Davin's responsibility, not his. Davin should be the man to protect her, as her betrothed.

Her future could never be a part of his. And when he regained his freedom, he wouldn't look back.

Kieran stepped outside, breathing in the morning air. His gaze stopped short when he saw Iseult standing a few paces outside Muirne's hut. Her hair was unbound, flowing about her shoulders, and her legs were bare. A rose-coloured *léine* and overdress clung to her slender body. She lowered a bucket and met his gaze. Concern creased her face, as though she'd worried about him. She didn't turn away like she should have. And neither did he.

As she filled her bucket with water from a rain barrel, he forced himself to go back inside the woodcarver's hut. He sat down upon the carver's bench, his palm curving over one of the gouges. With a whetstone, he sharpened the blade, letting the mindless task push away his thoughts of her.

His slavery would end, soon enough. And when he regained his freedom, he would leave Lismanagh and travel east, to make a new start.

Chapter Eleven

A few days later at sunset, the chieftain Alastar Ó Falvey called all the men to gather outside his dwelling. The council had convened, and they had come to a decision. They would ride out to meet the *Lochlannachs*, attacking them if necessary. They'd not wait for the enemy to strike first.

Davin stood at his father's side, his spirits heavy about what was to come. He'd grown up with these men, knew them all by name. And on the morrow, some would die.

'We ride to meet the Norsemen at dawn,' Alastar declared. 'The *Gaillabh* are passing too close to our boundaries, and I need men willing to defend our ringfort. Who among you will volunteer to keep your women and children safe?'

A roar of approval sounded from the men. Davin surveyed the crowd and saw Iseult standing next to her friend Niamh. Neither looked pleased. Niamh, in particular, glared at him as though he were responsible for the danger.

He didn't particularly want to go into battle, either, but

it was his duty. Only the young men like Orin, and the elderly, would stay behind. He and his tribesmen would form an impenetrable shield around their home, so that none of the invaders could cross it.

His father gathered groups of men together, assigning some as foot soldiers, others as archers. Each was given his choice of a weapon, and the men's spirits were high as they selected battle-axes and spears. As for himself, Davin preferred a sword.

Neasa summoned the slaves, ordering a large feast for the men. Barrels of ale were brought up from storage, and all were given as much as they wanted. Davin poured a cup for himself, carrying another to Iseult.

Though he wanted to be alone with her, to take her into his arms, he could see the hesitancy upon her face. She hadn't forgiven him for chaining Kieran; he could see it.

What else could he do to heal the breach between them? Though he did not believe his tribe would lose the fight, he didn't want ill feelings between them tonight.

'Would you like ale?' he asked, offering her the cup. She forced a smile, closing her hands around the goblet.

Then he stared at Niamh and nodded towards the door. An expression of annoyance flickered upon her face before she took the unspoken request and left them alone.

He wanted to say something to Iseult, anything to break the awkward silence. The cool distance in her eyes bothered him more, for it made her unreachable.

'Your bruises are fading,' he remarked, then wished he hadn't mentioned them. It would only conjure up memories of the night she'd been attacked.

'Yes.' She sipped the ale, her attentions elsewhere. He looked to see if there was something distracting her, but it seemed a deliberate move, not to meet his eyes.

He laid a hand across her shoulders, hoping she would turn and look at him. But though she did not pull away, it reminded him that she rarely initiated an embrace or a kiss. He'd thought it was because of what had happened with Murtagh. Now he wondered if the fault lay with him. Did she genuinely not want him? He'd never press his attentions on her, if it caused her discomfort.

He didn't want to lose her. He'd rather have a celibate marriage than live without Iseult at his side.

'I'll be leaving at dawn with the men,' he said. 'And I don't like what's happening between us. You're still angry with me.' His hand moved over to her nape, and at last she faced him.

'I'm afraid, Davin,' she admitted. 'Why must you fight them?'

'Because I believe in defending my tribe instead of letting the enemy come and take what he wants. Including you.'

Her shoulders lowered, her face troubled. 'Who will stay behind to defend us, if you and your men fall in battle?'

'We won't fail you,' he vowed. But in her eyes he saw the disbelief. It made him wonder what had changed. She was strangely quiet, almost suspicious of him. 'Why would you think I'd let anything happen to you?'

'If I had been taken,' she asked, 'would you have come to look for me?'

'Of course.' How could she think otherwise? 'I would not rest until I brought you home again. Never doubt that.' He drew her into his embrace, but she did not return it. 'You mean everything to me, Iseult. I would never stop looking for you.'

'And yet, you want me to stop looking for my son.' Accusation lined her tone, cool as ice.

So that was it. He wanted to exhale with relief, for at least he could do something about her anger. 'After this is over, I'll look with you for as long as you want,' he assured her.

Though he had hoped she would relinquish the search, it would take more time. He doubted if they would ever find the boy, as vast a land as Éireann was. Not a trace of Aidan had they seen. And he wasn't altogether disappointed about it.

The babe was not his, and he cringed at the idea of seeing a son that was not of his blood. It only reminded him that Iseult had shared her body with another man, and not himself. The jealous thoughts were wrong, he knew, but he could not deny them.

'When this is over, will you visit the slave markets for me?' she asked.

'Why?'

'I want to know if anyone sold Aidan into slavery. If they did, there might be a record.'

'It's been nearly a year,' he reminded her. 'I don't know if they would still have any news.' When her eyes would not meet his, he saw his chance dying. Quickly, he amended, 'But I'll try.'

'Swear to me.'

'I swear it.' He would do whatever it took to keep her. Davin took her palm in his, stroking her cold fingers. 'If there are answers to be had, I'll find them.'

Iseult squeezed his hand. 'I hope so.'

Niamh wondered why men felt the need to ride out in search of danger. They hadn't been attacked by anyone, had they? And she knew in her heart that many of the tribesmen would not return alive.

She watched each of them riding forth, and her gaze fell upon Davin Ó Falvey. Handsome as the sun, he was. A golden god of a man who had never noticed her, though she'd been fostered here for the past six years. She was like his little sister, always around.

He rode past her, his gaze upon the others. Quietly, he ensured that each man had his weapons and provisions. And her heart sank at the thought of him dying.

'Davin!' she called out, picking up her skirts as she ran forwards.

He offered her a kindly smile, one that a man would give to a child. 'What is it, Niamh?'

Don't go, she wanted to say. *Don't leave us.* But he had to, didn't he? As their future chieftain, it was his responsibility.

When she couldn't seem to gather her words together, he leaned down. 'Was there something you wanted?'

Yes. Many things. You especially.

But she couldn't say that, now, could she? 'I—I just wanted to wish you a safe journey,' she managed. 'Try not to get yourself killed.'

He was laughing at her, though he tried to hide it. 'I'll try.'

'Iseult would be devastated if she lost you.'

I would be devastated.

Davin reached out and touched the underside of her chin. 'It will be all right, Niamh. I intend to come back, after we've driven the raiders out.'

'Be sure that you do.' She nodded briskly and walked away. Good heavens, why did she always make such a fool of herself around Davin? She wanted to bash her head against the wall.

When she looked up, the slave was watching her. His black eyes saw what no one else did, her unspoken feelings. Colour flooded her cheeks.

A moment later, she caught his gaze elsewhere. Upon

Iseult. And, dear God, the look that passed between them was enough to set the ringfort ablaze. Though Iseult waved to the men, seemingly wishing Davin farewell, it was clear that she was fully aware of Kieran's attentions.

And her friend wasn't immune to them.

Well, now. That was something to think about, wasn't it?

When the men had gone, there was a palpable tension in the ringfort. Iseult had tried to go about her usual activities, but she had difficulty concentrating. The women milled about outside, most watching their surroundings as if expecting the Norsemen to come riding over the hillside with spears and battle cries.

As she passed the open door of the carver's hut, she saw Kieran inside. He was working steadily upon the dower chest, as if unconcerned by the possible raid. How could any man work at a time like this? She knew he'd been ordered to remain behind, along with the other slaves. But even they seemed preoccupied.

She strode a few steps further, then stopped. If Davin and his men could not defeat the Norsemen, the ringfort would not be spared. She and the others would die.

But she'd seen Kieran fight. Slave or not, he would know how to defend the fort. Slowly, she returned to his hut and stood at the entrance.

'You're blocking my light.' His voice remained clipped, while he gouged an intricate border along the edge of the chest. With steady hands, he appeared unconcerned that they would face a possible siege this day. He'd pulled his black hair into a leather thong, and his tunic was rumpled. Despite the carelessness of his appearance, she found it hard to tear her gaze away from him.

'Why work indoors? You'd have better light outside.'

'It's going to rain, and I've no wish to ruin the work I've begun.'

Her lips drew in a line. 'How can you sit and carve wood when we're going to be attacked?'

'There's nothing I can do about it, is there?' He cut another line from the oak, matching it to the first. Then he rubbed the section with butter, smoothing the finish. It seemed like a mindless task, continuing the carving around the rim.

'That isn't true at all. You know a great deal about defending a ringfort.'

He set the cloth down and regarded her. His brown eyes held impatience, the look of a man who expected her to leave. Well, she wouldn't. Not until she had his help.

'What do you want from me, Iseult?'

'I want you to help us, if Davin and his men should fail.' He had the knowledge, she was sure of it. If he would just leave the hut and join the other men, she would feel safer.

'If their forces cannot keep the invaders out, there's nothing I can do.'

When he picked up another piece of wood, she curled her fists. 'I don't believe you. I think you're being a coward.' She wanted to provoke him, to see a flash of anger. Anything but the calm acceptance.

Her words did just that. Kieran stood abruptly, his motion like a prowling animal. 'Practical, yes. Coward, no.'

'We aren't prepared for them,' Iseult argued. 'We need to organise ourselves. Davin put Orin and a few of the others in charge of the defences, but Orin is only a boy.'

'I am sure the older men will advise them.'

Why was he avoiding this fight? She laid her hand upon his, pleading. 'Help us.'

His warm skin stirred her consciousness. He took

another step closer, and his palm reached to her cheek, threading through her hair. She almost swayed on her feet, from the sensations overtaking her. She wanted to wind her arms around his neck and taste his kiss again.

It was so wrong to think of him in that way. But she couldn't seem to stop herself.

Kieran lowered his hand to her shoulder, before pulling away. 'Let Davin and his men do their duty. When it's over, you'll forget your fears.'

She wasn't so certain. In the past few weeks, she'd lost so much faith in her betrothed. Last night, she had sat with Davin for hours while the others partook in the feasting. All she'd felt was emptiness and disappointment in herself.

Davin had offered her everything, and yet, no matter what he did, she couldn't bring herself to want him. She was beginning to question whether she should go through with the marriage. He deserved a woman who could love him, not a woman who didn't know how to love.

She knew the desire she felt for Kieran was just that—a forbidden temptation that she would never act upon. But his very presence reminded her of what was missing with Davin.

She'd come here, hoping that Kieran would take the leadership and tell her what needed to be done. He had the instincts and the knowledge. If anything went astray, she wanted to rely upon him.

'Don't hide away, Kieran. We need you.'

He leaned up against the doorframe. 'I'm no hero, Iseult. Don't try to make me into one.'

Kieran was beginning to realise that staying at Lisma-nagh was impossible. Though it had only been a month, he could not remain any longer. If he stayed, he would take

Iseult to his bed. She got beneath his skin in a way no woman ever had, and his very presence endangered her.

She wanted him to defend her, to be her champion. Gods above, didn't she know what she was asking?

He couldn't save his own tribe. Why would it be any different with the Ó Falvey people? It was better if he left them alone.

A vision captured him, of the raiders taking Iseult. He pictured the men holding her down, and the thought made him want to sheathe his blade in their blood. A stinging sensation caught his attention. He'd been squeezing his knife so hard, the blade had cut into his thumb.

He didn't need to get involved in this. He knew the way these men fought, and it would not be a fair battle. Those who were foolish enough to cling to tribal methods of fighting were going to die. And so would the innocents.

His gaze fell upon the wooden figure of his brother. Egan had been a victim, just as these folk would be. He closed his eyes.

Just leave. Don't concern yourself with them.

The raid would provide the perfect opportunity to escape. No one would notice his absence, and by the time they discovered it, they would be unable to track him.

He threw together a bundle of provisions—a few packets of dried food, water, flint and a knife. Just enough to survive.

We need you, Iseult had said. The pleading look upon her face took apart all of his reasons for leaving. Could he turn his back, letting harm befall her?

Damn her for bringing him into this. Cursing, he threw the provisions across the room. If he allowed the tribe to be slaughtered without raising a hand, it made him no better than the raiders.

He armed himself with the few knives he had, mentally steeling himself for what was to come. The ringfort was unguarded, unprepared for an attack. It was up to him to change that.

Outside, it was unnaturally quiet. The overcast sky had transformed, and a bright sun hung over the ringfort. Kieran crossed the distance to the gates. Orin and Muirne's husband Hagen stood with spears gripped in their hands. The lad's face was smeared with dirt, his eyes glassy as though he hadn't slept. He was frozen with fear.

'Any word?' Kieran asked.

Orin shook his head. 'Nothing. I don't like it. Shouldn't they be back by now?'

'It's only been a few hours.' Kieran nodded to the small crowd staring outside the wall. 'I've an idea to improve our defences, Orin. If you wouldn't mind, you could be a help to me.'

The lad brightened and then tried to mask his enthusiasm with maturity. 'What can we do?'

'I'll need oil. A barrel, if you can spare it.' Kieran met Hagen's gaze. 'And a few men to dig a trench.' The older man's eyes gleamed, and a look of understanding passed between them.

'What do we need oil for?' Orin's face wrinkled in confusion.

'Just get it, lad,' Hagen ordered. 'I'll keep watch while both of you do what needs to be done.'

Iseult stayed beside Niamh, her hand palming a dagger. Every sense within her body was on alert. 'I can't stand this waiting,' she admitted.

'Me neither.' Niamh held a spear, awkwardly lifting it into the air. 'I don't even know how to use this. I'd sooner stab a man in his knee instead of his heart. And that's if I'm fortunate enough to hit him.'

Iseult still fumed over Kieran's refusal to help. What had she been expecting? That a slave could lead their defences? She was stupid to even think it. Everything about him had made her believe he was a warrior, or had been at one time. But she hadn't expected him to give up so easily.

'What are they doing?' Niamh asked, interrupting her thoughts. She pointed towards the gates where Kieran and Orin were standing.

The two men had lifted a barrel between them and were walking outside the ringfort without a single protest from Hagen. The older man let them pass, then resumed his position guarding the gate.

'Are they planning to send a barrel of ale to the enemy?' Iseult wondered aloud. She wasn't sure what to think.

The men disappeared beyond the rise of a hill and were gone for nearly two hours.

When they returned, Kieran had balanced the barrel upon one shoulder.

'I don't think that was ale,' Niamh replied. 'But Orin certainly looks pleased with himself.'

Iseult lowered her dagger. Kieran was watching her, his expression penetrating. He didn't take his eyes off her, and she shivered.

'Are you all right?' Niamh asked. 'You're flushed.' Then she stared back at Kieran, her voice growing suspicious. 'Iseult?'

'It's nothing,' she insisted. But her cheeks were burning.

Had he changed his mind? She wanted to believe it, but Kieran was unpredictable. 'I'm going to find out what they've done.'

Niamh cast a wary look and took her hand. 'I don't think you should talk with him. If Davin knew—'

'He's a slave, Niamh. Nothing more.' If she said it enough, perhaps she would start to believe it.

She crossed the ringfort and stopped in front of Kieran. Despite the bright day, a darkness seemed to shadow him. His black hair hung against his shoulders, the stubble of black beard outlining his cheeks. His skin had grown darker over the past few weeks as the sun transformed the landscape into spring. The lean, hollow look had gone, replaced by iron determination.

'I thought you weren't going to help us,' she said at last. Her voice came out more sharply than she'd intended. She took a breath and amended, 'If that's what you were doing, I mean.' She felt like kicking herself. There was no reason to be discomfited by Kieran.

He set the barrel down, not saying a word. Iseult gripped her fingers, feeling more and more foolish. Seconds later, Kieran turned his back on her and entered the woodcarver's hut. She had the choice of letting him go or following.

Curiosity overcame good sense. With a quick glance, she saw that no one was watching. It was easy enough to slip away from notice.

Once she was inside the hut, Kieran closed the door behind her. The intense darkness felt stifling. Only the coals from the fire remained to light the space.

'What did you do with the barrel?' she asked.

'Only what was necessary. There may be no need for it.'

He wasn't going to admit anything. Her exasperation rose even higher. 'I'm glad you decided to grow a conscience.'

'I haven't. I don't care about any of *them*,' he said suddenly. His low voice filled the space, sensual and deep.

Was he doing this for her? Her heartbeat quickened, and she took a step back towards the door, suddenly afraid to be alone with him.

'Who do you care about?' she whispered. 'Yourself?'

He reached out and unfastened the ribbon that held her braid. Letting it fall to the ground, her hair began to unravel around her shoulders.

His silent gesture was not the answer she'd expected. Dark brown eyes gazed upon her as if he wanted to devour her. Her skin blazed with awareness, and more than ever she knew she needed to open the door and get out.

'I'll stay long enough to keep you safe. And then I'm leaving.' His rough palm reached out to trace the outline of her jaw. She closed her eyes, entranced by his touch.

'Run away, Iseult,' he said. 'If you've the courage.'

'W-why?' she stammered.

'Because if you stay here, I'm going to kiss you goodbye.'

Chapter Twelve

So many thoughts passed through her mind, reasons why it was wrong to stay. Kieran was a slave, and she was betrothed to another man. Her hand closed upon the door, but she didn't open it.

Was it right to marry Davin? She didn't love him, but he would be a good husband. In the past few weeks, her doubts had grown stronger. Davin didn't want to find Aidan, not the way she did.

And Kieran had made no promises, no mention of what there was between them. Intense attraction and desire, little else. He was going to escape, given the opportunity. And heaven knew she wouldn't stop him.

Why was he looking at her that way? Like he wanted to remove every clothing barrier and fill her body with his own.

'You don't care anything about me,' she whispered, as he drew nearer.

'If that were true, I'd have left at dawn.' His hand moved to her braid, loosening the strands. 'You're the most beautiful woman I've ever seen.' With his hands he touched her forehead, moving down to her eyelids and the curve of her cheek. 'I've captured your spirit in wood. And I've tried to drive you out of my mind.'

He dipped low, tasting her lips softly. She had every opportunity to pull away from him. He tantalised her with the touch of his mouth upon hers. His work-roughened hands slid across her nape, spilling through her hair.

He smelled of wood, the clean scent of fresh shavings, and his kiss left no room for regrets. After this day, she'd never see him again. And so she surrendered to her desires.

She wound her arms around his neck, and he pulled her tightly against him. She felt his arousal against her stomach, her body rising to answer his call. He slid his thigh between her legs, balancing her weight. Her breath shattered at the pressure against her most sensitive part.

And he seemed to know it, too. He deepened the kiss, and she tasted his tongue against hers. His hands moved over her shoulders, down to her waist, caressing her.

Without thinking, she grasped his hand in hers. She needed him to touch her, needed him to fill the emptiness inside her. She placed his hand upon her breast, and instantly her nipple tightened with pleasure.

Kieran hissed beneath his breath, and his hungry gaze left no doubt of his own arousal. She had wanted him to ease the aching sensations, but instead, he brought his leg deeper between her thighs. A rush of moisture caught her, and she moaned as he moved himself against her centre.

'*Críost,*' he murmured, lowering his mouth to her throat. With his hands caressing her breasts, she couldn't breathe any more. She needed him desperately, and when he pulled her gown lower, he lifted her nipple and took her into his mouth.

The hot, drugging sensation went straight down to her core, and with a single move of his leg, a fiery rush caught her in a gripping release. So fast. She melted against him, clinging to him while his mouth caught hers in another intense kiss. Dark and forbidden, she tasted the temptation he offered. And wanted more.

When he broke free, her body trembled with needs she didn't understand. Never had she felt this way with a man. She almost wept, for this was the way it should have been with Davin.

He didn't speak a word, but his hands continued to stroke her. His palms filled with her breasts before he lifted her gown up again. 'Goodbye, *a mhuirnín*,' he murmured, kissing her one last time.

Tightness gathered in her throat, and she wanted so badly to cry. Her skin felt feverish, raging with need for him. He stepped away, and her knees shook.

Outside, shouts broke through the stillness. Iseult's pulse trembled, and Kieran lifted a finger to his lips. 'Stay here,' he warned. 'Don't come out until we know it's safe.'

Kieran grasped a knife, stepping outdoors into the blinding sun. In the distance, he saw the line of tribesmen and beyond them, the enemy. The sight cooled his ardour, centering his mind upon its purpose. He had to protect Iseult and use the opportunity to flee the ringfort.

He moved to the edge of the palisade, surveying the battle outside. The enemy forces were not as large as he'd thought. The *Lochlannachs* numbered about thirty, with three mounted horsemen. Kieran shielded his eyes, noting their weapons. Mostly spears and archers, but a few wielded the deadly double-bladed battle-axes. They wore iron-masked helms and carried large wooden shields with elaborate iron bosses in the centre.

Leading the men was the raider who had tried to seize Iseult. The same hostage who had let himself be captured, in order to better understand the ringfort's defences. Dressed in the armour of the *Lochlannachs*, it was clear that he was one of them.

Mentally Kieran adjusted the plan he'd formed. He signalled to Orin and Hagen, meeting them both just before the gates. 'We need archers. How many of your men and women can wield a bow?'

Hagen shrugged. 'Perhaps a dozen. Some of the younger boys can shoot.'

'You're going to need them.' Kieran nodded to the walls. 'Your only hope of surviving this attack is to shoot as many arrows as possible. Pick them off before they can get to the ringfort. But don't shoot our men.'

Hagen gave the orders, and Orin handed Kieran a bow and quiver. He returned to the woodcarver's hut where Iseult waited. She had bound her hair back up in the long braid and straightened her gown. She looked perfectly composed, not at all flustered by the way he'd touched her. Only her swollen lips gave evidence to their stolen moment.

Before he could breathe, she threw herself into his arms, holding tight. Even knowing he could not have her, could never be with her, he savoured the feeling. His palm caressed her back, while he imagined her bare skin against his own. More than anything in the world, he wanted to join his body with hers, and feel the fierce tremors of her release.

His mind filled up with a thousand reasons why he had to leave her behind. And yet, all he wanted to do was drag her to the back of the hut and satisfy his craving.

Damn it all, she made him want to live.

He closed his eyes, forcing himself to let her go. Iseult rested her palms upon his chest. 'What's happening?'

'We're about to be attacked.' Gently, he drew her hands away. 'Can you shoot a bow?'

'Not very well.'

'Do the best you can. We'll try to strike before they can reach our walls. With any hope, we'll fend them off.' He searched the hut for a length of linen and a small container of oil. When he found them, he tucked them away in a pouch at his waist.

'What about—?' She paled and tightened her lips. 'What about Davin and the others? Are they dead?'

'I don't know.'

The stricken, helpless look upon her face made him damn the consequences and pull her into his arms once more. She buried her face in his shoulder, and he stroked her hair. 'I won't let them harm you.'

'You're leaving,' she said.

'After it's over.' Because it was the right thing to do. Though he had sworn to endure the servitude until summer, no longer could he keep the vow. Not without endangering Iseult.

Perhaps it was a greater penance, having to let her go.

He memorised her face, her eyes that would haunt him after he'd gone. Then at last he released her. 'Wait a few moments and then follow me.'

Without looking back, he returned outside to his position along the palisade. There was no sign of the Ó Falvey tribesmen, only the line of enemy forces waiting to attack.

Orin joined him, his boyish face heavy with worry. 'We're going to die, aren't we?'

'We might.' Kieran wrapped a scrap of linen around the tip of an arrow and soaked it in oil. A short time later, he saw Iseult emerge, before she went to retrieve her own bow and arrows.

Desire pierced him at the sight of her, mingled with regrets. He had no choice but to let her go, for he had no future to offer.

'What do you want me to do?' Iseult asked, when she joined him. In her palm, she clutched a bow.

'How bad is your aim?'

She gave him a rueful smile. 'I rarely hit anything.'

Kieran took one of her arrows and wrapped the tip in linen, soaking it in oil. 'If they come towards the hillside, light this with a torch. Even if you strike a man's leg or arm, the fire will injure him.'

Her expression remained uncertain, but she nodded. Kieran turned to Orin. 'Have the others take their positions around the palisade. Every side must remain guarded.'

'And we'll survive?' Orin's voice revealed his fear.

Kieran fitted his arrow to the bow. 'It's our best chance. If they break into the ringfort, abandon it. Take sanctuary among the trees, and don't try to fight them. They are here for conquest and looting, not your death.'

Even so, the young man looked as though he might lose his mid-day meal. His hands shook upon the bow, and tension gripped every muscle. Kieran set his hand upon Orin's shoulder. 'Just concentrate on one man at a time. You'll manage. There are enough of us to hold them off.'

A brutal battle cry pierced the air, and a moment later, the Norsemen charged towards the ringfort. They wore leather armour and iron helms with nose guards. Experienced fighters they were, men who gloried in battle.

Kieran waited until they were in range and dipped his first arrow into the torch. He aimed at one of the mounted soldiers, stretching the bowstring taut. With a hiss, the flaming arrow struck its mark, setting the horseman ablaze.

Iseult turned her head away, grimacing. Though Kieran kept sending arrow after arrow, her hands shook. She'd never killed a man, nor did she want to. The clawing memory of the raider's attack sank deep into her mind.

'We need your bow, Iseult,' Kieran said. 'Don't let your fear control you.'

With shaking hands, she followed his instructions for lighting an arrow. She stretched the bowstring, trying not to think of what she was about to do. Then a warm palm settled on her spine. 'Keep your thoughts steady. Aim and shoot.'

The touch of his hand upon her skin seemed to calm her, and she drew strength from him. Though she loathed what she was about to do, she understood that if she did not kill these men, they would kill her.

Despite the heavy losses, the raiders kept coming. With wooden shields raised in a full line, the arrows no longer penetrated flesh. The flames attacked the wood, but the Norsemen showed no sign of retreat.

'Orin.' Kieran signalled to the young man. 'It's time.'

Time for what? Iseult wondered. Both men wrapped their arrows with linen, soaking the tips in oil. Instead of lighting the arrows, they made several more. Both men went to each side of the ringfort, distributing the arrows to Hagen and another to Niamh. Iseult hadn't realised her friend was also fighting among them.

With his hand raised, Kieran ordered them to light their arrows. Iseult stepped back and watched as he held everyone's attention.

By Saint Brigid, this man had never been a slave. He was leading her tribesman as surely as if he were Alastar or Davin. They seemed to sense his knowledge, and no one argued. When he called out the command to shoot, they released flaming arrows into the grass.

Instantly, a ring of fire surrounded the ringfort. The oil. He'd built a fiery boundary around them, one that no raiders could penetrate. The invaders stopped short, and at that moment Davin's men appeared on the opposite side.

Relief flooded through her at the sight of Davin and the others. With swords and spears, they attacked the enemy, while from the ringfort Kieran ordered a steady stream of arrows.

They were winning the battle. Iseult's arms ached and her inner forearm stung from the bowstring. Beside her, Orin's face gleamed with triumph.

And when she looked towards Kieran once again, he wasn't there. Her heart bled, for she knew he'd taken the opportunity to leave. He hadn't said a word to her, and it stung to realise he had truly gone.

It felt empty without him. Iseult forced herself to continue shooting arrows, and a moment later, she saw Kieran outside the ringfort, armed with a knife and torch. He swung the torch at a Norseman, using the blade to take his enemy's life. When the raider fell, Kieran seized the double-edged sword, hacking a path to freedom. In time, he disappeared over the opposite side of the hill.

Hagen joined alongside them, and it was then that Orin noticed Kieran's absence. 'Where is Kieran?' he asked.

'He…joined Davin and the other men in the battle,' she lied.

Orin nodded with satisfaction. 'Good. Davin could use him at his side.'

Iseult tried to smile, but couldn't bring one to her lips. Hagen turned to the pair, his long greying hair hanging against his broad shoulders. He slung his bow over one arm, pointing at the remains of the battle. 'That slave was a warrior. Mark my words. He's seen fighting of this sort many times.'

'I believe it.' Orin lowered his own bow, and they stood watching the remains of the battle. Though the fiery ring still burned, Iseult saw that the men had dug a shallow trench to prevent the flames from spreading further.

She leaned up against the palisade, her knees beginning to shake. Kieran was truly gone. It froze her senses, just to think of it. Though he had been with their tribe only a few weeks, he had awakened a dormant part of her spirit. She wanted to weep, but knew she did not deserve to mourn what had never been. Sinking against the palisade wall, she closed her eyes to the remains of the battle, wanting to disappear.

Niamh approached, her face looking worried. 'Are you all right, Iseult?'

No, she wanted to say. 'Just shaky. I'll be well enough in a few minutes.'

Deena and a few of the women waited near the gates for hours, before the first of the tribesmen arrived, both the wounded and the dead. Cearul had not survived the battle, along with half a dozen others. Davin walked with a limp, his face covered in blood and dirt. His eyes were weary, but he was alive.

Iseult broke into tears at the sight of him. Her weeping was not thankfulness for his well-being, but instead the worst guilt she could have felt. Anger at herself, anger at Kieran for leaving, and grief for those who had died. His arms were around her in moments, and his low voice murmured words of comfort and endearments.

When the last body was brought in, the sight nearly took her to her knees. Kieran was carried by two men, his face ashen. A makeshift bandage covered his side, stained with blood.

'Is he—?' Her voice would hardly form the words, such terror struck her.

'No. But he took a sword that was meant for me. I'd be dead if he weren't fighting at my side.' The solemnity of Davin's voice revealed his debt.

He was supposed to escape. Iseult's legs trembled, and she clung to Davin to keep from screaming. Her mind and soul were torn apart, between the two men she cared for.

'If it weren't for him, we would have died here as well,' Iseult managed. 'The raiders broke past your men and attacked.'

'We saw the fires. Thank God he started them.' Davin led her away from the wounded, towards his family's hut. 'I am granting him his freedom in return for what he did here. If he lives.'

Another tear slid down her cheek, for if Kieran didn't live, his freedom meant nothing at all.

When they reached his dwelling, Davin embraced her, stroking her hair. 'We will say a Mass this evening, of thankfulness. And in memory of those who perished.'

Iseult couldn't stop her tears. It wasn't right to marry Davin, not any more. But how could she explain? It was not as though Kieran wanted her. He hadn't even suggested taking her with him. Pain cut through her, for she no longer understood her own feelings.

'I will see you later,' she said quietly, giving his hand a squeeze. 'I think I'll go and help Deena. She'll have her hands full with the wounded.'

When Davin had gone, it was all she could do to keep her steps even. She needed to know if Kieran was all right. The idea of him dying made her numb inside.

She opened the door to the sick hut and found chaos. Men were crying out in pain while Deena walked from one tribesman to the next. Niamh was helping her, and Iseult stood out of the way.

'Do you want another pair of hands?' she asked.

'What I need is a larger space,' Deena answered. 'The men are too close together, and none can heal with these conditions.'

'Should we move some of them?'

'After I've treated those with minor wounds. They can return to their homes and we'll see what we have left.'

'How is Kieran?' Iseult asked gravely.

Deena shook her head. 'If he makes it through the night, it will be a miracle. The sword cut him across the ribs. I've stitched him up, but if the wound becomes poisoned, he'll die.'

Iseult's heartbeat quickened with fear. She stepped across the wounded and knelt beside Kieran. She took his hand, and as soon as she touched his cold flesh, she sensed the danger.

'You saved us,' she murmured beneath her breath, knowing he could not hear her. 'I'll always be grateful for it.' Her thumb traced small circles over the back of his hand. 'Davin granted you your freedom. You saved his life.'

She swallowed hard, bitter tears drowning her eyes. Leaning down, she saw his eyes flicker. And she whispered one last truth.

'I'm not going to marry him.'

Chapter Thirteen

The pain ripped through Kieran so badly, he wished the sword had ended his life. He wanted to let go, to sink into the nothingness that beckoned. But he felt a woman's hand touching his, her fingers interlaced with his own. Sweet and fragrant, he recognised Iseult's unique scent immediately. And somehow it gave him strength, having her near. He kept his eyes closed, fighting against the brutal agony that threatened to drag him under.

'Davin is looking for you,' he heard Deena say.

'I know. I'll come soon.' A cool compress settled upon his forehead. He smelled pungent herbs, and a wooden cup touched his mouth.

'Drink. It will help you sleep,' Iseult urged. He choked down the bitter brew, forcing his eyes open. If he was going to die this night, he wanted to remember her face.

'I'll return later,' she murmured. Deep blue eyes held worry, her mouth unsmiling. She had bound her hair, but a few sunny strands escaped, framing her face. God, she was beautiful.

And she wasn't his. Never would be, despite what she'd

said. She'd been speaking foolishness when she'd said earlier that she wasn't going to marry Davin. The chieftain's son would make a good husband for her. Davin would take care of her and protect her the way he couldn't.

His head felt as heavy as stone. Although he had his freedom now, it meant less than he'd thought it would. Like a hollow shell, he had no one to share it with. The thought of returning home was an impossible vision.

A gnarled hand touched him, and he managed to raise his eyelids. Deena spread a cooling herbal mixture upon his wounds, and it made it easier to give in to the sleeping draught.

'She cares for you,' Deena said. 'You'd best watch yourself, slave.'

'She belongs with Davin.' He winced when she touched the sword wound, wrapping a bandage around his ribs.

'Aye, she is betrothed to him. But why did she come to tend you, instead of Davin?' The healer's knowing glance pierced him.

Kieran struggled to breathe, pain lancing his side. 'I don't know.'

The lie fell from his mouth, but he suspected that Iseult's feelings were as tangled as his own.

Deena sat back to regard him. 'Do you love her?'

He said nothing, closing his eyes as if he hadn't heard the words. Though he wanted Iseult for himself, she was fully out of his reach.

'Well?' she prompted again.

'Stop your prying, woman.'

Deena laughed and leaned forwards, lowering her voice. 'If you want to win her heart, find her son. A man who loved her would seek the answers she cannot find.'

Kieran turned his face away from the healer, sinking into sleep. And in his dreams, the face of his brother haunted him.

That night, Iseult stood at Davin's side in the cool stone chapel while their priest, Father Aengus, said a special Mass for the dead. The Latin words washed over her, familiar and comforting. But when she knelt to pray among the tribesmen and women, she found herself praying for Kieran. She murmured the silent words, both for him and for her missing son. *God keep them both.*

Afterwards, Davin led her back to his dwelling. Iseult forced herself to go with him, though she wanted to return to the sick hut. Her thoughts roiled with guilt, for she was betraying Davin by keeping silent about her feelings for Kieran.

But if she admitted the truth, Davin would kill Kieran. The only way to protect him was to hold her tongue.

When they arrived, Neasa approached them from the far side of the chapel. The woman wore her hair bound up in a fine linen veil, and her grey eyes held solemn accusations.

'Davin, your father wants to see you.' She smiled warmly, embracing her son. 'He wants your help in inspecting the damage. Iseult and I will direct the meal preparations while you're gone.'

Davin lifted her palm to his lips. 'I'm sorry, *a stór.* I'll return soon.' The heat and longing in his eyes drove an invisible knife into her heart. Somehow, she forced a smile.

Neasa waited until he'd joined Alastar at the opposite end of the fort before she spoke. 'I saw you earlier,' she accused. 'You went to the slave's hut alone during the battle.'

It was clear what Neasa was implying. Iseult could not deny it, but what could she say? She chose her words carefully. 'I did, yes. And without Kieran's help, all of us would have died in the battle. You know it as well as I. I went to gain his help.'

'You were alone with him. And when Davin learns of it—'

Iseult cut her off. 'He will not learn of it.' Fear gripped her by the throat. She fully intended to break off the betrothal, but not until Kieran had recovered from his wounds. His life depended upon her silence. 'Nor will he hear lies from you.'

Neasa's face turned bright with fury. 'I would tell him nothing but the truth.'

'As I intend to do, once Kieran has gone.' She took a deep breath. 'Hold your silence, and you will get what you long for most of all.'

'How could you presume to know what I long for?'

'You want me to break my betrothal with Davin,' she predicted. To her embarrassment, her voice shook. The strange finality of her decision hurt. Davin was her friend, a man who loved her. Leaving him meant breaking his heart, even if it was the right thing to do.

'And you would do this?' Neasa grew still, her face tightening with disbelief.

'I want what is best for him,' Iseult managed. And knowing what she felt for Kieran, it was best not to marry Davin. It would only hurt both of them. 'And I no longer think I would make a good wife for him.'

Neasa's hand moved to her heart. 'It is because of the slave. You're protecting him.'

Iseult shook her head. 'He saved my life and the life of everyone here. He has earned his freedom, not accusations that could cost him his life.'

Neasa remained unconvinced. 'Are you leaving with him?'

'No.' She had no intention of betraying Davin any more than she already had. 'I'll return home to my family. Alone.'

The crack in her heart split open a little wider, knowing that she would not see Kieran again. Seeing him near death in Deena's hut made her soul bleed.

Neasa stepped back. 'He deserves to know what you did. You owe him your confession.'

'What is there to confess?' Iseult's anger rose within her. 'That I do not love him the way he deserves to be loved?'

'That you shared your body with that slave while he was away in battle.'

'I did nothing of the sort. You can believe whatever you like in your own narrow mind. I'll be leaving soon, and that's all that matters to you.'

Neasa didn't smile, but opened the door. 'Go in. Davin will be expecting to see you after he returns. Though I'd be as happy if you left now.'

Iseult stepped across the threshold. Inside, the warm interior smelled of roasted fish and stewed cherries. Several female slaves worked to prepare the meal, and Iseult chose a place beside one of the low tables to wait.

Thankfully, it was not long before Davin reappeared. She rose to greet him, and he embraced her warmly, kissing her cheek. 'I'd like for us to take our meal outside. I want to have a private celebration with you.'

Dire warnings resounded in Iseult's mind. She had hoped to avoid hurting Davin's feelings, but if she went with him, he would want to press his affections upon her.

'Have you eaten?' he asked.

The thought of food made her stomach churn. 'I'm not hungry,' she admitted.

'Neither am I.' He leaned down and kissed the soft spot of her neck. 'Not for food, anyway.' His warm hand moved over her spine in a silent invitation.

Iseult moved away from him, her face on fire. She didn't want him to touch her, but neither could she admit the truth. Not until Kieran had healed and was gone.

'Is something wrong?'

She shook her head, not facing him. 'I'd rather go outside.'

Davin followed her, but when they were away from his parents' home, she realised her mistake. He thought she wanted to be alone with him. His arms wound around her waist, and she could feel his desire. Her throat closed up with fear and guilt.

'I am glad that you were all right after the battle,' she said, trying to keep him distanced. 'I was afraid for you.'

'I would not have let them harm you.' Davin's grasp tightened around her. 'There is something else we learned. The hostages we took were Norse spies, not Sullivans.' His hand traced the spot on her cheek where the bruise was still fading. 'You were fortunate Kieran was there to keep you safe.'

She nodded, not trusting herself to speak.

'God blessed our battle and made us victorious,' Davin continued.

'I only wish we hadn't lost so many men.'

His face sobered. She didn't want to think of the images he carried with him, watching his own men die. With a heavy heart, she broke away from his embrace. 'It's been a long night for both of us. I think it's best if I return home.'

Regret clouded his face, and his hand closed upon her nape. 'I will see you on the morrow.'

After she left, she walked slowly back to Muirne's hut. As the moon rose above the ringfort, she stopped to gaze over the wall at the charred grasses. The heavy scent of smoke and ashes coated the air. Her palm curled over the wood of the palisade, splinters cutting into her skin. Soon she would leave this place.

And then what?

Over the past year, she'd continued her search for Aidan, but had done little else. She had followed in the path of other women, cooking and weaving. Mindlessly becoming more and more of a shadow.

If she returned home, would she lose herself entirely? Iseult raised her face to the sky, taking a deep breath. More than anything, she wished Kieran would take her with him.

She'd never met a man with more intensity. And he'd wanted her. The day of the battle, there was no denying it. She had revelled in his touch, the way she never could with Davin. Even now she craved being with him. Was it only desire? Or something more?

The old impulses sparked. She sensed that if Kieran ever let go of the nightmares that haunted him, there was a man of true worth beneath it all. Someone worth fighting for.

It was time to be honest with herself, and to stop hiding behind her grief for Aidan. Though she would never cease the search for her son, neither could she let Kieran go. Not without learning what he felt for her.

She halted in front of the sick hut, a tangle of thoughts running through her head. The door opened, and Deena stepped outside.

'He's asleep,' she said. Her kindly face held understanding, and Iseult wished she could go into the older woman's arms for comfort.

'How is the wound?'

'I've treated it as best I can. Pray for him, and he may be spared.' Her gaze turned troubled. 'Did you see Davin?'

Iseult inclined her head. 'I did. And I would like to see Kieran now.'

'Do you think it wise?'

From the knowing look in Deena's eyes, Iseult wavered. 'I need to know that he will live.'

'That is in God's hands.' Nonetheless, Deena opened the door. 'Would you like some camomile tea?'

'I would, yes.' Iseult stepped inside, and the comforting scent of healing herbs surrounded her. Coals glowed upon the hearth, warming the interior. Three men slept upon pallets, Kieran's being the furthest away. Iseult walked towards him, and knelt down. Deena had removed his tunic, leaving only the linen bandages upon his torso.

Though he had not the immense strength of some of the other tribesmen, rigid muscles moulded his chest. Lean and sinewy, he was no less dangerous than brawny men such as Cearul. She closed her eyes, for Cearul was numbered among the dead.

She wanted to touch Kieran's skin, to feel his heartbeat beneath her fingertips. But she'd not disturb him.

'Iseult?' Deena held out a steaming clay mug.

She stepped across the bodies of the men, accepting the hot drink. The healer gestured for her to sit down upon one of the log stools. Iseult sipped at the sweet blend, tasting the camomile.

'Why did you come back?' Deena prompted.

'To see about the men.' She kept her voice neutral, but the healer seemed to see through her façade.

'Iseult, you tread upon dangerous ground,' the healer warned.

She tore her gaze away from Kieran, for it was clear

Deena had already guessed the truth. 'What would you do, were you in my place?'

'I would tell Davin.'

'And so I shall. But not until Kieran has healed.' She gazed over at him once again. 'Davin would kill him otherwise.'

'You cannot protect the slave,' Deena cautioned. 'The longer you wait, the worse it will become.'

Iseult took another sip of the tea. 'I won't let his life be forfeit, if I say anything to Davin. Kieran might desire me, but he would never take me with him. There is nothing for us.' She looked back at Deena. 'Will his wounds heal before Bealtaine?'

The woman shrugged. 'If he does not die of a fever, he would be well enough to leave. It would be dangerous to travel, though.'

Iseult finished her tea and stood. 'I must return to Muirne's. Let me know if anything changes. Else I will come back on the morrow.' She embraced the older woman.

'You should tell Kieran of your feelings for him, Iseult.'

'I can't.' She raised her *brat* to cover her head. 'For I don't know what I feel.'

'You're in love with him.' Deena squeezed her hand. 'And he deserves to know it.'

A bright burning stung her eyes, and Iseult shook her head. 'It would change nothing.'

'It might change everything.'

Chapter Fourteen

Death had not taken him, but instead had left Kieran with pain beyond anything he'd ever experienced. Even a fortnight later, he was not well enough to leave Lismanagh. Though Davin had granted his freedom, his wounds imprisoned him here.

Deena had moved him back into the carver's hut, and she visited him each day, inspecting him with the precision of a commander. She had spread foul-smelling concoctions upon his wound, and so far he had managed to recover.

But Iseult had not come. Not since that night. He was glad she'd listened to him, though he'd felt the loss of her presence. He needed to know that she would be safe, that someone would protect her. Especially since that man could never be himself.

Though Deena had encouraged him to rest, he disliked being idle. He sharpened his tools and renewed his work upon the dower chest. As each day passed, he carved an interlocking design that incorporated both Irish and ancient Norse patterns. Though he was still too weak to travel, he would finish as much of it as possible before he left.

And each time Iseult saw it, she would remember him.

At night, he'd spent hours working on another piece of yew. Though it was not as detailed as the carving of Iseult, the task occupied his hands. Seeing the face emerge pained him, for it brought forth memories he'd locked away for several moons.

A shadow blocked his light in the doorway. His heart quickened at the sight of Iseult. She wore a gown of almost pure white, with a cream overdress. Tiny stitches of rose thread formed embroidered flowers upon the overdress.

'Why did you come?' He set down the chisel, startled to see her.

'Because I couldn't stay away any longer.' She moved to stand behind him. Gently, she laid her hands upon his shoulders. The touch, light as a kiss, brought a ripple of guilt into his conscience.

Gods, she was driving him to madness. If she were his, he'd pull her down to his lap, plundering the sweetness of her mouth. He would close the door, no matter that it was daylight outside. She would lie upon his pallet, and he'd savour the time alone with her.

Instead, he took her hands and removed them gently. 'You're betrothed to Davin.' The reminder was as much to himself as to her.

'Only until you're healed.'

He heard the note of hope within her voice. And though it made him want to pull her into his arms, holding her close, it was a dream that could never be. He was a slave, a man without a home. A man with nothing to give.

'Iseult—'

'Don't.' She braved a smile through the glimmer of tears. 'I know what you're going to say. And I'm not ready to hear it yet.' She stepped away and ran her slim fingers over the dower chest. 'This is beautiful.'

'It will be finished in time for your wedding.' He couldn't let her hold onto false hopes.

Iseult's expression dimmed. 'I won't be marrying Davin.'

He reached out and took her wrist. 'You should.' He couldn't let her throw away her future, not on a man like him. 'He'll take care of you.'

'He's not the man I want,' she murmured. The pain upon her face made him long to say something. He wanted her more than he'd ever thought it was possible to want a woman. But already he'd let himself get too close to her. Allowing himself to feel anything towards Iseult would only make it harder to leave her. And leave, he must.

Before he could speak, she interrupted him. 'I don't want your pity. I know that you don't care for me. But I won't hurt Davin by pretending he's someone else.'

Kieran struggled to rise to his feet, using the table for balance. He hated seeing her misery, knowing he was the cause of it.

'You're wrong.' He closed his eyes, leaning down until his nose touched hers. Iseult stood so close, their breath mingled. Her lips parted, an open invitation to kiss her. But he did not. He savoured the last few moments before he stepped backwards. 'But I can't give you what you want.'

A tear escaped her blue eyes, and the sight cut him down. She looked so damned fragile, as though she would shatter. And her sadness was because of him.

'What is it you think I want?'

'A home. A family and people who love you.'

She lowered her chin. 'None of that matters.'

He cupped her cheek, sliding his fingers behind the

curve of her ear. 'It matters. I know what it is to be alone. And it wouldn't suit you.'

'I wouldn't be alone. You would be with me. It's enough.'

He shook his head. 'I'm not a man worth saving, Iseult. I've committed more sins than any priest could ever absolve.'

'Is that why you sold yourself into slavery?' she asked. 'Do you really believe yourself undeserving of happiness?'

He tucked a strand of hair behind her ear. 'Go back to him, Iseult. Let him give you the life I can't.'

She shook her head. 'I've lied to him these past few weeks in order to save your life. I stayed away from you, to protect you. I won't lie to him any more.' Anger glittered in her eyes, overpowering the tears. 'As soon as you've left Lismanagh, I'm going to tell him the truth.'

Her gaze lowered to his bandaged side. 'You'd better leave as soon as you're able. Because if you're still here when I end the betrothal, Davin will kill you.'

The day before Bealtaine, the atmosphere transformed from one of mourning to one of celebration. Though none could forget the men who had died during the invasion weeks ago, the rituals were held sacred. The dawning of spring and the prayers for a good harvest were far too important.

Iseult had spent most of the day baking bread until perspiration dampened her hair. When she removed the last loaf from the pan upon the hearth, she wiped her brow and stepped outside.

Young men carried cut hawthorn, while the women cast secretive glances, watching to see who would lay branches across their homes as a sign of affection. Many would wed tomorrow eve, some handfasting for a year and a day. And Iseult was expected to be among them.

Her heart sank. She had hoped to tell Davin long ago, but Kieran had not been well enough to leave.

Today. It had to be today. She would send Deena to warn Kieran and make him leave. She covered her eyes from the sun, calming her racing heart. Not since that day had she seen Kieran. Although he remained at Lismanagh, she had already lost him. And it hurt, like a sword slicing across her own ribs. Cutting out her heart.

'You've been avoiding me.'

Iseult jerked with surprise when Davin came up from behind her. His hands wrapped around her waist in a soft embrace.

'I've been helping with the wounded men and with the Bealtaine preparations.' She tried to keep her voice even, but inwardly she was shaking. The warmth of his hands felt like a brand of possession.

'What about our wedding preparations?' He turned her to face him. 'We've waited a long time, *a ghrá*.' In his eyes she saw such anticipation, she loathed herself for what she had to do.

Tell him now. He deserved no less than her full honesty.

'Davin, I—'

He cut her off, kissing her deeply as though he'd been repressing his own desires for weeks. There could be no doubt that he wanted her.

'I cannot wait for tomorrow eve,' he murmured huskily. When he drew back, she was shaking. Her mouth felt bruised, her feelings raw. *I can't do this. I can't wed him.*

'Kieran brought the dower chest to me this morn.' He wrapped her hair around his wrist, holding her captive. 'It's the finest work I've ever seen.'

'Is it?' She hadn't known he had accomplished so much.

With his injury, she didn't think it was possible. She forced a smile, as though she were pleased to hear it.

'A pity he won't be staying with us. His talent is unmatched.'

'Has he left?' Please, God, please. Let him be gone.

'I don't know. I asked him to stay until after Bealtaine.' Davin shrugged. 'But he has his freedom. He can go or stay as it pleases him.'

She had to know. The sooner he was gone, the sooner she could break her betrothal.

'I must go,' she apologised. 'I've promised to help Muirne. Perhaps I'll see you later.'

She intended to break the betrothal in private. She didn't want him to endure the same humiliation she had gone through when Murtagh had abandoned her on their wedding day.

Though she knew Davin would fight for her to change her mind, in the end he could not force her to wed him.

He leaned down and kissed her cheek. 'I cannot wait until tomorrow eve.'

Iseult nodded, her face flaming as she turned to go. 'Goodbye, Davin.'

She walked towards Muirne's hut, not stopping when she passed the woodcarver's dwelling. The door was closed, as if he'd left already. The thought filled her with such emptiness, she wanted to throw the door open and see for herself.

But she forced herself to keep walking. With her head down, she almost didn't see Deena waving towards her.

'Iseult!' the healer called out. When she stopped, Deena beckoned closer.

'What is it?'

Deena lowered her voice. 'He left a short time ago. I thought you might wish to know.'

Iseult didn't have to ask whom Deena meant. 'Where?'

'Eastward, near the forest. He's on foot, so you may be able to catch up to him.'

There was no reason to go after Kieran. Already they had spoken their farewells. And yet, the thought of never seeing him again was akin to tearing out her heart. Her body tensed with the loss, and on impulse she hugged the healer. 'Thank you, Deena.'

The old woman's eyes turned kind. 'Go to him. You can take my mare, to save time.'

One last chance to say goodbye. It was wrong, and yet she needed a stolen moment in his arms, a memory to carry with her.

It took only moments to lift a blanket over the animal's back and mount. Iseult urged the mare forwards, pausing briefly at the ringfort gate to speak with one of the guards. 'I am going to bring back some herbs for Deena.'

The guardsman did not protest, but waved her onwards. As soon as she cleared the ringfort, Iseult urged the animal to go faster. In the distance, she saw the lone figure of Kieran.

She held tightly to the reins, her knees gripping the mare for balance. When she reached him at last, she recognised the forest where they had gone to collect wood so many weeks ago. It was here that he'd rescued her from the *Lochlannachs*. She shivered at the reminder, drawing the horse to a stop.

Kieran glanced back at her, his face unreadable. Iseult dismounted, leading the mare towards him.

'Why did you come, Iseult?' His eyes, dark as walnut, stared into hers. He didn't welcome her, nor behave as if he wanted to see her.

An aching emptiness seemed to swallow her. She didn't trust her voice to speak. When he stepped into the shadows and into the forest, her throat closed up. Then he turned and held out his hand, seeming to guess what she could not say.

'Does he know?'

She shook her head, lowering her chin. 'Not yet. I plan to tell him after you've gone.' She tethered the mare to a nearby tree. 'I needed to see you one last time.'

His palm stroked the side of her cheek. She closed her eyes, drinking in his touch. Though his hands were rough, he aroused her with the simple touch of her face.

The last of the dying sunlight spilled through the trees, casting a golden glow behind him. His black hair was bound away from his face, his dark brown eyes gazing at her with an unfathomable expression.

He drew her to him, his warm body sheltering hers. 'Let Davin take care of you,' he urged softly. 'I need to know that you'll be safe.'

'I'd rather have you take care of me.' His heartbeat thundered beneath her cheek, and Iseult closed her eyes, drawing comfort from him. When there was a long silence, she lifted her head. 'But I can't have that, can I?'

He shook his head. She'd expected him to refuse her, but it still bruised her feelings. Though it tore at her to say it, she had to know the truth. 'Is there nothing between us, Kieran?'

He stared at her with heated intensity, as though he wanted to touch her, but would not. 'What is between us is forbidden.'

'I know it,' she murmured. 'But I need to be with you. One last time.' Iseult pressed her hands to his face. He had drawn a blade over his face, shaving off the roughened stubble. Most of the tribesmen wore long curling beards, in contrast. She found that she liked seeing the angles of his face, the strong jaw and firm mouth.

She stood on tiptoe and raised her lips to his. Smooth

and warm, he responded to her. His hands smoothed a path down her spine. Her breasts tightened, and she opened her mouth slightly.

He tantalised her with the kiss, tempting her into madness. When his tongue slid inside, she grasped his shoulders for balance. Warm male hands slid down to her hips, dragging her so close she could feel his arousal. He broke free of her mouth, finding the soft places upon her neck until she shivered.

'You're the only man who's ever made me feel this way,' she whispered, bringing her hands beneath his tunic. It was true. Even the night she'd shared with Murtagh had been awkward, nothing like the intense needs Kieran kindled inside her.

Careful to avoid his healing wound, she stroked his pectoral muscles. She explored his skin, trying to memorise every ridge, every part of him.

'I wanted you from the first moment I saw you.' His hand moved down her thigh, grasping at the fabric of her gown until he touched her leg. She gasped at the sensation of his hand moving up her bare skin. 'You've invaded my dreams.'

She couldn't stop trembling, especially when he paused at the juncture between her thighs. Knowing that his hand was right there, poised to touch her, set her body afire. 'What—?' Saint Brigid, she couldn't seem to form a coherent thought with the sensations pouring through her. He lowered her gown to her waist, baring her breasts before him.

'What do you dream of?' she managed shakily. She felt exposed, completely defenceless. Cool air brushed over her nipples.

With that, he slid a finger inside her. Iseult melted against him, her womanhood wet with wanting him. His mouth bent down to drop a soft kiss upon her nipple.

'I think you know what I dream of.' His expression was feral. His thumb found the small centre of her womanhood, and a spicy pleasure broke over her as he stroked it. She tried to grasp his head, to kiss him again. She needed for him to feel the same thing she did.

'I'm aching for you,' she breathed. His answer was to lay her body upon the mossy forest ground, covering her breast with his mouth. He suckled hard until a flood of burning need came crashing through. Iseult's hands dragged through his hair, and she arched her back when he slid another finger inside her, caressing her.

When he would not stop the intimate torment, she touched her hand to the hard ridge inside his trews. A groan came from his throat, and she caressed the length of him. Pleasure for pleasure, she stroked him until he began moving his fingers in a rhythm inside her.

'Please, Kieran. I can't bear it.' More than anything she wanted him to join with her, to feel his body as a part of her own.

He raised his head from her breast. 'I'm going to pleasure you like no man has ever done before.'

She cried out when his hand began to move in imitation of the act she craved. Of its own accord, her body shook with need. He bit her nipple gently, stroking the tip with his tongue.

She moved her hand over his erection, gripping him through the rough wool of his trews.

'Witch,' he whispered against her skin. 'You've cast your spell upon me.'

The fire building inside her body blazed as his fingers continued to move inside of her. She moaned, helpless as his mouth ravaged hers, his thumb pushing her higher until flames of release erupted. She shuddered violently, riding the wave until she rested limp upon the ground.

Oh, it was wicked to be touched this way. But no longer did she feel bound to Davin. She had never shared this with him, nor had she given him her heart. In this moment with Kieran, she felt awakened.

'Make love to me,' she urged, reaching for the ties of his trews.

But he stopped her, holding her wrists firm. And shook his head. 'I've already touched you, far more than I should have.'

He wrapped her tightly into his arms, holding her close. The aching inside cracked apart as she wept. It was almost worse, knowing what she was giving up. Her heart was raw, while the thought of living without him was unbearable.

'I don't want to stay behind,' she whispered.

'I'm not the kind of man you should be with, *a mhuirnín*.' He eased himself into a seated position, closing his eyes slightly with the pain from his ribs.

The words were a physical blow. It took all of her strength to hold herself together. 'I can't change the way I feel. And I wouldn't want to.'

Taking a deep breath, she rearranged her gown. 'Where will you go?'

He adjusted his own clothing and rose to his feet. 'Wherever I find a place for myself.'

'You should return to your family. Let them know you are alive.'

He lifted his belongings from the leather sack upon the ground. 'They would rather see me dead.'

'Why?'

He leaned against one of the trees, silent for a while. For so long he had held his secrets from her.

'I'd like to know the truth,' she said, touching his shoulder. 'If it would ease your pain…'

'I don't need your pity, Iseult. Let it be.'

He was closing himself off to her, and she fought against it. 'It doesn't matter what happened in the past. I know your family would want to see you again.' She drew back, and added, 'Just as I would give anything to see Aidan.'

His brown eyes softened, and he wiped another tear from her cheek. 'I'll find him for you, Iseult. Your son.'

She grew still, her heart beating a little faster. His offer was not made lightly. She sensed that he would not stop until the answers were found. 'What if he's dead?'

'If he is, I'll let you know it.' He reached into his pouch and pulled out a piece of wrapped linen. 'I should have given this to you earlier, but it wasn't finished. Perhaps you'd like it now.'

She accepted the linen and felt something hard within it. Pulling back the cloth, she revealed a wood carving of a child's face. Her hands shook as she studied the boy. It wasn't Aidan, but the carving represented all she had lost.

'Thank you.' She pressed it to her heart. It meant everything, holding something he'd made with his own hands. She didn't know why he'd carved it, but the piece touched her deeply.

'You must return to the ringfort,' he said. 'They'll be looking for you.'

'I know.' She reached up and straightened his tunic. 'Be safe, Kieran. May God watch over you.'

He regarded her with an intense solemnity. 'I meant what I said. Let your mind be at ease, and do not search for Aidan. If your son is anywhere to be found, I'll seek him for you.'

'Why?' The terrible emptiness, the fear of never seeing him again caught in her throat. 'He isn't your son.'

He leaned down, touching his forehead to hers. 'He's your heart. And it's something I can give you.'

She gripped him fiercely, and their mouths tangled in one last kiss.

'Farewell, *a mhuirnín*.'

Chapter Fifteen

Iseult walked alongside the mare, leading the animal back to the ringfort. She had no desire to go any faster. Kieran was truly gone this time, and there were not enough tears to ease the pain she felt. Worst of all, she had to face Davin.

She couldn't think of anything to say to him. Her skin chilled, and she stopped a moment, resting her head against the mare's back. Though she hated hurting him, it was right to end the betrothal.

Her lips felt tender from Kieran's kiss, her body still lush with warmth. Would to God she could ride towards him and leave everything else behind.

Instead, she forced herself to mount the mare and return to Lismanagh. It would take time to pack her belongings and prepare for the journey back to her family. They would not be pleased to see her. Her father would have to return the bride price Davin had paid.

Strange, to think of new beginnings. Though she did not intend to abandon her own search for Aidan, she believed Kieran's vow to help her. The seeds of faith took root inside her, along with confidence in him.

Inside the ringfort, men and women continued to bustle with the preparations for Bealtaine. Delicious scents rose from the homes, and she marvelled at the greenery and flowers everywhere.

She returned Deena's horse, leading the mare to a trough of water before walking back to Muirne's hut. Amid the thatching, she saw branches of hawthorn and knew they were from Davin.

'There you are!' Muirne beamed when she saw her. 'Come and see the gifts he's sent!'

Iseult didn't need to ask who 'he' was. And when she saw the dower chest, her heart sank.

Muirne's foster-sons rushed over, half-bouncing with excitement. Glendon cried out, 'Open it, Iseult! I want to see what he gave you.'

'And me!' Bartley chimed in. Both boys hovered over the chest, their eyes gleaming as though they expected it to be filled with honey cakes.

Muirne ushered the boys out of the way. 'Now, lads, let her open it.' She turned a discerning eye upon Iseult. 'What's happened?'

'It's nothing.' Iseult touched the elaborate carving upon the lid, remembering the way Kieran had watched her before forming her image out of wood. She ran her fingers over one of the curves, the way she had touched his body only hours ago. She suppressed a shiver.

Taking a breath, she opened the lid. Inside, she smelled lilacs from a bundle of dried flowers wrapped in linen. Gowns of blue, crimson, rose and cream lay inside. Muirne exclaimed over the exquisite fabric.

'He's traded for these,' she said, lifting one of the gowns. 'This is silk. Perhaps from Byzantium.' She held the piece almost reverently.

Iseult closed her eyes in dismay. He'd spent a fortune upon her. She'd never expected this, and her guilt trebled. With shaking hands, she packed the gowns away, closing the lid. No longer could she wait to end the betrothal. It had to be now.

'May I speak with you?'

Davin turned from the horses and saw Iseult standing before him. She had left her hair unbound, a reddish-gold curtain that fell down to her hips. The evening air was cool, sending strands of auburn hair against Iseult's face. Her cream overdress fell in graceful folds over the saffron *léine* beneath it. She held herself like a queen instead of a black-smith's daughter. And yet her lips did not smile.

His instincts sharpened. She had been unhappy for several weeks now, ever since the battle against the *Lochlannachs*. He suspected that whatever bothered her would not be welcome news.

'Of course.' He poured the bucket of oats into a trough for the horses, patting his gelding Lir. 'Did you receive the chest I sent to Muirne's?'

'Yes, thank you.' There was no smile upon her cheeks, but a faint colour rose. Had he done something wrong? Her words were far too polite. Most women would have been overjoyed at the treasures he'd bought. He'd wanted to gift her with exotic fabrics, silks that were worthy of her beauty. But she was behaving in a manner he'd not seen before, as though she were hiding something from him.

Ugly suspicions darkened in his mind. Davin recalled a conversation he wasn't supposed to overhear, between his mother and father last night. Neasa had claimed she'd seen Iseult sneaking into Kieran's hut.

Davin had dismissed it, for his mother's animosity

towards his bride was clear. It was only Neasa's way of stirring up trouble. Iseult had hardly looked at Kieran. She seemed to avoid him at every moment. Not only that, but he'd learned that the woodcarver had already left.

Perhaps she'd had some bad news regarding her son. 'Is this about Aidan?'

'No. It's something else.' She took his hand in hers and led him towards the gates of the ringfort. He accompanied her, noting how cold her fingers were. The moon rose above the ringfort, stark and white against the darkened sky. Torches flickered in the wind.

When they reached the hillside, she led him down until they were completely alone. She sat upon the grassy knoll, tucking her bare feet beneath her skirts.

'You're unhappy,' he said, sitting beside her. 'I can see it in your face.' He'd hoped she would relax and deny it. Instead, she lowered her gaze.

The sinking feeling in the pit of his stomach worsened. Had she ever been happy here? Always leaving the ringfort in search of her son, never content. And even when he showed her affection, she seemed uneasy. His consternation increased while he wondered what he could say to make her feel better.

'It's nothing you've done. You've been the kindest man to me.' She let go of his hand, drawing her knees up. In the moonlight, her profile was pale, uncertain. 'But I can't marry you.'

Like an axe, her words severed his intended response. It was the last thing he'd expected. 'What do you mean?'

'You deserve a better wife than I can be to you. It would be wrong.'

Panic overrode him. He sensed their betrothal crumbling, and he struggled to hold the pieces together. 'You're the only wife I want.' He drew his hand around her shoulders, but Iseult did not respond. The wall of ice had returned, and he didn't know what to do.

A heaviness seemed to encircle his heart as he pulled his hand away. 'What has happened? Only yestereve, you were still planning to wed me at Bealtaine.'

'I think I've always known it was wrong,' she whispered. 'I tried to convince myself that I could love you. You were everything a husband should be, everything I thought I wanted.' Even as she spoke the words, she would not look at him.

His skin drew taut, his nerves growing more suspicious. 'But something made you change your mind.' He ventured a guess. 'It's Kieran, isn't it?'

He'd expected her to laugh or deny it. Instead, her face transformed into guilt. Though she tried to veil it, Davin could see the fear in her eyes. And frightened she should be, for his rage boiled with the need for violence against the slave. His mother had been right.

His knuckles curled into fists, his throat tight with anger. How could she betray him like this? He'd given her his full trust, never believing she would behave dishonourably. 'You're in love with him.'

'He's gone, Davin.' A tear rolled down her cheek. 'Whatever he chooses to do with his life has nothing to do with us.'

Disgust filled him at the sight of her tears. 'He seduced you, didn't he? All the time when he was carving your likeness.' They had planned this together. She'd waited until the slave had gone before telling him.

Iseult turned scarlet and rose to her feet. 'You're wrong. Never did I share his bed, and you needn't treat me like a woman who would lie with any man.'

'You lay with Murtagh and bore his child.'

'That was years ago. It has nothing to do with right now.'

'Never once have you shared my bed,' he pointed out. 'Though we were betrothed.'

'Did you think it was your right?' She crossed her arms, her eyes sparking with fury.

'It was my right more than his.' Davin stood, grasping her firmly by the waist. She struggled, but he held her fast. He wanted her to fear him, wanted her to feel as helpless as she made him feel right now. 'You were promised to me long before you met him.'

'Kieran is no longer a threat to you. I don't know where he's gone, and it doesn't matter. I will return home to my family.'

'If he dares show his face to me again, I will kill him.' He meant it. Nothing would give him greater pleasure than to drive his blade into Kieran's chest. It didn't matter if they had never been lovers. He could see that Iseult had given the slave her heart. And she didn't love him.

'I'll send the chest back,' she said, her voice dull. 'You can give it to the woman you marry.'

He released her. 'That woman was supposed to be you.'

'I won't marry you,' she said quietly. 'It was wrong of me to think I could.'

'You never gave us a chance.' Her words carved invisible wounds into his stomach. 'You gave more of yourself to Murtagh and that…*slave* than you ever did to me.'

'Don't lower yourself, Davin.' She stepped away from him. 'Find another woman and forget about me.'

'I'm still in love with you. And I won't let you go.'

She looked away. 'One day you'll know I'm letting you go because I care for you. Wedding you would be a mistake for both of us.'

'And what of Kieran?' He didn't for a moment believe that she was going home. Icy jealousy made him want to tear the man apart.

She raised a tear-stained face to him, fully meeting his eyes. 'There is no future for me with Kieran. We both know it.'

The loss of her cut into him so deeply, he felt the desperate need to ask her again. Though he loathed the thought of begging, he couldn't stand by and watch her go. He still loved her. Still needed her. 'I would wait for you, Iseult.'

She shook her head sadly and reached out to touch his cheek. 'Don't.'

The crack of a whip struck through the morning stillness. Kieran remained hidden in the crowd, trying to keep his mind detached from the brutality of the slave market. Only this past winter, he had stood naked before a crowd such as this one. He'd fought to free himself, only to receive the lash upon his spine.

His hand went to his pouch to where the frail sheet of parchment rested, the proof of his freedom. No doubt Iseult would have told Davin by now of her decision. Several weeks had passed since Bealtaine.

When he looked upon the faces of the slaves, he thought of his earlier vow. Thirteen weeks, he'd sworn to endure as penance. But he'd been unable to keep the promise. With each day he'd remained at Lismanagh, his desire for Iseult increased. Giving her up was worse than enduring any form of slavery.

He wouldn't let himself dwell upon the vision of her face, nor her soft sighs of pleasure when he'd touched her. He had the memory of her. It would have to be enough.

Kieran dragged his attention back to the slave auction,

never taking his hand off the dagger. Women and men were sold off one by one, fear and uncertainty in their faces. Children wept when they were pulled away from their mothers. His gut twisted at the sight of a young adolescent boy, a dark-haired lad the same age as Egan. All were too old to be Iseult's son.

His hands shook, curling over the cold metal of his weapon. The scars upon his back, though long healed, seemed to ache with memory. No one should have to suffer this way, nor lose their freedom. Though he offered a prayer for them, he hadn't a coin to his name, nothing to save any of the slaves from their fate.

He swore a silent vow, never to keep a slave of his own. Not so long as he breathed.

Almost an hour passed until the remaining slaves were sold. The Norse slave trader Bodvar handled the auction, calling out the merits of each man, woman and child. Kieran waited until the crowd dispersed, and Bodvar finished counting his silver. The trader had long reddish hair that hung to his waist, tied back with a thong. A thick curling beard rested upon his chest, and his narrow eyes focused upon the coins.

Finally, Kieran stepped forward. When his shadow darkened Bodvar's line of sight, the Norseman looked up. A thin smile spread over his face.

'I always thought you'd escape, Kieran Ó Brannon. None of the others had your strength.'

'I am a free man now,' he replied, withdrawing the parchment from his pouch as proof.

Bodvar shrugged and crossed his arms. 'You're too late to purchase a slave of your own. But if you've silver, I might be persuaded to find a woman for you among my own slaves.'

Kieran ignored the remark. 'I'm looking for a young boy, two years of age. Stolen from his mother last summer. He has black hair, and his mother named him Aidan.'

The Norseman finished tying off his purse of silver and bound it to his waist. 'Haven't seen him.'

'You see hundreds of boys like him everywhere you travel. This one came not far from here. From the Mac-Fergus clan.'

Bodvar stood. 'If he was taken from his own clan, it was either raiders or one of their own kin. Someone who needed silver, who wanted to be rid of the boy.'

Kieran considered the possibility, along with the difficulties it posed. 'I intend to find him.'

Bodvar laughed. 'You'll never find him, and well you know it.'

Kieran did not respond. To Bodvar, a child was nothing more than a nuisance and hardly worth a profit. There was nothing more to gain by speaking to him. But Iseult's family was another matter. There might be answers within her own clan.

He quelled the rising hope of seeing her again. Iseult had made her choices, and they had nothing to do with him. Likely she had wed Davin after all. He'd told Iseult to keep her betrothal, for at least she would be safe. But the thought of Davin caressing her bare skin made him clench his dagger as though it were a man's throat.

He continued walking east, though his feet ached from the journey. When it grew too dark to go any further, he built a fire on the lee side of a hill and warmed himself. As he leaned back to sleep, Iseult's face haunted him once more. He wanted to see her. He itched to touch her skin, to thread his hands through the silk of her hair.

Would that he could suppress the memories. Iseult Mac-Fergus could never belong to him, not with a life such as this.

She had urged him to return home, to seek his family once more. Never. They would not forgive him for what had happened to Egan. How could they, when he couldn't forgive himself?

No, he had no place where he belonged. He would keep his promise to Iseult and find her son.

And after that, it didn't matter where he went.

Chapter Sixteen

A furious rain pounded down from the skies. Iseult clung to her mare, praying that she was on the right path home. Dark clouds shrouded the countryside, making it difficult to see past the mist. She kept her mount along the path of the river, both for the water source and to keep herself from becoming lost.

Her life was packed away in two bundles. She'd left behind her dower chest and everything Davin had given her. For the past three days she'd travelled alone. Beneath her *brat*, she shivered.

She'd slipped away in the early morning, telling only Deena of her intent to leave. She was afraid Davin wouldn't let her go, otherwise.

Her body ached from the effort of holding onto the mare. Though it was nearing sunset, she was almost home. She clung to the thought, craving the familiarity of her family's dwelling. The land shifted to the meadows she knew, the thatched wattle and daub huts of friends. And in the distance stood the gates of their ringfort.

Iseult leaned her head down upon the horse's mane and

wept. Exhaustion permeated her body, tempting her with the promise of sleep. She reached inside her cloak to touch the wooden figure of her son, as if she could somehow be nearer to Kieran.

Would he truly carry out his promise to find Aidan? Though she wanted to believe it, she was afraid to let herself hope. As she stared out at the desolate landscape, she prayed for both of them.

With a signal to the mare, she continued onward. On the outskirts of the ringfort stood the blacksmith's hut, belonging to her father. Though it was made of stone, he kept the work space open to the elements to avoid the dangers of fire. Due to the rain, she suspected he would be staying inside their home this day.

No one guarded the gates, and Iseult smelled the musty aroma of peat burning as she drew near. She dismounted and led the horse inside the ringfort. Her wet gown clung to her skin, causing her to shiver with cold. Although the rain had slowed, she longed to be inside, warming herself before a fire.

She brought the mare to her family's dwelling, a circular stone hut with a thatched roof. After loosening the ties that bound her belongings, she led the animal to a sheltered lean-to. She rubbed the mare down, then gave her grain and water.

Iseult hesitated before knocking upon the door, unsure of what her parents would say. But when the door opened, her father's face broke into a smile. His hair had grown thinner, and he'd cut it short to his shoulders. In the months since she'd seen him last, the fair strands had faded almost to grey. Rory pulled her into a bone-crushing hug, laughing heartily.

'Iseult, *a iníon*, it's good to see you.' He brought her inside, and she saw her mother sitting by the fire, her needle moving through a woollen garment. Unlike Da, her mother did not get up to embrace her. Instead, Caitleen's mouth drew into a disapproving line, and she continued sewing.

'We received your message about delaying the wedding,' Rory said, guiding her to sit down. He poured her a cup of mead, which Iseult accepted gratefully. 'I can't say as I understand why, but that's for the two of you to decide, I suppose. And where is Davin? Seeing to the horses?'

'He is still at Lismanagh, I expect.' Her glance flickered towards Caitleen, who still had not voiced a single word of welcome.

'He let you come alone?' Rory was aghast at her admission. 'I can't believe it.'

Iseult faltered a moment, but managed to gather her thoughts together. She had hoped for more time before telling them the truth. Best to get it over with, she supposed. 'I decided not to marry him, Da,' she admitted quietly. 'I would not have made him a good wife.'

Her mother's hands stopped moving, her eyes glittering with anger. 'I knew you were too foolish to know a strong match when we found it for you. A more ungrateful girl I've never met.'

'Caitleen—' her father warned.

'Well, she is. Davin Ó Falvey was the best marriage we could have arranged for her, and she turned him away.' Caitleen dropped her mending. 'If she wants to go and marry a farmer, so be it. I won't be responsible for her future any more.'

'Iseult may choose whatever man she wishes,' Rory argued. 'She does not need a chieftain for a husband.'

Caitleen shook her head, returning her attention to her sewing. 'You wouldn't understand.'

Iseult kept her spine straight, not letting her mother see

how much the words hurt. 'May I stay with you for a time, Da?' she asked quietly.

Rory put his arm around her shoulders. 'Of course. You are always welcome here.' But his eyes turned bitter when he glanced at his wife.

Though Caitleen might have given birth to her, Iseult had never been close to her mother. She didn't understand why her father remained married to the woman. Caitleen had never forgiven him for being content as a blacksmith, her ambitions ever rising.

'Have you a *léine* I could borrow?' she asked her mother quietly. All of her clothing was soaked from the hard rain and would take time to dry.

Wordlessly, her mother opened a trunk and handed her a gown. Iseult thanked her and moved behind a small partition, stripping off her clothing. When she stood naked, her mind recalled Kieran's touch upon her body. She regretted none of it. She wished desperately to feel his arms around her, to smell the faint hint of wood that surrounded him. To lie in his arms and to love him.

Saint Brigid, it was lonely without him. She pulled the dry *léine* over her body, but the clothing did little to make her feel better. From her cloak, she withdrew the wooden carving, for at least she had something that had been close to Kieran. She ran the edge of her thumb over the carved lines, before at last putting it away.

When she joined her father by the fire, Rory handed her a bowl of mutton stew. She picked at the food, though she hadn't eaten since this morn.

'Have you learned anything about Aidan?' she asked.

Her father shook his head. 'I wish I had better news for you, *a stór*. But no one has seen or heard anything about your son.'

'Could he have been taken into slavery?' she asked, staring hard at the fire. Her eyes remained dry, her feelings drawn tight by the barest sense of control.

'I don't believe so. Usually only the Norsemen capture slaves. We've seen none of the foreigners nearby.'

He didn't know. Iseult set her bowl down, her blood racing at the thought of the *Lochlannachs*. If the raiders had anything to do with Aidan's disappearance, she had to find them.

'The raiders landed on the far side of the bay only weeks ago,' she admitted. 'They attacked Lismanagh.'

'Was anyone hurt?' Rory asked. He took the bowl from her, worry creasing his face.

'We lost some of the tribesmen. Several were…wounded.' The blade of memory slashed her again as she thought of Kieran.

She swallowed hard, closing off her mind from the bitterness. 'I should search again,' she said. 'You've not seen the *Lochlannachs* this far inland?'

'No.'

Her mother set her mending aside and poured herself a cup of mead. 'Let him go, Iseult. It's been a year. You should forget about Aidan.'

Such a choking rage filled her, she could barely speak. Never would she consider such a thing. 'He is of my flesh and blood,' Iseult argued. 'I cannot forget about him. And I will find out what happened and whether or not he lives.'

Her mother sighed. 'You'll never marry, then. No man of worth would claim the boy, even if you did find him.'

'Caitleen, enough.' Her father sent his wife a dark warning. To Iseult he added, 'I know you grieve. And if you want to search again, I'll take you myself.'

'Thank you, Da.' She embraced him again, grateful that he, at least, understood her.

Davin Ó Falvey sat in front of the land he'd chosen for his bride. Without Iseult, his days were empty. The sun warmed his skin, but he hardly felt its rays.

He'd gone over their separation a thousand times in his mind, wondering what he could have done or said to make things different. He'd never loved any woman this way and couldn't imagine letting her go.

Gods, if he'd known what was happening between them, he'd have sent the slave away. Or worse. His hand moved down to his knife, fingering the hilt.

But now she'd gone. Without a farewell, with no word to anyone except Deena, she'd left him. To her family, Deena claimed, but he didn't believe her.

They'd made a fool of him, and the anger seethed inside.

His foster-brother Orin approached, his feet kicking against the dust. Almost as though he were afraid to speak.

'What is it?' Davin snapped.

'Your father has been asking for you. He wants your opinion on a few matters.'

Davin's jaw clenched. Alastar had no need of his opinions. His father had always done as he pleased, when it came to matters concerning the tribe. 'He's the chieftain. Let him make the decisions.'

Orin folded his arms, staring at the dirt. 'It isn't about that. He's arranged for you to meet another bride. He's going to visit the Donovan clan, and he wants to you accompany him.'

Damn his father's interference. 'I'll marry a woman of my choosing or not at all.'

'It's a good alliance, so he said.' Orin glanced towards their dwelling. 'At least meet with her.'

He refused to consider it, caring nothing for a chieftain's daughter whose status equalled his own. He would have Iseult or no one at all.

'He can go alone,' he said, dismissing his foster-brother. 'I'll not wed her.' He strode over to the palisade wall, staring eastward. What had happened to Iseult?

He had to know if she'd betrayed him. Jealousy reared inside, boiling his anger to the breaking point. He moved towards the stable of horses, a plan forming in his mind.

'Where are you going?' Orin asked.

'I've a journey of my own to make.' He'd go and visit Iseult's parents. Then he'd know if she had told him the truth.

'I don't think that's such a good idea.' Orin eyed him with suspicion. 'Your father—'

'—does not control my actions,' Davin finished. 'I will choose my bride, not him.' And though it might be futile to dream of Iseult, he hadn't given up hope. 'I am going to visit the MacFergus clan.'

'Don't do this, Davin,' Orin urged. 'She made her choice.'

Davin tensed, unwilling to accept it. 'A woman can change her mind.'

And he intended to do anything necessary to win her back. She belonged to him and no one else.

A single moon had waned, and Kieran travelled to the MacFergus lands to ask questions about Aidan. Without a horse, it took a great deal of time to reach his destination, but he didn't mind the solitude. Each passing day renewed his endurance and strength. No longer did the nightmares of Egan plague him, but the loss of Iseult caught him at unexpected moments.

When he'd cleaned a fish for dinner the other night, he thought of her lost wager. Even when he worked upon a simple carved spoon, he could see her face in his mind, the clear beauty that would never be his.

When at last Kieran reached the clan's holdings, he remained hidden for several days. Watching them, searching for those who might have arranged for Aidan's disappearance. The quest for her son gave him a sense of purpose.

And then, unexpectedly, he'd caught a glimpse of her. Why was she here? Had she come alone?

Though he did not reveal his presence to her, remaining camped in the forest, he watched her. Like a starving man, he satisfied his need to see her.

She walked through the fields, her slender figure ghostly in the way she moved. This evening, she wore white, a gown that accentuated her ethereal beauty. A fey spirit, one who captivated him.

She wasn't happy. He could see the loneliness in her face, the discontent. He leaned up against a birch tree, deliberating whether to walk into the clearing.

But what would he say? That he had found a trace of her son? That he needed her to confirm the boy's identity?

Troubled questions flooded his mind. Had she wed Davin? Was he with her now? Though he had not seen his former master, it didn't mean that Iseult was free to speak with him.

He wanted to talk to her. Even if he couldn't touch her, just to look upon her face would be enough. The rim of the sun edged the horizon, the sky growing darker.

He held his position, surprised when she walked towards the forest. When she reached the base of the hill, she stopped before the grove and held a small dagger in her hand. So close, his heartbeat quickened.

'I know someone is there,' she called out. 'Show yourself.'

He didn't move. A long moment passed before she entered the trees. Her braid hung down her back, her skirts dragging upon the ground. She clenched the dagger, her eyes discerning.

Then her gaze fell upon him and the dagger slipped from her palm, striking the dirt.

'You came back.'

His hand curled around a birch sapling, to keep himself from moving towards her. She stood no more than a few arm lengths from him, but neither moved. He wanted to embrace her, to show her how much he'd missed her. But he held himself back, for she was likely another man's wife. He'd wanted that for her, a safe place to live and a man who loved her in the way she deserved.

'I may have found Aidan,' he said at last.

Iseult's hand went to her mouth, her eyes filling with tears. A mixture of hope and fear masked her face, but she managed to gather her composure. 'Is he alive?'

'I believe he is. But I cannot know whether it is him for certain.'

The tears spilled over her cheeks then, her hands shaking. He wanted so badly to hold her, but his feet remained rooted.

'Take me to him,' she begged. 'We can go now.'

'It's too far, and we'll lose daylight soon. Dawn at the earliest.'

A curse fell from her lips, her mouth tight with a frown. 'If we must.' She retrieved the dagger and pulled the edges of her *brat* closer for warmth. 'Come and share an evening meal with us. I don't know where you've taken shelter, but my family could—'

'Don't worry about me, Iseult. I'll make camp here.' He still didn't know if Davin had accompanied her, and he had no desire to lay eyes upon the man.

She touched his shoulder. 'Kieran, don't turn me away. I haven't seen you in so long.'

Her fingertips seared him. He was half-witted to believe that time would diminish his need for her. Even now, he wanted to ravage her, to clasp her slender body against his own, until she understood his fierce desires.

But not if she belonged to another man.

'Did you marry him?' The words escaped him with the desperate need to know.

She shook her head. 'I couldn't. Not after what I felt for you.'

Hope and elation blazed through him. A fleeting second later, she kissed his mouth. It was so sudden, he might have imagined the warmth of her lips. 'Meet me in the black-smith's hut later,' she murmured.

Before he could say a word, she hurried back to the ringfort. Kieran lowered his head against the birch, knowing he was about to make the gravest of mistakes. Did he really believe he could spend a night alone with her, without joining his body with hers?

She deserved a far better man than himself. The problem was convincing her to accept the truth.

Iseult waited in the blacksmith's hut, a fire flickering against the twilight. She had told her father not to expect her home for several days.

Rory had reddened. 'I don't like it, Iseult. Whether or not this man Kieran has news of Aidan, I don't want you travelling alone with him.'

'He saved my life from *Lochlannachs*.' She laid her hands upon his arm. 'I trust him, Da. And you needn't worry about me.'

He grunted, passing her the basket of food she'd packed. 'He's the reason you didn't marry Davin, isn't he?'

She could not meet his gaze. 'One of many reasons. He…means a great deal to me.'

Her father sighed and shook his head. 'You always did follow your heart, Iseult.' He opened the door for her and added, 'Take one of my horses, if you have the need.'

She kissed his cheek in thanks and donned her cloak. After securing the supplies to the horses, she led both of them outside. Silvery stars dotted the night sky, the summer evening turning cooler. When she arrived at the blacksmith's hut, she tethered the horses for the night. She built a fire and settled back to wait, leaning back against the stone wall.

Would he come at all? She could hardly believe he had returned. Even so, he seemed like a stranger. She had kissed him on impulse, hoping to thaw the dispassionate barrier he exuded. It had only startled him, and he hadn't kissed her back.

She covered her cheeks with her palms. Was she being foolish again? A ball of hurt gathered in her stomach, for she was afraid it would be like loving Murtagh all over again. Kieran might touch her with desire, but did she hold a place in his heart? She clenched her hands together, the doubts multiplying.

But then he arrived. Dying sunlight silhouetted his form, and she studied him more closely. He'd grown stronger since she'd seen him last. His dark hair still needed to be trimmed, but his face had lost the hungry planes. He wore a different tunic, a nondescript shade of brown that helped him blend into his surroundings. She wondered where it came from.

In his hands, he carried a string of fish.

'You haven't lost your skill, I see,' she remarked with a smile, rising to her feet. 'Am I supposed to clean those?'

'I'll take care of them.' He didn't respond to her teasing.

Her attempt at humour faded, and awkwardness silenced her voice. She didn't know what to say, for it was the first time Davin was not a barrier between them.

Always there had been forbidden desire. But she wondered if she truly knew Kieran.

She took one of the fish from him, needing something to occupy her hands. Using a wooden plank, she unsheathed her own knife and helped him prepare the food.

He offered no conversation, no contact at all. As his knife moved over the fish, his muscles appeared tense, his face strained. Almost as if he didn't want to be here. When she could bear it no longer, she asked, 'What happened after you left Lismanagh? Where did you go?'

'I went to see the slave traders.'

She nicked her finger upon the knife, gasping at the pain. Kieran came up beside her, setting his own blade down. 'What happened?'

'It's nothing.' But her heart thundered at the thought of what he'd learned about Aidan.

His hand moved to her waist while he examined the cut. She tried to stop the bleeding, but to no avail.

'I'll wrap it for you.' He brought a bucket of water over, lifting a dipper. The cold water spilled over her finger, washing the blood away. Kieran tore a strip of cloth from his tunic. 'Sit down.'

He gestured towards a tree stump, and Iseult sat, trying to gather herself back together. The sight of the cut made her dizzy, and she forced herself to look away. 'It's not deep. You needn't worry.'

He knelt down, taking her hand in his. Gently, he wrapped the cloth around the cut, tying off the ends. Iseult didn't move, afraid he would pull away from her. No longer did she feel the sting of the cut. Instead, her awareness centred upon him. The way his dark eyes looked upon her, the roughness of his hands. She smelled the familiar scent of wood, and her gaze moved to his firm mouth. There was hesitancy in his expression and veiled desire.

Without speaking, she lowered her forehead to his, needing to be close to him. Though it was only an innocent movement, his warm skin made her remember everything about the last time he'd touched her. He inhaled a breath, as though fighting for control. Her hair fell across his shoulders, and he leaned his cheek against her own.

If she turned her face, his mouth would be upon hers.

Chapter Seventeen

So long he'd waited to touch her. Kieran was afraid of letting himself get too close, for fear he'd lose control. He desired her so badly, his hands were trembling.

Gods above, he didn't want to frighten her. But the intensity of his need dominated all thoughts. Only a thread of control kept him from laying her body upon the ground and driving her to madness with the pleasure he wanted to give. A woman like Iseult deserved tenderness. He fought to keep the raw urges under control.

'Your son wasn't there, Iseult.' When he voiced the words, her arms moved around his neck. He held her close, offering her the comfort she needed. 'He wasn't among the slaves.'

'Tell me what you discovered. Did you see him?'

Within her questions, he sensed the terrible fear. 'I don't know if it's him.' But he had strong suspicions. Every instinct told him that he'd found her son. But even if it were so, she would be hurt by what he'd learned.

'On the morrow, I'll take you there. I believe the boy I found is Aidan.' He removed the fish from the fire and prepared a portion for her, setting it upon a wooden plank.

Iseult accepted the food, picking at it without any true appetite. He suspected she wanted to go after Aidan now, even though it was impossible in the darkness.

The night air blew over her face, skimmed with the fragrance of summer. The peat smoke, familiar and comforting, eased him while they ate in silence. He watched her, the way shadows outlined the soft line of her jaw. The way her hair fell across her back in a silken web.

Without speaking a word, his gaze travelled over her body with an unspoken hunger. But if he made a single move towards her, he wouldn't stop. His imagination envisioned pushing aside the linen gown, touching her and stroking her to a fever pitch.

Iseult withdrew a flask of wine from the basket, along with two clay cups. 'How did you find Aidan?'

'I watched the members of your clan. Only a few people had the motives to have the child taken away.'

She handed him a cup of wine, and he drained it far too quickly. The wine did nothing to assuage his lust, nor did it dull the frustration building inside.

Her face became strained. 'I've asked everyone in the ringfort and in the surrounding area. No one saw anything.'

'Perhaps you didn't ask the right questions, *a mhuirnín*.' Kieran cleaned his knife and sheathed it in his belt. 'Or the right people.'

'What do you mean? Who told you where he was?'

He hesitated, not knowing if she was ready to hear the truth. He didn't want her to be hurt by what he'd learned. 'Does it matter?'

'Don't keep secrets from me. Not about this.' She slammed the pitcher down, anger brewing in her eyes. 'He's my son, and I deserve to know what happened.'

'You do,' he admitted. 'But you won't like the answers.'

'Don't try to protect me. The only thing that matters is Aidan.' Her fingers curled up against her palms. 'Tell me what you know.'

He met her fury with a steadfast gaze. Whether or not she was ready to hear it, he would grant her the truth. 'I followed a man who travelled a day's journey from here. He brought food and supplies to a foster-family who had a small boy with them. Then he returned here and was paid by your mother.'

Iseult stared at him before nodding slowly. She reached down beside her father's anvil and picked up a scrap piece of iron. For a moment, she held the metal within her palm until it warmed. Then she hurled it against the shelter, the metal clanging against the stone. Fury ripped through her, for she knew he spoke the truth. Caitleen had hated the news of her pregnancy, claiming that no man of worth would wed her. When Murtagh had not shown up on their wedding day, she'd thought her mother was right.

She whirled, running towards the ringfort. A terrible anger flooded through her. If she'd had a weapon, she'd be tempted to strike out at her own mother.

Kieran caught her, holding her back. 'Wait, Iseult.'

'Don't tell me to wait,' she snapped. 'For over a year, I've wept for my son. She deserves to know the same pain I've suffered.'

'It won't change the past.'

Perhaps not. But she intended to confront Caitleen for what she'd done. 'Stay here.'

Her anger blinded her with each step. How could Caitleen have done it? Her own mother, the woman who had given her life. And for what? A narrow-minded view that a man like Davin wouldn't have her if she'd borne a child? She didn't want to believe it, though her heart suspected otherwise.

She pushed onward until at last she opened the door to her parents' hut. Rory looked up from his meal. 'What is it, Iseult?'

She ignored her father and strode up to Caitleen. 'You took him from me. My own son.' The accusations spilled from her lips, while she waited for her mother to deny it.

Caitleen blanched, her hand going to her mouth. But she did not speak. Her silence damned her as surely as any words.

'Why?' Iseult demanded. 'He was your blood, just as I am.'

'I did him no harm,' Caitleen said. 'His foster-parents are known to me.'

'I wept for him,' Iseult said. 'Each night I blamed myself for not watching him closely enough. I thought it was my fault.'

'I wanted you to have a better marriage,' Caitleen said. 'You were so enamoured of Aidan, you never saw the way Davin watched you. I saw a chance for you, and I took it.'

Rory's face was outraged. 'Have you no heart at all, Caitleen?'

Caitleen gripped her hands. 'I did what I thought was best.'

Iseult was shaking. She struggled to cool her emotions, but right now she couldn't breathe from the anger inside.

'I don't wish to see you again,' she said at last. Turning her back, she pushed her way out the door.

'Iseult!' her father called out.

'I am leaving with Kieran,' she said, 'to find my son.' She turned her gaze to his. 'I won't be returning here.'

The sympathy on Rory's face was genuine. 'I didn't know what she'd done,' he said. 'Believe me, daughter.'

She did. The ageing planes of his face showed his sincerity, but, more than that, she knew her father would never do anything to hurt her.

'Be well, my father.'

She raised her *brat* over her head, clasping it beneath her chin with one hand. The wind whipped at her face while she returned to the blacksmith's hut, barely holding herself together. Her own mother. After all this time.

When she found Kieran waiting, she walked into his arms. Only then did she release the anguish inside her, needing his strength. Ragged sobs tore from her throat, the disappointment in her mother. And in herself for not seeing the truth sooner.

He reached out and brushed a tear away, framing her face with his palms. 'I am sorry for causing you such pain, *a mhuirnín.*'

'You can't know what it is to lose a child,' she accused, retreating from his embrace. Nothing compared to the fierce loss, nor the gaping hole inside her heart.

'I know what it is to lose a brother. A brother I should have protected.'

It wasn't the same, not at all. And yet, it was the first time he had ever offered anything about his past. She sensed the heaviness in his voice, the reluctance to speak of it as he pulled away. She sat down, pulling her knees up while he picked up a cup of wine. 'What happened to your brother?'

Kieran drank, as if gathering strength from the cup. 'It was late winter. Our harvest was poor, and there wasn't enough food to last everyone. So many of them starved to death.'

He held out his hand to her, and she took it. The warmth of his palm caressed hers, offering comfort even as he relayed his own suffering. 'We couldn't bury those who died. The ground was too frozen.' He lowered his gaze, still holding her hands. 'We lost four men, eight women and seven children last winter.'

Iseult moved closer, leaning against him. 'What of your own family?'

'We had few provisions, the same as the others. Sometimes I gave my share of food to my sisters, or to Egan, my brother. They were younger. Not as strong.

'Then the raiders came. *Lochlannachs*, like the ones we fought here. They plundered our supplies, stealing our grain and setting fire to our homes. I fought alongside my father and my uncles. But we hadn't the strength to stop them.'

'Did your brother Egan die in the battle?'

Kieran's face grew grave. 'I wish he had. It would have been more merciful.' He shook his head. 'They took him, along with my sisters and a few of the others. Planning to sell them as slaves or keep them as hostages, I suppose.'

His hand moved through her hair idly as he spoke. 'I fought for my sisters, and saved them from captivity. The raiders left with Egan.'

The back of his hand rested upon her nape. The touch of his skin seemed to burn against her, sparking feelings she wanted to deny.

'I followed them to their camp alone. I offered to trade myself into slavery, thinking they would let my brother go.' He shook his head. 'I was stupid to believe they would accept my bargain. Arrogant to think that my fighting strength was worth more than my brother's life.' He met her gaze with such fury, such pain, she wanted to weep for him.

'What did they do to him?'

He expelled a mocking laugh. 'They agreed to my bargain. And when they went to cut his ropes, they slit his throat instead. I watched him die in front of me. They sent a bag of grain to my father, in exchange for both of us.'

She couldn't imagine such a horror. But she recognised his pain, as deep as her own. She almost said, *It wasn't your fault*. The words stilled upon her lips, for she knew his guilt as surely as she had believed herself responsible for not protecting Aidan.

'I'm sorry.' Her hands moved around his neck, and she kissed him, offering comfort in the best way she knew how.

He returned the kiss, his mouth gentle against hers. No longer the fierce, forbidden embrace, but instead his touch assuaged her grief. The tenderness moved her in a way nothing else had.

Kieran raised her to stand before him, never ceasing the kiss. In his arms, she leaned against him while her skin felt unbearably hot, her lips almost numb from kissing him. She needed more, craved his body upon hers.

He pulled back, his eyes dark with passion. 'Did Davin touch you on Bealtaine?'

'No.' Her blood raced within her skin at Kieran's jealousy, her breasts tightening. Her gown felt confining, the sensitive tips erect from the rough fabric. Staring into his eyes, she spoke the truth. 'I wanted no man but you.'

To prove it, she reached up and loosened the ties of his tunic. He pulled it over his head, revealing golden skin and taut muscles. No longer did he have the gaunt appearance of hunger. Instead, he held a subdued strength. Iseult palmed his torso, pressing kisses against his neck.

Kieran's self-control was about to snap. The scent of her surrounded him. Like wild honey, he craved the taste of her. She enslaved him with invisible chains of need.

'Iseult,' he breathed, kissing her palms, 'is this what you want?' He wanted nothing but honesty between them. 'I am a man without a tribe. There is nothing I can give you. No home, no future.'

She moved so close, the rigid tips of her breasts brushed against his chest. He ached with the sweet torment, exhaling sharply.

'Then give me yourself,' she whispered. 'It will be enough.'

Slowly, she unbound her overdress and *léine*, sliding the clothing from her shoulders until she stood bare before him. Her skin appeared creamy in the summer night, her reddish-gold hair falling in waves down to curved hips. Rounded breasts held firm, erect nipples that he longed to touch.

Her mouth touched his, and he was completely lost. He kissed her with reverence, wanting her to know how she humbled him.

He didn't deserve her, couldn't possibly become the man she wanted him to be. And yet somehow none of it mattered this night.

There was no pallet to lay her upon, so he arranged their garments into a soft pile. She knelt beside him, drawing him upon her body.

'Kiss me again,' she ordered.

He did, releasing the hunger that flared up inside. His body ached with the need to sheathe himself inside her, but he wanted to fulfil every dream she'd ever had. With his mouth, he kissed every part of her skin, circling her breast with his tongue. When he reached the hardened nipple, he bit it gently, teasing her until she shivered.

His hand moved between her thighs, coaxing her to open for him. The wetness that met his touch made him groan. Instinctively, she moved against his hand, and he slipped a finger inside. A shuddering gasp released from her mouth.

'Kieran,' she whispered, palming his hips as he moved

his length against her. She closed her eyes, trying to pull him closer.

'We have all night,' he promised. He tasted the warm skin of her ribcage, moving down her stomach. When he raised her knees up, she shivered. Vulnerable and exposed to him.

'You won't think of anything else but this.' He lowered his mouth to taste her woman's flesh, and Iseult's breath came in ragged gasps. With his tongue, he moved against the most sensitive part of her body, stroking it until she moaned.

Belenus, but he wanted to watch her shatter. He licked her sensitive flesh, tasting the honey of her womanhood while rubbing the tips of her breasts with his thumb and forefingers. She moved against him, her body reaching for the release he wanted to give.

Mine. The word echoed within him, the impossible need to possess her. He no longer cared that it was wrong to become her lover, to steal away her very breath and heart. He needed this. By God, he would mark her until she would never again make love to a man without remembering him.

When he sucked hard against her swollen folds, she cried out. Wild shudders racked her body, as she rode the wave of pleasure.

She opened her eyes, her skin flushed and ready for him. 'My turn.'

Sweet God. Though he hadn't intended it, she took his erection into her slender fingers. Squeezing his length, she caressed him, rubbing her thumb over the tip. He was helpless to do anything but obey her, his own body consumed by cravings. She laid him back on to the clothing, straddling his waist.

'When you were a slave, I imagined this.' She kissed his throat, her hands stroking his chest. With her hands, she trapped his wrists away from his body.

'I am still your slave.' Not a lie. He'd do anything for her, and the sweet torment only inspired a greater desire. Kieran leaned up to her breast, hanging in front of his mouth like a ripe fruit. Taking her nipple into his mouth, he used his mouth to pleasure her.

But she turned the sensations back upon him when she sheathed his manhood inside her wetness. Kieran gripped her hips, groaning at the feel of her body caressing him. Every inch of him strained at the warmth of her. He nearly lost control at that very second, for she was better than anything he'd ever dreamed of.

When she moved against him, he grew harder. Her hair slid over her shoulders, tickling his skin as she rose up and then sheathed herself again. It was like dying slowly, and he revelled in every moment of it. He lifted her, increasing the tempo until he touched her very core.

As if he could touch her heart.

Iseult cried out at the friction, riding him as he pulled her hips against his. Her body squeezed him, as she found another release, pulling against him with another flood of moisture.

He needed more. Rolling her over, he drove himself inside, trying with each stroke to brand her as his. Though never could she truly belong to him, he didn't want her to ever forget what there was between them.

She tightened her legs around his waist, her breath hitching as she met him stroke for stroke. When her mouth met his once more in a fierce kiss of possession, he spilled himself inside her. The aftershocks pulsed through him, his body trembling.

He lay upon her, silent. Neither spoke, though Iseult pressed a kiss upon his chest. The fire crackled upon the hearth, a stark glow against the starlight. He caressed her hip, reluctantly withdrawing from inside her body.

Iseult wrapped her arms around his neck. Against his chest he could feel her bare breasts, and the sensation stirred him. She touched his face, her eyes turning serious. 'After we find Aidan, where will you go?'

He shook his head. 'I don't know.'

'You still will not return to your family?'

'I can't.' He couldn't face them, not after what had happened to Egan. 'And they won't want to see me.'

'Do they know about your brother?'

'They know. And I've no wish to see them because of it.'

She sat up, caressing her hand over his chest. 'And so now your mother has lost both of her sons.'

'She has her daughters to comfort her,' he argued.

'Until they leave and marry.' She withdrew her hand from his skin. He twined his fingers in hers, needing to touch her.

'I think your mother would welcome your home-coming,' she continued. 'Why not give it a chance?'

He shook his head. She didn't understand what it would be like. His people had suffered a great deal, and he pre-ferred to leave the past behind.

'Were you the chieftain's son?' she asked.

'I was.' And for that reason, his shame went even deeper. The people had expected him to become their leader one day. He shouldered the burden for each life that was lost, for it was a chieftain's duty to provide for everyone.

He'd seen his father Marcas sitting alone and staring out at the devastating rot upon the fields. The bleakness in Marcas's eyes made him wish he could do something to help.

Iseult drew her knees up, her face pensive. 'I thought as much. You never did act like a slave.' Her lips curved upwards. 'I believed you were a warrior.' She reached out and touched his arm, using both palms to encircle the thick muscle.

Though it seemed impossible, his body was already stirring to life at her caress. 'I could fight as well as the next man,' he admitted. 'But my father wanted me to lead them.'

'Is your father still alive?'

'I don't know.' His father had raged at him when Kieran had gone after Egan, threatening to cut him off. Muttered curses had been the last farewell he'd heard. The curses had worked, judging from the kind of life he'd led in the past season.

Iseult didn't ask him anything further, and he was grateful for it. 'What happened after I left you with Davin?' he asked.

'I came here.'

'And Davin let you go?'

'I slipped out alone, before dawn.' She reached out and donned her *léine*. 'Only Deena knew where I was.'

The idea of Iseult travelling alone stopped him cold. She could have been attacked or hurt. Even stolen away, had the *Lochlannachs* found her.

She knelt down with her feet hidden beneath the gown, looking as innocent as a child. Against the light of the hearth, her hair turned fiery red. Gods, she took his breath away. Why she wanted a man like him, he'd never understand.

'Don't go back to Lismanagh,' he warned. Rising to his feet, he donned his trews. With both of them clothed, the intimacy disappeared.

'I won't,' she promised. Then she stood and wrapped her arms around his waist, laying her cheek against his chest. Kieran gripped her so hard, it felt as though he were saying goodbye to her once again.

'We'll find Aidan,' he said. 'No matter how long it takes.' He meant the vow. He wanted to give her that gift, to see the joy upon her face.

Iseult pressed a soft kiss upon his mouth, and he held her close, wondering how he would ever find the strength to let her go again.

They rode for most of the morning in silence. During the journey, Iseult emptied her mind of everything, trying hard not to let herself hope. But she thought of her baby son, wondering if he would still remember her. If Aidan saw her, would he run away crying? Her throat clenched up with unshed tears. It was almost worse, not knowing if he were truly alive or not.

Kieran led them further east, towards the midlands where the mountains evolved into hills. She had never travelled this far before, and the unfamiliarity made her uneasy. Sheep grazed throughout the meadows, with only an occasional abbey or tiny *rath* to mark the landscape.

At midday, they stopped to eat. Iseult dismounted from her horse, reaching towards the provisions for food. She struggled to untie the sack, and Kieran came up behind her, his hands covering hers upon the knots.

'Let me.'

She should have moved aside to give him better access. Instead, she stayed where she was, her body attuned to his. She felt the warmth of his skin behind her, the faint smell of wood surrounding him. He untied the knots, his arms embracing her waist. When the rope fell free, Iseult turned towards him. Her palms rested against his torso, and she lifted her face to his.

'We'll be there in a few hours more,' he said. His brown eyes watched her with unspoken need. And yet, he didn't touch her.

Move away, Iseult. The more time she spent with Kieran, the more her defences dissolved. No matter how badly she wanted him, he wasn't a man with a future to give her. It wasn't wise to let herself love him.

She leaned her head against his broad chest, and his breath rose upon her nape. He was unravelling her sensibilities, taking her sense of reason apart. He was going to leave, but they had these last few days together. Was there harm in acting upon her desires?

His hand caressed the side of her face, a dark hunger rising in his eyes. 'Was there something else you needed?'

I need you.

She didn't speak, letting her actions answer for her. Her hands moved beneath his tunic, touching his bare skin. She traced rigid muscles and a scar that ran across his ribs. Raising herself up on her tiptoes, she touched her lips to his.

His mouth covered hers, kissing her with unsuppressed heat. Work-roughened hands caressed her waist, sliding down her skirts to touch her thigh. Slowly, intimately, he slid his palms over her bottom, bringing her close to him.

Iseult wound her arms around his neck, her body melting against the feeling of his hands upon her. He kissed her again, his tongue invading her mouth the way his body had joined with hers the night before.

'I wasn't going to touch you,' he whispered, his mouth moving over her skin.

'I know,' she replied, shivering when his hands slid up her thigh and towards the place where she wanted him most. She moaned when his fingers rubbed the fabric of her gown against the nub of her womanhood. 'But I wanted you to.'

One last, stolen moment. A chance to be with him before she could remember all of the reasons why they shouldn't be together.

His kiss became wild, a tangle of tongues and lips. Like a craving, she couldn't get enough of him.

'I shouldn't do this, either.' He unfastened his trews and lifted her up, wrapping her legs around his waist. A moment later, he penetrated her, and she cried out at the sensation of him stretching her. Her breasts swelled, the nipples tightening as he plunged deep inside.

His mouth ravaged hers, and all the while he kept up a steady rhythm, pumping inside her. Desire built up so tightly, she clutched at the back of his hair.

He slowed down suddenly, watching her with hooded eyes. Lifting her slowly, she felt every inch of him before he filled her again. It was torment and heaven at the same time.

Grinding her hips against him, she tried to make him increase the tempo, but instead he impaled her with such lingering strokes, she bit her lips to keep from crying out.

She closed her eyes, fighting against herself. *Don't love him, don't love him.* He wasn't going to stay. It was foolishness to lose her heart over this man.

But her body welcomed his, joining as though they were meant to be together. He caressed her with each stroke, as though he wanted to mark her for his own.

The wave caught her so unawares, she convulsed against him, crying out in fulfilment. A few strokes more, and his own release followed.

Kieran lowered her to the grass, still inside her. She couldn't catch her breath, couldn't move with the satisfaction he'd given her. Physically, they could not have been closer.

With swollen lips, she kissed him again, blinking to hold her feelings together. 'If we find—' She closed her eyes, trying to hold the pieces of her optimism together. 'No, *after* we find Aidan,' she amended, 'I don't want you to leave us.'

He looked away, as if the grass were infinitely more fascinating. 'Iseult—'

'Let me finish. You say that you can offer us no future.'

She hesitated, unsure of whether to reveal so much of herself to him. 'But I want to go wherever you do. Be with you, no matter what befalls us.'

Kieran withdrew from her body, his face showing no emotion. As he straightened his clothing, he said, 'You don't know what you are asking.'

'I'm asking you to give me a chance. I—' She caught herself before she spoke words that revealed too much of her feelings. 'I care for you.'

His arm caught her around the waist. 'Look at me, Iseult.' His face was hard, unforgiving. 'There are no second chances for men like me. I am nothing.'

'Do you think I care whether you're a slave or a king? It doesn't matter.'

'It does, Iseult. It matters to me.' There was absolute conviction in his voice. She hadn't known that he would deny himself a wife and family if he couldn't provide for them.

If he loved you, it wouldn't matter whether or not he had land, her heart warned. It was devastatingly clear that he didn't care enough.

He released her, and her skin felt the loss of his warmth. She took another step backwards, her throat burning. Suddenly, she felt so weary, she wanted to sink down and close her eyes.

'After we find Aidan, I want you to forget about me,' Kieran said. 'Find a man who will give you the home and children you deserve.'

'I've found the man I want,' she said, her throat so tight she wanted to weep. 'But you won't give us a chance.'

'No, I won't.' His voice was a blade of anger. 'I won't force you to endure the life I've chosen.'

But why would he choose such a bleak existence? He didn't have to live that way.

'If I'm with you, I don't care.' Though she fought with her words, trying to change his mind, she could see the futility. And it hurt worse than she'd ever imagined.

A shaking anger began inside her. She was so very tired of being left behind, abandoned by the men she loved.

There was resignation upon Kieran's face. 'One day you'll find a man who can make you happy. Then you'll see—'

'Don't try to convince me. You've made your choice.'

Kieran let her walk away. There was nothing more to be said. She wouldn't understand his reasons.

Death had been his companion for so long, he didn't want to be responsible for anyone any more. It was best not to stay in one place, not to have a family again. They were better off without him.

Iseult needed to live among a tribe, for the sake of her son. It wasn't fair, asking her to give up everything. *Críost*, he could sense her pain. He loathed himself for making her feel this way.

She stood near the horse with her head bowed. He drew closer, reaching out to embrace her from behind. A moment later, he froze, letting his hands fall away. He'd hurt her enough.

'We're going to find your son today,' he said. 'I swear it.'

She nodded, but when she turned to him, there was no hope upon her face. Only disappointment. He told himself that it would be different when she found Aidan.

She would have her son; after that, she would forget about him.

Chapter Eighteen

Iseult could hardly concentrate as they drew closer to the tiny plot of land in the distance. Hope brimmed up inside, though she tried to keep it at bay. She wanted to see Aidan again, so badly.

She shielded her eyes from the sun, staring hard for the sight of a small boy. He would be walking by now, running, even. His soft baby curves would have thinned into the face of a child.

As Kieran led the way, she recited a litany of prayers. When he slowed the pace at last, she spied a lone settlement in the distance.

Iseult urged her mare faster, unable to wait even a few minutes more. The circular stone hut was large enough to provide a comfortable home, certainly not a poor family. Surrounding the homestead were even rows of grain sprouting within the furrows.

Let him be here. God, please.

When at last she reached the dwelling, her hopes froze. Something felt wrong. She could not smell a hearth burning. And there should have been animals—geese and pigs, cows and horses. Although wooden pens were built around the hut, they were empty.

Kieran drew his horse to a stop, his gaze frowning. He sensed it, too.

Iseult closed her eyes, the prayers dying upon her lips. Even as she hurried towards the dwelling, the voices of doubt taunted her. *What did you think? That you would find him, after all this time?*

The hut stood empty. Though peat ashes remained in the hearth, there were no pallets, no family belongings. If Aidan had ever lived in this house, he was gone now.

She spun around and saw Kieran standing in the doorway. 'Where are they?'

He shook his head, disbelief marking his features. 'I saw a family living here, only a sennight ago. Your mother's servant brought them supplies.'

'Did you see Aidan?'

'I saw the family. A woman and man, along with their children.'

'That isn't what I asked. Did you see *my son*? Black hair, blue eyes.' She blurted out the description, as though it would mean something to Kieran. But of course, it didn't.

He reached out and took her hand in his. 'I believe he was here. I've no doubt that Caitleen arranged for his fostering with this family.'

Iseult pushed her way back outside, not wanting to hear what Kieran had thought. Her anger rose up, drowning her in helpless frustration. She'd believed him. Built her hopes up, thinking that she would hold Aidan in her arms again.

She couldn't see, from the tears streaming down her face. And when Kieran tried to offer her comfort, tried to pull her into his arms, she wouldn't let him. 'You never saw him. You don't know he was ever here.'

'It was the most likely place. But we'll find him.'

'We?' Her tears choked in the back of her throat. 'There is no "we". You already said you don't want me to stay with you.' She gave free rein to her feelings, letting them spill out. 'Even if I'd found him, you'd still leave.'

And that was the final blow. Kieran claimed that he would find Aidan, that he wanted to help her. But in the end, he, like Murtagh, would go.

She couldn't bear it again. And the longer she stayed with Kieran, the worse it would be when he finally left. For Kieran didn't love her. Not enough to let go of his past and make a home for them. She understood that nothing she said would make a difference to him. Until he believed it was possible to build a life together, they had nothing.

'We can ask the other villagers,' Kieran offered. 'They might know where the family has gone. There's still hope.' His hand moved to frame her jaw, his thumb wiping a tear away. 'Don't give up on your faith. Not when you're so close.'

She covered his hand, wishing she could carry the memory of his touch forever. But it was better to stop now, than to make the heartache even worse.

'I'll never give up on Aidan,' she promised. Lifting her gaze to his, she continued, 'But I can't go on looking with you,' she whispered. 'It hurts too much.'

He lowered his forehead to touch hers. 'I'm sorry. I wanted to find him for you.' In his voice, she heard the resignation. He wasn't going to fight for her, nor try to convince her to stay with him.

'Do you want me to take you home?' His hand reached to her nape, caressing the tension.

She couldn't go home. Not to Caitleen, knowing what her mother had done.

But there was one place she could go. A place where she could make her own choices. A place where someone loved her desperately.

'Take me back to Lismanagh.'

Watching her leave was one of the hardest things he'd ever done. Time slowed, and Kieran committed to memory the beauty of her face. Her hair that tangled around her shoulders like a fading sunrise. The sadness in her eyes when she believed he didn't want her.

Far from it. He wanted her more than he'd ever wanted any woman. Branna paled in comparison to Iseult.

When he'd said goodbye, he'd wanted to hold her tight, feel her lips against his, one last time. But she'd held herself apart, not letting him close.

The rejection took him by surprise, bruising his pride. She'd made her decision. She'd chosen to return to Davin Ó Falvey, a man who would take care of her in the way he never could.

A surge of possession caught him by surprise. He'd thought he was doing the right thing by letting her go. But the truth was, he didn't like it. He wanted her to stay with him while they searched for Aidan, for however long that might be.

She had disappeared inside the entrance, and he felt like an intruder spying on her. But he had to ensure her safety.

Kieran crept to the edge of the fort, continuing to watch her through the thin crevices. When Davin emerged to greet her, a look of startled happiness spread over his face. He opened his arms and welcomed Iseult with a warm embrace.

Kieran wasn't prepared for the fist of jealousy that caught him in the gut. *She's mine.* A growl caught in his throat. He wanted to smash through the wooden palisade and demand that Davin get away from her.

God in heaven, he was a fool for letting her go. And though he wasn't at all the right man for her, this wasn't over.

Far from it.

You chose this. You were the one who told her there was no future.

It was the truth, wasn't it? He had nothing to give. Why would she want to stay with a man like him? Once, he had been their tribe's greatest warrior, following in the footsteps of his father. He'd fallen so far, he didn't feel that he could ever be the man he once was.

Fight for her, a voice inside him urged.

He gripped one of the wooden supports on the palisade, squeezing so hard, splinters dug into his palms. It would mean returning home, rebuilding what was lost. Facing his family.

He'd never planned on going back to Duncarrick. He didn't want to see the blame in his father's eyes for Egan's death.

His father had loved his youngest son best of all, for the lad's smile never failed to charm those around him. Egan had looked up to him, constantly emulating Kieran's actions. It had humbled him instead of being an irritation. He'd wanted to be worthy of the pedestal his brother had set him upon.

But now, Egan was gone.

Could he return home again? He didn't know if his tribe had forgiven him. It had been so long since he'd been to Duncarrick. As an outcast, they might ask him to leave.

Kieran stood and strode back to his horse, his mind piecing

together his plans. Iseult's son meant everything to her, and he intended to get the child back, no matter what the cost.

And after that, he would find a way to give her the happiness she'd only dreamed of.

Iseult sat inside the woodcarver's hut, staring at the tools Kieran had left behind. It was the middle of the night, and she had nothing but an oil lamp to light the darkness. Memories of Kieran drew her within.

She ran her fingers over the handles, remembering the hands that had created life out of wood. She remembered Kieran's hands caressing her, as though he treasured her.

She laid her head down upon the table, eyes dry. There were no tears left to cry any more, not after a fortnight without him.

She didn't regret her choice. Davin had been overjoyed to see her, though he didn't pressure her into anything more than friendship. During the days, he handled the needs of the tribe, working alongside his father the chieftain. In the evenings, he spent time walking with her. Not once had he spoken of Kieran, though his presence hung between them.

She reached inside a fold of her *léine*, her hands curling across a carved piece of wood. Her thumb grazed each rise and swell of the wood, the details of the young boy's face. Though it was not Aidan, the figure of the boy brought her comfort.

One day I'll find you, she promised her son. Perhaps Davin could help her. Or her father Rory.

Would Kieran continue to look? She wanted to believe it, though she had released him from any obligation. Sweet Jesu, she missed him. Though it had only been a few days they'd spent together, it felt like years were gone from her life.

You'll get over him, she told herself. She'd endured the pain of losing Murtagh, though now she understood it had been more embarrassment than heartache. She hardly thought of him any more.

Forgetting about Kieran would take far longer. She thought of his strong hands, his attention to detail in both his woodcarvings and the way he touched her. Her body shivered in sudden warmth and remembrance.

He had the most courage of any man she'd ever known. And yet underneath his fierce shield was a man who had suffered great loss. She understood him, for she had known the same pain.

An outside noise caught her attention, and Iseult stiffened as the door opened. She relaxed at the sight of her friend Niamh.

'What are you doing here?' Niamh whispered. 'I saw the light from your lamp. Is everything all right'

Iseult nodded, mustering a faint smile. 'I'm fine. I just…felt the need to bc here.'

'You're so pale.' Her friend put an arm around her. 'Have you eaten anything?'

She couldn't remember. Shrugging, she didn't protest when Niamh handed her a hard piece of bread. It tasted stale, but she ate it out of courtesy.

'You should go home,' Iseult urged, after she'd finished the food. 'It's late.'

'As should you.'

'I will. After I've spent a little more time here.' She picked up the figure Kieran had carved for her and put it away. The yew was smooth and polished, though the image of the boy was not finished.

Niamh sighed and sent her a knowing look. 'Are you in love with him?'

Iseult rested her chin upon her hands. 'Not with Davin.'

But her friend understood whom she meant. 'What will you do?'

Her thoughts drifted back to Kieran. The bleakness of her life these past few weeks made it hurt even more to think of him. She woke up each morning, wishing to see his face. Even if she could never feel his arms around her again, it cut her heart to shreds worrying about him.

'There's nothing I can do. He's gone.' She met Niamh's gaze, and her friend embraced her.

'Maybe he'll come back for you,' Niamh offered.

She didn't dare let herself hope for that. 'Maybe,' was all she said.

The door swung open, and Davin ducked inside. His fair hair hung ragged against his neck, his clothes thrown on as if in a hurry. 'I thought I might find you here.'

He kept his tone soft, but Iseult didn't miss the jealousy within it.

Niamh moved beside her, taking her hand. Bless her. Iseult raised weary eyes, afraid of what Davin might say.

'Do you want me to stay?' her friend asked.

'I'd like to speak with Iseult alone.' Davin gave a pointed look towards the door, but Niamh held her ground.

'I wasn't asking you. Iseult?'

It wasn't fair to put Niamh in the middle, not when Davin wanted nothing but a conversation. 'It's all right. I'll speak with you on the morrow.'

When her friend had left, Davin closed the door. His expression was grim, his eyes empty. 'Even now, you go to him.'

He sat down, staring at the empty hearth. 'I thought if you were away from him, you'd forget him. The way you did Murtagh.'

'There was nothing between Murtagh and myself, save the one night we were lovers.' She sat beside him, leaning her cheek against her hand.

Davin looked as haggard as she felt, and when he raked a hand through his hair, she caught sight of his grief. 'You love him, don't you?'

She nodded slowly. The look of anguish upon his face startled her. And she realised that Davin had never stopped caring for her.

'I'm sorry for what I did.' He reached out to take her hand. His fingers closed over hers in the lightest caress. 'I know that I can't change your heart. But I'd like to ask for a second chance.'

She didn't answer for a long moment. The air inside the hut seemed to resonate with Kieran's presence. He was here, with her, despite his physical absence.

Could she ever go back to Davin, after this?

'I'll think about it.' She could promise nothing more.

Sometimes men didn't know what was best for them. And Niamh had decided that the time had come to actively pursue Davin Ó Falvey. Though she had tried to gain his notice after Iseult had gone, he'd been so wrapped up in his own misery, it was too soon for him to even consider it.

But now time was running out. With Iseult back again, Davin was sliding back into his former lovesick self.

Couldn't the man see that Iseult was in love with Kieran? And couldn't he turn his attention to her, instead? Though she doubted there was even the faintest chance, this would be her last attempt.

Niamh armed herself with courage and a full ewer of ale. Likely her luck would improve if Davin were completely drunk.

He'd gone to the stables that evening after the meal, to tend his gelding Lir. Niamh waited to be sure no one was watching and followed him, carrying the ale and two clay mugs. Though she normally did not enjoy ale, preferring wine, she supposed she'd have to suffer through it. Davin likely wouldn't want to drink alone.

Inside the stables, he smoothed the flanks of his horse, murmuring in a low voice.

'I brought you some ale,' Niamh said, pouring him a cup.

'In the stables?' Davin frowned, sniffing the brew.

'Why not?' She set the ewer down and behaved as if people normally drank ale amidst the horses.

He wasn't at all fooled. 'Was there something you wanted?'

Only for you to look upon me in the same way as you do Iseult. The man was blind, never seeing what was right in front of him. But Niamh did not speak her innermost thoughts.

She leaned up against a wooden stall, sipping her own mug of ale. It tasted as terrible as she remembered, but she managed to choke it down. 'Why not tell me what's troubling you?' she suggested. 'I'm a good listener.'

Davin's lips curved in a patronising smile. 'I won't burden you with our tribe's needs, Niamh.'

Liar. He wasn't thinking of the tribe at all.

'You're thinking of Iseult,' Niamh predicted, keeping her voice light, as if the answer didn't matter. 'She is very beautiful.'

The way I'm not. But then, she'd come to terms with her plain face. She couldn't do anything about what God had given her, so she'd have to make the most of her wits.

Davin took a long drink of ale and looked around the stable, as if hoping to escape once again.

'You still love her, don't you?' Niamh had no qualms about asking a direct question. When he nodded slowly, the pain was evident in his eyes. Fool that she was, she found him attractive. And she was drawn to his wounded, misguided heart.

She took his cup from him and refilled it once more. 'You're a good man, Davin Ó Falvey, even if you've made some mistakes.'

'And what mistakes would those be?'

Niamh held out her hand, counting off her fingers. 'Let me see. Not looking for Iseult's son, bullying her when she tried to leave, threatening to kill Kieran…shall I go on?'

Davin reached for the ewer and refilled his mug. In the shadows of the barn, his gold hair appeared darker. His cheeks were stony, his blue eyes haggard. 'I did what I thought was right.'

Niamh rolled her eyes. 'You were stupid, that's what. The choice has to be hers.'

He drained the mug of ale. 'Are you trying to make me feel better? Because if you are, it's not working.'

'I'm simply stating the truth.' She refilled his mug again and found him staring at her. Those blue eyes, intelligent and honest, made her transform from a sensible young woman into the worst sort of halfwit. What she wouldn't give to be kissed by a man such as him. Someone who knew what a woman dreamed of.

Davin shook his head, gripping the mug as though it were a man's throat. 'Things didn't end well between us. I almost went after her.' He expelled a rough laugh. 'That would have been pitiful, wouldn't it? But I'm afraid I won't be able to make things right. I said terrible things to her.'

Oh, saints above. He was treating her as his confessor, wanting advice. This was going terribly wrong.

'Well, don't worry. I'm sure you'll find another woman to wed.' She drank her own mug of ale and found that the taste wasn't so bad. Then again, her head was feeling a trifle muzzy.

'Why are you so intent on me finding a wife?' His voice had mellowed, and he filled both of their cups again. The ale sloshed over the sides, spattering onto the dirt floor.

'You're a fine-looking man. I think you deserve to be happy.' She complimented him as if she were speaking of the weather. Thank heavens, she wasn't flushing. But Davin looked as though he wanted to bolt from the stables.

'Oh, don't worry,' she continued. 'I'm not expecting you to say the same for me. I'm plain-faced, and well I know it.'

He set down his mug and reached out to touch a strand of her hair. She didn't breathe, couldn't move when he fingered the brown curl. 'You aren't that plain.'

Polite words, empty words they were. She knew it. 'But not as beautiful as Iseult.'

He didn't deny it, as she'd expected. Brightly, she added, 'I do hope you find happiness, though. With a woman who cares about you.'

Like me. But she didn't say it. Her quest was hopeless, and she might as well abandon it.

'I think we've finished the ale,' she said, holding her spinning head with a hand.

'There isn't enough ale in Éireann to make me forget about her,' Davin grumbled, raising the empty ewer.

He'd lost count of how much he'd drunk, but it hadn't drowned the memory of Iseult and Kieran. She really did love the slave. He could see it in the wistful expression on her face, in the way she touched Kieran's tools. She wanted to be with him.

And the thought of the two of them together made him want to stab something.

Niamh sank against the stable wall, tucking her feet beneath her *léine*. 'I think I drank too much.' She fumbled with her hair absently, then unbraided it. The long brown length spilled across her shoulders in soft waves. In the fading sunset, her hair had a golden halo.

He couldn't help but notice the way her gown moulded to generous curves. Though her face was not as fair as Iseult's, Niamh had an interesting smile.

'Why didn't you go after them?' she asked. 'Kieran and Iseult, I mean.'

The effects of the ale made the stable sway. He sat down beside her, leaning back for balance. 'I don't know. I should have.' He propped his hand up on one knee. The ale hadn't dulled his senses enough, and his restlessness continued. 'Why did you really come here, Niamh?'

Guilt flushed her face, followed by stubbornness. 'Because I wanted to help you forget about her,' she whispered.

In her eyes, he saw a storm of troubled emotions. And something more…a longing. It startled him, to see a woman who desired him.

He'd known Niamh for many years, but never had she stirred any feelings in him. She'd been a friend, someone who was always there.

'What do you want from me, Niamh?' he asked.

'I want you to let her go.' She rested her palms on his shoulders. The touch of her hands startled him, evoking sensations he'd locked away for so long.

'And if I did?' he asked.

She lifted her knuckles to the growth of beard upon his cheeks, grazing it softly. 'Then there might be a chance that you'd find love again. Somewhere unexpected.'

Not once had she spoken her feelings, though they were

as transparent as water. He took her palm in his, aware that the ale had relaxed him more than it should have. Never would he have touched her otherwise.

But she had not pushed him. And he found her intriguing to look at. With a thumb, he brushed the edge of her mouth, watching her response. The flesh upon her skin rose up in goose bumps.

He leaned in, angling his mouth to taste her lips. The sweetness of her innocence allured him, and when she welcomed his kiss, he deepened it.

Her cheeks flamed scarlet when at last he drew back. 'I've been kissed before. But never by the man I wanted.' A chagrined smile tipped her mouth. 'Thank you for taking pity upon me.'

She rose and fled the stables before he could answer. It hadn't been pity at all.

And that, perhaps, was the greatest surprise of all.

Chapter Nineteen

Kieran smelled the smoke for miles before he reached the settlement. Once it had been a *catháir*, a ringfort made of stone. Now all that remained were ashes. Sounds mingled, of children crying and mothers trying to hush them.

Familiar sounds, of people dying. Like a living nightmare, it was like stepping back in time to the aftermath of his own tribe's raid. Kieran suppressed a shudder as he dismounted and tethered his mount. Whether it was Norsemen or another clan didn't matter. What mattered was the survivors.

Small huts dotted the land, until he reached the centre point where they were clustered together. What he found appalled him.

The bodies of slain men rested upon the ground, their bodies stiffened before anyone could bury them. Women, too, lay dead. The living folk were huddled together, soothing children and talking amongst themselves. Their stares pierced right through him, suspicious and fearful.

It was like walking amidst his own people and being unable to help. There was a sense of chaos, a lack of leadership. No one was giving orders, nor making decisions on what was to be done. Women and children spoke in low voices, each waiting for someone else to take command.

It was presumptuous to step into such a role, though Kieran knew what needed to happen first. But perhaps, once he acted, they would follow.

Without speaking a word, he found a spade leaning against one of the huts near a garden. After choosing a spot, he began to dig a shallow grave. The dull wooden tool bit into the damp earth and as the dirt began to pile up, he found himself remembering the tribe members they had lost.

Declan. Séan. Siobhan.

Some had died from hunger, others from the raiders who had struck them down. The simple task of digging a grave released the grief he'd held back for so long. He hacked at the earth, giving rein to the anger and frustration. He had lived, while his closest friends had died. And Egan.

The people watched him in silence, before another young woman joined him with her digging stick. Then an older woman and a child barely over the age of eight. Together they worked to bury the dead. Kieran kept his head lowered so they would not look upon his face. He poured himself into the gruelling work, letting it ease him in a way nothing else could.

When the last spade of earth covered the last body, his palms were blistered and his mind blessedly empty. The sun had gone down hours earlier, and they had worked by torchlight.

He leaned against the spade, wiping his brow with his sleeve.

'You must be thirsty,' an older woman said, offering a dripping skin of water. 'I am Rosaleen Murphy. Who are you, lad, and who sent you?'

'I am Kieran Ó Brannon.' He took a long drink of water, never minding that it was stale, and handed it back to Rosaleen. For a moment, he almost called himself a slave. But he'd earned back his freedom. He thought of telling her he was a woodcarver. But in the end, the truth came out.

'I am a chieftain's son and a warrior,' he said. Her head nodded with approval, and he continued. 'I came in search of Aidan MacFergus. His mother Iseult has been looking for him over the past year, and I am here on her behalf. I believe he was fostered among you.'

Though he had not seen the child, he had followed the family's path here. Nearly two moons had passed since he'd left Iseult. Each day he thought of her, and he needed to see her again. But not before he found Aidan.

Rosaleen crossed herself. 'Bless the saints that you've come to us. Both of Aidan's foster-parents are dead. They fled here when the raiders arrived, but did not survive the attack.' She bowed her head in respect. 'They were among those we buried just now.'

Kieran kept his face expressionless, though inwardly his heart was pounding. 'Is the boy all right?'

'I'll take you to him,' Rosaleen offered. 'Aidan and his foster-sister need someone to look after them.'

He followed her to one of the stone huts. The thatch had burned away, and they had spread a canvas covering atop one segment to provide shelter. At least ten children were inside, ranging in age from babies to those nearing adolescence. The din of noise was mostly from whining younger children who wanted food.

'Aidan,' Rosaleen called out. 'Come here, sweeting. And you, Shannon. This man has come to take care of both of you.'

Both? Kieran nearly denied it, but a young girl around

the age of eight came forward, holding the hand of a black-haired lad. Aidan. Iseult's son.

A hollow feeling invaded him, humbling him at the sight. She should be here to see the boy. It should be Iseult holding out her arms, weeping with gratitude.

And then panic set in. He knew nothing about children. He'd paid no attention at all to the young ones and hadn't the faintest idea of how to take care of them.

'Rosaleen—'

'I'll find a place for the three of you to spend the night. You'll want to talk before you take them to Aidan's mother.' Rosaleen embraced the two children, smoothing the girl's fair hair. 'Shannon has been fostered with Aidan for the past year. I promised her I wouldn't part her from her brother. He's all she has left, since her parents died last season.'

The elderly woman sent him such a strong look that he could not deny this child his protection. He hadn't planned on two children, but what else could he do?

'I'm a stranger to them,' he found himself saying. 'Perhaps you'd want to send someone along as an escort.' But as soon as the words left his mouth, he realised the futility. The children far outnumbered the living adults. Those who remained were elderly or nursing mothers.

Rosaleen took a child in each hand. 'You came to us as a stranger. And you helped us bury those who did not survive the raid. I don't know whose prayers were responsible for bringing you here, but I'm a woman of faith. I know a good man when I see one. And I know that Aidan is a MacFergus, for his foster-mother told me.' She gave a weary smile and placed Aidan's hand in his right palm, Shannon's in his left. 'Now, I'll get you settled for the night and you can begin your journey on the morrow.'

Their fingers were incredibly small within his hands. Aidan's mouth trembled with fear, and Shannon stared down at the ground.

As he followed Rosaleen, Kieran found himself voicing a prayer of his own.

Please, God, don't let them cry.

This couldn't be happening. Not again.

Iseult's hand moved down to her stomach. Her mind cried out with the unfairness of it all, but no longer could she deny the truth. She had not had her woman's flow since she'd seen Kieran last.

Another child grew within her womb.

She wanted to cry out with frustration, knowing that Fate had cursed her again with a living reminder of a man's rejection.

The last time, Murtagh had known about the child and had abandoned her on their wedding day. Her family and friends had witnessed her shame, and she'd endured six more months of stares, gossip, and humiliation before she'd held Aidan in her arms.

And once she had, the sight of her son had made her forget everything else.

Would it be the same with this babe? Would a tiny fist clasp her thumb, her heart melting at the sight of the child's solemn trust?

No. It would be worse this time, because she'd see Kieran's face in the babe's features. Each day she would know that he hadn't loved her enough to take her with him. And even if she wanted to tell him about the child, how could she find him? He could be anywhere in Éireann.

Saint Brigid, what could she do? She had tried so hard to forget about him, making a new life for herself here.

And just as before, she would bear a child given by a man who'd left her.

'Iseult?' Davin's arrival interrupted her thoughts. Iseult snatched her hand away from her womb, as if he'd guess. 'I came to ask if you wanted to join us. Niamh, Orin and myself are going to take the boat out.' He smiled warmly. 'Perhaps we'll make another wager on who can catch the most fish.'

Without warning, she burst into tears. There was no way to hold back the sobs at the mention of fishing. That was the day she'd begun falling in love with Kieran.

Poor Davin had no idea what he'd walked into. He put an arm around her, and Iseult buried her face in his chest, needing the comfort of a friend. She wept for Kieran, for her unborn child, and, most of all, for the guilt at not wanting this babe.

She didn't know how she'd endure it again.

Davin stroked her hair, holding her close until she managed to stop her tears. Iseult raised a weary face to his, afraid of the questions he'd ask.

'I won't make you clean the fish this time,' he said softly.

A choked laugh came from throat. 'That's not why I was weeping.' She took a breath, wiping away her tears. 'Go on without me. I don't really feel like fishing.'

'All right.' His hand pressed against her lower back, his palm a steady reminder that he was here for her. He didn't ask a single question. And for that reason, she admitted the reason for her outburst.

'Kieran's child grows within me,' she confessed.

Davin held very still, his face grim with shock. She waited for him to shout at her, to recoil in disgust.

'I don't know what to do,' she whispered. 'I've been so stupid.'

'You'll marry me,' he said. 'And I'll take care of you the way I always wanted to.'

It was on her tongue to refuse him, for she didn't love him. Her love belonged to Kieran, even if he was far from here. Even if she could never hold his heart.

Instead, she heard herself say, 'All right.'

The choice became an act of rebellion. A way of proving to herself that she would not be alone this time. Kieran might not want her to be part of his life, but another man did.

And though her conscience cried out that it was wrong to use Davin in this way, she told herself she didn't care. This child would have a father.

When Davin embraced her, she didn't pull away. She would learn to fall in love with him.

He deserved nothing less.

The journey to Lismanagh was long enough on his own. With two children in tow, it took an eternity. Kieran stopped for the night, wishing it were possible to continue travelling in the dark. He wanted to reach Iseult as soon as possible. She'd waited so long to find her son, he didn't want her to have to wait any longer.

In his visions, he pictured her happiness, and in it, he found a sense of his own peace. The unsettling question was what he should say to her. How could he convince her to come away with him? He didn't want to watch another man take care of her, or love her. And knowing that Davin was doing just that increased the need to travel faster.

He was running low on provisions, but had not taken the time to stop and hunt. Instead, he split his food between the children. He'd gone hungry before; it meant nothing to him. At dawn he would replenish their travel stores and satisfy his hunger.

But it had not escaped Shannon's notice.

'What are *you* eating?' she demanded, after she'd nearly finished her portion of bread.

He rubbed down the horse's back, using a bit of dried grass since he had nothing else. When she repeated her question, he glared at her. 'I eat little girls who ask too many questions.'

Shannon frowned right back at him. 'That isn't funny.' A moment later, she tore off a small piece of bread and pressed it into his palm. 'I'll share.'

The tiny scrap of bread was hardly more than a mouthful. He knew she hadn't had enough to eat, from what little he'd provided. Her tiny offering humbled him. No one had ever tried to take care of him. No one, save Iseult.

A slight tug on his tunic caught his attention. Aidan reached up and handed him a soggy bite of his own bread. Then the boy trotted back to sit near the fire. Though the bread looked like the sorriest bit of food, Kieran couldn't very well refuse it. Instead, he ate both pieces. And they filled him up in a way he hadn't expected.

'You're not very good at this, are you?' Shannon said, tossing a stick on to the fire he'd built. 'Being a foster-father, I mean.'

'I'm not your foster-father. I'm taking Aidan to his mother. If you're good, I'll try to find you a nice family while we're at Lismanagh.'

'I'm glad.' She nodded her head, accepting his word. 'You aren't good at taking care of children.'

Though she had spoken matter of factly, he took umbrage at the statement. True, he wasn't very good at it. But he could protect them well enough. He almost voiced a protest but stopped himself.

Shannon was trying to provoke him. For what purpose,

he didn't know, but she really did remind him of his sisters. Not at all intimidated, she seemed ready to take advantage of him at every opportunity.

He hadn't expected to like this wisp of a girl. But something about her insistence that he was a terrible guardian made him want to prove otherwise. It was likely her reason for being so contrary.

Aidan whined, rubbing his eyes.

'He needs to go to sleep,' Shannon informed him.

'Then he should just close his eyes.'

At that pronouncement, the boy's whining turned into tears. 'Want Rosaleen,' he sobbed.

Kieran glanced skywards, wondering if this was meant to be part of his penance. Not a moment's peace had he attained since leaving the *catháir*. If Iseult were here, she would know what to do. He imagined she'd pull Aidan into her arms and cuddle the boy, whispering endearments as she rocked him.

Damn it all, he missed her. He sensed that Iseult would be a wonderful mother, able to meet their needs without a second thought. He envisioned her tucking them into their pallets, pressing a kiss upon their foreheads. And then he'd tell her to come and kiss him goodnight.

But not on the forehead. The wicked image conjured up vivid memories of her body, of feeling her softness beneath him.

Loneliness sliced at him. She'd left him, of her own choice. She didn't want him any more, not unless he promised her a life together.

Didn't she know how much he wanted that? What wouldn't he give to wake beside her each morning, to know that she would be with him always? The emptiness in his heart was drowned out by Aidan's shrieking.

'What does he want?' Kieran demanded.

Shannon cringed at his sharp tone, and he wished he'd held his patience a little better. But what was he supposed to do? He'd fed the child, given him a warm fire. Aidan would be with his mother, soon enough.

'He can't sleep on the ground,' Shannon pointed out. 'Make a bed for him out of your cloak and some leaves.'

It wasn't a bad idea. He set Shannon to the task of piling up dried leaves, and he spread his cloak atop them when she'd found enough.

'Go to sleep,' he commanded the boy, lifting Aidan on to the cloak. The boy hiccoughed, his shoulders shaking as he gulped for air.

Shannon laid down beside Aidan and rubbed his back. At the simple touch, the boy's crying grew softer. 'He misses our foster-mother,' she said. 'Maybe you could tell us a story. That's what she used to do.'

A story. What did he know of stories? The only tales he knew involved men being slain for glory upon a battlefield. Not exactly reassuring to a child.

'I don't know any,' he admitted.

'Yes, you do. Tell us a story about a warrior and a princess.' Shannon snuggled up beside her brother. 'Make one up.'

'If I do, will you go to sleep?' Both heads bobbed in agreement.

Kieran wanted to groan. He wasn't a bard. It was time for the children to sleep, and that should have been good enough. He didn't need to waste time with a useless story.

'Once, long ago, there lived a princess and a warrior. They were happy together. And that's the end.' He leaned back against a birch tree and closed his eyes, feigning sleep.

A stunned silence met his grand tale before Shannon blurted out, 'That's the worst story I ever heard.'

'You never said how long it had to be. Now, both of you, go to sleep.'

A faint snort caught his attention, and he saw Aidan's mouth smirking. The sight of the child's smile speared his heart, for it was Iseult's smile. So rare it was, and so precious.

Tomorrow, he reminded himself. Tomorrow they would reach Lismanagh, and he would see her again. He'd give her what she'd been missing most of all.

But he couldn't quell the thought that it wouldn't be enough.

Chapter Twenty

Rory MacFergus was the worst sort of fool. Iseult wouldn't at all like him meddling in her business.

A wedding. After everything she'd been through, after casting Davin aside once before, she planned to marry him now? He didn't believe a word of it.

He'd told her so, to her face, when he'd gone to Lismanagh. Iseult had put on a false smile as though she were excited about the festivities.

But she was lying to him. He knew it, for as her father he'd always been able to see the truth in her eyes. She didn't love Davin Ó Falvey. Not the way she loved her woodcarver.

And where Kieran had gone, he didn't know. What he did know was that the carver made his daughter's face flush with love. He'd never seen her so happy before. And something had happened to drive the two of them apart. He intended to find out exactly what it was.

He'd decided to track down Kieran, starting with the Murphy lands where Aidan had been fostered. It was as good a place as any.

Likely he'd come all this way for naught. He was going soft in the head, sure enough. The chances of him actually finding Kieran Ó Brannon were remote, not to mention that Iseult would be livid at his interfering.

But what if the woodcarver didn't know about the wedding?

That would be a problem, now, wouldn't it? Kieran couldn't stop Iseult from marrying the wrong man if he knew nothing about it.

Rory shielded his eyes from the sunset, knowing he'd have to make camp soon enough. He took a drink from his water skin, studying the winding path that led towards the Murphy lands.

Then suddenly, over the rise of a hill, he scented stale peat smoke. A fire that had gone cold. He narrowed his gaze, seeing the silhouette of a figure ahead. He couldn't make out whether or not it was the woodcarver.

Spurring his horse forwards, Rory moved towards the tiny spiral of smoke until he reached the source. When he saw Kieran sitting before the fire, all the blood seemed to drain from his face.

'Mary, Mother of God,' he breathed.

The carver was leaning up against a large oak tree beside an enormous pile of leaves. Two children slept upon his cloak. He recognised Aidan, who was resting his head in Kieran's lap. The girl he didn't know, but she was holding the carver's hand in sleep.

Kieran's eyes snapped open, but he relaxed when he recognised Rory. His neck was stiff and he didn't know how he'd dozed off when it was still early evening. The exhaustion of the past few days had caught up with him.

'It's only me, lad,' Rory said in a low voice, dismounting. He tethered his mount and, while he tended to his horse, a smile caught his mouth. 'Looks as though you've your hands full. Is that my young grandson, Aidan?'

'It is,' Kieran confirmed. He, too, kept his voice quiet. The children had been tired, but unable to relax. Aidan had started crying again after the story, and Kieran had only managed to make him cease by sitting next to the boy. One thing had led to another, and before he knew what had happened, both children were snuggled up against him for warmth.

Rory lowered the reins and walked quietly over to stand before the child. His face softened at the sight of the boy. 'It's been so long since I've seen him. But it's him, sure enough. He has Iseult's face and Murtagh's hair.'

The mention of Iseult's former lover made Kieran involuntarily clench his fist. Shannon's eyes snapped open, and Kieran realised he'd hurt her hand. 'It's nothing,' he murmured, softening his grip. 'Go back to sleep.' He released her hand and touched her hair.

'Who is that?' Shannon whispered, pointing to Rory.

'Aidan's grandsire. You'll speak with him in the morning.' Kieran exerted a gentle pressure on her head until Shannon curled up against him, burying her face in his cloak.

He regarded Iseult's father with all seriousness. 'Why are you here?'

'I came to talk to you about Iseult.' Rory withdrew a flask from his supplies and took a drink before passing it over.

Kieran sipped the lukewarm mead as if nothing were amiss, but Rory's words unnerved him. 'What's happened?'

'Now, don't worry,' Rory continued. 'She's all right.' He sank down, letting out a grunt when he leaned up against a fallen log. 'But she's given Davin her promise to marry him.'

Marry? Why would she agree to wed Davin again?

Was the man threatening her? The thought made Kieran want to snarl.

He gently extracted himself from the children, his mind racing. Damn it all, he didn't want another man to have her. *He* wanted her.

'What do you plan to do about it?' Rory asked.

'What do you think I'll do?' he growled. It tempted him to ride into Lismanagh and simply carry her off, like one of the raiders. She might forgive him for it. Eventually.

He'd let her go to Davin, believing he had nothing to offer. He was wrong. He had her son, the child of her heart. And whether or not he could make a life for them, he was nothing but a coward if he didn't try.

'When will they wed?' he asked.

'Two days hence.'

Kieran expelled the breath he'd been holding. It was enough time to reach Lismanagh before the wedding.

What he didn't know was why she had decided to marry Davin. And whether or not she would give him another chance.

The next evening, Iseult's nerves were strung tightly. She couldn't bring herself to eat anything, not even for the sake of her babe. Last night, she had argued with Davin's mother until she wanted to bury herself beneath a coverlet and never come out.

Neasa wanted to prevent this wedding at all costs. But Iseult hadn't succumbed to the intimidation, nor the threats.

Today was meant to be a day of happiness. Why, then, did she feel like weeping again? Not even her best friend Niamh had come to see her. Iseult didn't know what was wrong, but she missed her friend.

'Come here, *a chara*,' Muirne urged. She held up an

antelope comb and bade her sit down. 'Let me arrange your hair for you.'

Iseult relaxed while Muirne combed her hair and braided it, chattering about all manner of things. The interior of the hut smelled delicious from the bread they had baked, using the best grains of the season.

Although the celebrating and feasting had been going on all day, Iseult had kept to herself during the festivities. The weariness of pregnancy was taking its toll, though none of the people, save Davin, were aware of it.

'There. Now you look like a bride.' Muirne beamed and hugged her. 'And your gown is perfect for the occasion.' Iseult raised a hand and touched the intricate braids which wound around her forehead and nape into a crown. Her long hair spilled down her back, and she wore a violet silk overdress and cream *léine*. They had been among the garments Davin had given as part of her bride price. She had asked Muirne to choose a gown, for she'd been unable to look at the carved dower chest without her emotions spilling over.

A slight knock at the door caught their attention. Young Bartley burst in with garlands of flowers in his hands. 'Davin sent these!' the boy exclaimed, shoving them into Iseult's hands.

Muirne swatted her foster-son away, laughing as Bartley tried to snatch a crumb from one of the fresh loaves. 'Go on with you.'

Iseult lifted the garland of wildflowers, yellow gorse and purple heather, and set it upon her hair. When the last touches were finished, Muirne took her hands.

'You don't look very happy, Iseult. Are you remembering the wedding with Murtagh?'

No. She'd been thinking of Kieran. Wondering if he had

gone home again or whether he'd kept his vow to find Aidan. She had begged Davin to send men to the place they had searched before, but they'd found nothing. Not a trace of her son.

Just accept it. He's gone. You're not going to find him, and you may as well start a new life with Davin.

A heaviness rested within her heart, but she believed she was doing the right thing by marrying Davin.

'I'll be all right,' she whispered to Muirne. And she would. Davin wanted to take care of her and the baby, and that was enough. It had to be.

'Let us go.'

'We're not stopping.' Kieran urged the horse as fast as it was able, while Shannon begged and pleaded.

'I have to. Or I'll wet my gown.'

'Don't you dare.' He tightened his grip around both children, wishing to God he had left them with Rory so he could ride to Lismanagh at a faster pace. But in his mind, he'd always imagined meeting Iseult with Aidan in his arms. He didn't want to go to her empty-handed, not after he'd sworn to find the boy.

Now he regretted his decision to send Rory on ahead, to try to stop the wedding. He should have gone.

'Kieran, please.' Shannon gripped her knees, her voice quivering.

'We stopped at the noon meal. You should have taken care of matters then.'

'I didn't have to go, then,' she whimpered.

Damn it. He didn't have time for this.

'Make it quick,' he barked, slowing the horse and letting her down. Shannon raced towards the woods, disappearing into the thicket.

The sun was already sinking lower on to the horizon. It had taken all of yesterday and all of today to make it this far.

And the wedding was today. Kieran gritted his teeth, wishing to God there was a way to travel faster. For all he knew, he might already be too late. When at last Shannon returned, he urged the horse faster.

As if to mock them, the skies released a downpour. Heavy rain beat down upon them, muddying the grass and soaking their clothes. The day just couldn't get any worse. His only consolation was that no one else would be celebrating in this weather.

Both children howled at the weather, and he removed his cloak. Keeping his arms tightly around them, he gave Shannon the garment to raise over their heads.

'Why are we travelling so fast?' she complained.

'Do you remember the story I told you, about the warrior and the princess?'

'That wasn't a story at all.'

'The princess is about to marry someone else. This warrior has to go and stop her.'

Shannon turned to stare at him. 'It's a true story?'

He nodded.

She seemed to think about it for a moment longer. In all seriousness, she added, 'Then you'd better hurry up. Your princess won't want to wait on you.'

'I can't do this!' Niamh protested.

Rory crossed his arms. 'It won't take long. Just do as I've asked, and it will all be well.'

'You're asking the impossible. I don't know how.'

Rory winked. 'Oh, I think you do know, lass. And you know how important this is. Get Deena to help you.'

Niamh wrung her hands. 'Are you sure? Because I don't think it's a good idea.'

'More than anything in my life.' Rory turned around. 'Now go and find Davin.'

Niamh raised troubled eyes to his. 'He won't like it. Why won't you just tell him the truth?'

'Because I'm an old fool who likes a bit of romance at a wedding.' He touched the underside of her chin. 'I have faith in you, Niamh.'

The young woman sighed. 'So be it. But if anything goes wrong, it will be upon your shoulders.'

The air was damp from the rain, the atmosphere not at all welcoming for a wedding. Perhaps it was an ill omen.

Iseult walked outside, to where a small crowd of tribesmen and women gathered. Several other women, like herself, were crowned with garlands of flowers. The men waited on the opposite side with the priest, their faces eager with anticipation.

But there was no sign of Davin. She stood with the other unmarried women, her gaze seeking him. As one couple after another paired off and spoke their vows, she waited for him to appear.

Nothing.

He'll come, her instincts told her. Davin would never abandon you. He cares too much.

Didn't he? Unbidden doubts rose up, for he knew about the unborn child in her womb.

The priest smiled at her, and Iseult stepped forward. At any moment now, Davin would appear. Though she kept a serene expression on her face, it grew strained as each minute passed. The priest could not begin the wedding Mass for the other couples until she and Davin had spoken their vows.

Where was he?

People had begun to talk, and the couples who had joined hands were watching her. When she looked over at Davin's mother Neasa, the woman's expression was as confused as her own. There was no smirk of satisfaction. Neasa hadn't known anything about it, which made her even more uneasy. Iseult forced herself to look straight ahead, not meeting anyone's gaze.

When the rain began again, lightly falling upon her face, she was thankful for it. At least it veiled her tears.

Why had he done this? He, of all people, knew the humiliation she'd suffered when Murtagh had not shown up for their wedding. And now, he'd done the same to her.

Davin wasn't going to come. He had never intended to wed her. She swallowed back the flood of tears, furious at herself for thinking she could trust him. This was his means of revenge. He was the only man who'd known about her unborn babe. And just as he didn't want Aidan, he didn't want to be a father to this child.

She waited while the rain soaked through her gown and finally motioned for the others to go on inside the stone church. They could begin the Mass without her.

As each man, woman, and child passed, she felt their stares and their pity. When they were inside, she ripped off the sodden garland of gorse and heather, tossing it to the ground.

'Iseult? Do you want me to wait with you?' Her father kept his voice gentle, but he was the last man she wanted to see right now.

'No. Go and celebrate the Mass with the others. I want to be alone right now.'

'It's raining,' he reminded her. 'You shouldn't be out here in the dampness.'

With leaden steps, she trod her way through the mud until she reached the mound of hostages. Her heart felt as cold as the stone, unable to think of anything past her own pain.

She rested her forehead against her wrist, ignoring the wetness of the rain. This was truly the worst day she'd ever known.

Though a part of her wanted to believe that something had happened to prevent Davin from coming, the cynical voice inside reminded her that he was a jealous man. He'd been furious when he'd learned that she loved Kieran.

No, Davin wasn't going to come and take care of her. The only person she could rely on was herself. The weight of loneliness bore down upon her at the thought.

The sound of voices interrupted her. Children's voices, along with a familiar baritone.

'Stop arguing, both of you,' the man commanded. 'Take my hands and we'll go inside.'

Iseult raised her face from the stone and saw Kieran standing there. His dark hair fell across his shoulders, his expression threatening. Drops of water shone upon his face, while his clothing was drenched from the rain.

When she saw the small hand holding his, her heart cracked apart. It was him. Her son Aidan.

Iseult's knees crumbled like sand, and the tears flooded her face. He'd kept his word. Kieran had found her son and somehow brought him back to her. She picked up her skirts and ran towards the boy, crouching down when she reached his side.

His face, the one she'd dreamed of for the past year, had lost some of its baby roundness. Dark, fine-textured hair framed his jaw, and he stared at her with blue eyes that mirrored her own.

Suspicion darkened his gaze, and there was no recognition. 'You don't remember me, do you?' she whispered. 'I'm your mother.'

The boy shook his head, but Kieran caught his wrist and placed the tiny hand in hers.

More than anything, she wanted to pull Aidan into her arms and hold him tight. She wanted to touch his silky dark hair and marvel at the sight of him. But she was afraid of frightening him.

'He'll remember you in time,' Kieran said.

Iseult couldn't find her voice, but managed a nod. Slowly she stood, though she kept her grip tight upon Aidan's hand. 'You came back.'

'I keep my promises.'

She waited for him to embrace her. She needed the feel of his arms around her. But he made no move. She couldn't read his expression, didn't know what he was feeling.

'Thank you for bringing Aidan to me,' she said at last.

He only nodded. Again, she waited for him to pull her into his arms. To say something, anything of what he was thinking. The earth seemed to drop beneath her feet when he didn't.

He came for you, she reminded herself. Surely that had to mean something. She forced away the self-doubts and faced him.

'Did you wed him?' he asked in a tight voice. Only then did she see the raw fear he'd been hiding. And she wondered if there might be a chance for them.

'No. He didn't come.'

Kieran stepped forward, his hand reaching up to caress her cheek. 'Then will you let me take his place?'

Chapter Twenty-One

She started trembling then, afraid to touch him. Afraid that she was hearing things.

'Let me become your husband,' Kieran murmured. 'Let me take care of you and Aidan.'

She slid her arm around his neck, blinded by the tears. 'I didn't think you wanted me any more. I thought—'

He cut off her words with a kiss, healing the hurt and easing her in a way nothing else could. She clung to him, feeling his strength even as he cherished her.

'I think I'd have carried you away from here, even if you had wed him,' he said gruffly.

She raised her palm to his face. 'Know that I will follow you wherever you go.'

'Why did you agree to wed him?' He kept her in a tight embrace, as if afraid to let her go.

She broke away then, holding his hand and resting it upon her womb. 'Because he promised to take care of me. And our unborn babe.'

When she looked into his eyes, Kieran felt as if he'd been struck across the head with a *bata*. His lips moved, but no sound came forth. All the air seemed to leave his lungs, his heart pounding.

A child. His own flesh and blood growing inside of her womb.

Kieran was moved by the sudden urge to touch her again, as though he could feel the life growing within her body. 'Our child.' He repeated the words, unable to believe them. He couldn't get his mind around it, though he knew she spoke the truth.

'Yes. Ours.' She kept her hand in his, her other hand linked in Aidan's. Kieran suddenly realised he'd forgotten completely about the children. Glancing around, he saw Shannon lurking near the palisade wall.

'Come here,' he said to her.

Shannon bit her lip, a wary expression in her eyes. When she reached his side, he introduced her to Iseult as Aidan's foster-sister. Shannon mumbled a greeting, but kept her gaze downwards. The worried crease upon her mouth didn't relax. 'Was I a good girl?'

He didn't know what she was talking about. 'Good enough for what?'

Her hopeful eyes met his. When he didn't understand what she was hinting at, she broke free of his hand. 'It doesn't matter.'

With a little shrug, she went over to stand by the gate. Lost and lonely, it struck him suddenly what she meant.

He crossed the ringfort, leaving Iseult with her son. Crouching down, he rested his wrist upon his knee. 'You should know, I'm not good at telling stories. I've never been around children much. I'd make a terrible foster-father.'

Hope swelled in her eyes. 'You might get better.'

He kept silent, as though thinking about it. 'We'd need someone to help us with Aidan. I don't suppose you—'

She flew into his arms, gripping him as though he were the last man in the world. And the most startling warmth spread over him. He gave her a slight squeeze before leading her back to Iseult.

'Shannon has agreed to help us with Aidan.'

Iseult exchanged a knowing glance with him, but he didn't care. It had been so long since he'd taken care of others. Now he'd gone from no children to nearly three.

Iseult carried Aidan on her hip, while he led Shannon with his other hand. Side by side, they walked to the chapel.

'I'm surprised Davin didn't come,' Iseult remarked. 'But glad of it.'

A man coughed from near the chapel, and Kieran suddenly spied Rory. His broad face brightened. 'I see you found each other.'

'I'm going to wed her and take her back to Duncarrick,' Kieran said.

Rory nodded with approval. 'And she'll be more than a woodcarver's bride, I imagine.'

'She's a princess,' Shannon piped in.

At Iseult's blush, Kieran agreed. 'One day, perhaps.'

To Rory, he added, 'My thanks for delaying the wedding.'

The older man looked guilty, all of a sudden. 'Well, you'd best give your thanks to Niamh. It was her doing, what with Davin and all.'

Iseult stared hard at her father. 'What do you mean, "with Davin and all"?'

Rory failed to look innocent. 'I won't say I'm sorry for it. You're far happier with this man than with Davin. Niamh and I simply did what was necessary to keep you from wedding the wrong man.'

Iseult was horrified. 'Da, what did you do?'

* * *

Davin awoke in the stables with the worst headache he'd ever had. Woozy and sick, he tried to clear his head, but couldn't make sense of a single thought.

His first vision was of a woman's skirts. He blinked hard and then recognised Niamh sitting across from him. Her hands were folded, her mouth moving rapidly in prayer.

When she spied him, she crossed herself. 'Oh, thank God. I was afraid I'd killed you.'

He struggled to sit up, and just then realised that his hands and feet were trussed with rope. 'What is going on?'

Niamh bit her lip, rushing to his side. With a knife, she sawed through his bonds. When she was finished, she looked him square in the face. 'I won't lie to you. This isn't the way I would have planned it, but Rory wanted to be sure you didn't wed Iseult. He asked me to keep you away from the wedding. I mixed up a sleeping draught with the bilberries I gave you earlier. Then I tied you up.'

How exactly was a man supposed to respond to that? He ought to be angry, but right now thoughts kept slipping from his mind like sand. 'Is Iseult all right?'

Niamh nodded. 'She wed Kieran. He's going to take her back to his homeland. Oh, and he found Aidan for her.'

Davin didn't know what to say. Iseult had gone and married someone else. He felt as if he'd taken a blow to his stomach.

He should be shouting at Niamh, raving for what she'd done. Instead, he stared at her. 'Was this truly necessary?'

Niamh clasped her hands together in her lap, looking miserable. 'I didn't think it was,' she murmured. 'I've always thought you were a man of honour. Someone who would do the right thing.'

There was a time when he'd wanted to kill Kieran. But now, it hardly seemed worth the effort. Whether he wanted it to be true or not, Iseult loved the man. And Kieran had given her back her son.

'I don't suppose I'm really the man you think I am,' he said with a sigh. 'I still love her.'

'Do you love her enough to give her up?' Niamh asked.

He lowered his head, the effects of the herbs making it difficult to form the words. 'I haven't a choice. She's carrying his babe.'

Niamh took his hand in hers. 'Let her go, Davin.' She raised his hand, warming it against her face. And though her face had not the beauty of Iseult's, he did not find it wanting. He could look upon Niamh's face and draw comfort from it.

'I might,' he murmured.

Inside the small tent, Kieran pulled her near, his palms covering her shoulders. Iseult could hardly believe he was with her once more, that he was now her husband.

Kieran nipped at her mouth, a teasing kiss that tempted her. She stifled her laugh when he pressed her down onto their pallet. 'Shh, or you'll wake the children.'

'They're in another tent,' he replied. 'And no one will take better care of Aidan than Shannon.'

He threaded his hand through her hair. 'When I first saw you, I was lost. You were every forbidden dream I could imagine.' He lowered his nose to hers, framing her face with his fingertips. 'I love you, *a mhuirnín*. Would that I had a kingdom to give you.'

'I never cared about that,' she murmured. 'I would rather be wife to a slave than live without you.'

She lifted away her overdress, letting the violet fabric

drop to the ground. The *léine* slid over one shoulder, baring her skin. 'Do you want me, Kieran?'

'More than life itself.' He loosened the belt at his side, lifting away his own tunic. Iseult's eyes widened at the sight of his bare chest. He'd trained hard these past few moons, rebuilding the muscles he'd lost. She hardly recognised the warrior standing before her. Handsome and rugged, he took her breath away.

'Never doubt that I want you.' He closed the distance, placing her hands upon him. She touched his shoulders, running her fingers over his skin. Her thumb grazed his nipple, and he jerked as though she'd burned him.

She closed her eyes, breathing in the masculine scent of him, the faint wood that always seemed to emanate from his skin. And now she could revel in the fact that this man belonged to her, for always.

'Touch me.' She needed to feel his body against hers, to know that he was real.

'For this night, I am yours to command.' He removed the rest of his clothing, fitting her body to his. Skin to skin, he ignited her cravings. His hands moved over every inch of her body, stroking her until she moaned with need.

She pressed a kiss against his chest, feeling the pounding of his heart beneath her lips. Kieran palmed her bottom, lifting her up and wrapping her legs around his waist. He carried her thus, teasing the cleft of her womanhood with his hardened length before taking her down upon the pallet.

He whispered endearments, keeping her on top so that he rested between her thighs. Already her body was wet, ready to receive him. 'I dreamed of you,' he said.

'And I missed you,' was her answer.

His warm mouth kindled an aching desire, such a need

that she craved him more than she thought possible. She leaned down, until the tips of her breasts touched his chest. Lips, tongue and mouth tormented her, building the fire inside. She lowered herself onto him, bringing the tip of his erection inside her warmth.

In one swift motion, he drove deeply inside, shocking her with the sensation. She moaned at the contact, and when his mouth took her nipple, the heat rose even higher.

'I love you,' she murmured.

Kieran's eyes darkened with possession, and he pressed his thumb against her womanhood, stroking her arousal while moving himself in and out. The pressure heightened, torturous in the way he drew out the response from her. He lifted her hips and turned her onto her back, pulling her against him.

'Don't ever leave me again.'

'Never.' As if to seal the vow, he filled her again, driving her body into madness. She wrapped her legs around his waist, closing her eyes so he would not see her frustration.

'Look at me,' he commanded. He kissed her eyelids, his fingers tracing her cheeks. 'Iseult.'

At last she did, and in his face she saw the rough need. He slowed the tempo of his penetration, as if to soften his assertion. 'I'll never let you go.'

He bent her knees, pushing them back until he could go no deeper. Every inch of him filled her, and she cried out as he quickened the pace, the rigid length rubbing against her most sensitive place. When his mouth took her nipple again, he bit it gently, causing a rush of moisture between her thighs.

Her release was within reach, the pounding of his body driving her to even higher excitement. Then suddenly, the dam burst, and wave after wave of pleasure flooded her. Her cheeks were wet with tears, and he continued the driving force, bringing forth yet another tremor of wildness.

'I can't,' she whispered, unable to stand any more of the intensity.

'You will.' And like her master, he continued the fierce penetration until she wept with the blissful sensations sweeping over her.

Finally, he roared out his own release, clasping her to him. Her heart raced, her thighs still trembling from the aftershocks. Kieran rested upon her, their bodies damp with sweat.

One hand lingered upon her breasts, and he cupped the heavy weight. 'You're looking beautiful, *a stór*,' he murmured, tracing his hand down the dip in her waist over the slight swelling.

'I'll take care of you. And our children.' His hand moved over her swelling abdomen. 'I love you.'

Her eyes blurred with tears of joy and healing. As the sun brightened the darkness of their tent, she lifted her face towards it. For nothing could dim the happiness inside her.

Epilogue

Kieran hadn't broken his fast, his stomach too churned to bother with food. He anchored their boat near the shoreline, and Shannon splashed eagerly behind him, not waiting for him to carry her. Aidan followed suit, crowing at the cold water when it wasn't as warm as he'd expected.

When he lifted Iseult to the shore, she grimaced at her rounded stomach. 'In another month, you won't be able to carry me.'

'Then I'll train harder,' was his response. He didn't tell her that he marvelled at the sight of her changing body, knowing that his child grew within her.

She stopped walking, even as the children raced ahead. 'It doesn't matter what happens, Kieran. I'll love you, even if your family turns you away.'

'I hope it doesn't come to that.'

The dark fields lay fallow, stripped of their golden bounty. He absorbed the familiar sights, watching Iseult's face as she saw them for the first time. In the distance stood his father's ringfort, a circle of nine thatched huts resting atop the hillside. His tribesmen had repaired the wooden palisade, but Kieran could still see weaknesses in the structure.

'This is Duncarrick,' he told her. But as a child he had imagined a new name. He'd called it Laochre, a variant of *Laochra*, for a band of warriors. He'd envisioned himself as a mighty king, ruling over a vast land.

A rueful smile touched his lips. Childish dreams, indeed. The only claim to territory he had was a small island, hardly more than a hundred acres, given to him by his great-grandsire. Nothing stood there, save grass and stones. Unfit for farming, with a rocky coastline, no one else had wanted it.

'Is that your father's land?' Iseult asked.

He nodded. 'Marcas is the chieftain.' Glancing seawards he added, 'But the island is mine. Or at least, it was. Ennisleigh is its name.'

As a child, he'd swum the small channel a few times, when a boat was unavailable. A few nights, he'd even slept out of doors, watching the stars scattered like salt upon a dusky blanket.

The island held a wealth of memories. He stared at the land, wishing it belonged to him still. He could think of no better place for their children and foster-children.

Unless his father turned him away.

And though Iseult claimed she would go with him, whether he was a slave or a king, he wanted to give her his birthright. He wanted to rebuild, with her at his side.

When he reached the outer fosse, Kieran trudged up the hill towards the enclosure. Peat smoke hung above the dwellings, and he paused before the gate. No one guarded it, and he wondered why. Moments later, he entered.

One of his kinsmen, Steafán, stopped short as though he'd seen one of the *sidhe dubh*, an evil spirit. His cousin was thin, but he no longer held the look of a starving man. With long hair pulled back in a leather thong and a brown beard that touched his chest, he was starting to regain his former strength.

Kieran continued striding forwards, Iseult's hand in his, while the children hung behind. At last, his kinsman's shoulders lowered in relief and he hastened forward to welcome him. 'It is you. I wondered if you would ever return.'

Kieran accepted Steafán's embrace, clapping his cousin on the shoulder. 'For now.'

'We didn't think we'd see you alive again.'

'I doubted it myself.' Though the pain of losing Egan had not fully diminished, it was easier to live with the guilt.

'Would you like to join us for a small meal? My wife could offer some pottage or—'

Kieran shook his head. 'Thank you, but no. I should go and greet my family.'

'Your father will want to see you.' Steafán's expression turned grim. 'He has not been well these past few weeks.'

Kieran didn't want to hear any more. 'We'll go and see them now.' He bade his cousin a good morn and squared his shoulders. He knew not what sort of welcome he would receive, if any at all.

When he reached his parents' home, the door stood open to let in the daylight. He saw his mother Eithne stirring a large iron pot. She looked at least ten years older than when he'd last seen her. Grey streaks lined her deep brown hair, and wrinkles edged her eyes and mouth.

'*Dia dhúit*, Mother,' he greeted her. Eithne whirled around, her mouth dropping open. Seconds later, her eyes filled with tears. She opened her arms to him, weeping softly as he let her pull his head down against her neck. 'You're home. Blessed saints, you're home.'

'I've missed you,' he said quietly, returning his mother's fierce embrace. She kissed his cheek and wiped the tears away from her face. Quietly, he introduced Iseult and the children.

Eithne's smile widened. 'Marcas, come and see. It's our Kieran. He's alive.'

Marcas sat beside a low table, unmoving. Unlike Eithne, he appeared exactly the same. Leathery skin stretched across a dark-bearded jaw, his face framed by black hair touched with silver.

Every muscle in his body tensed as Kieran approached his father. He prepared himself for his father's wrath, or possibly cold silence.

He wasn't prepared to see the grief upon Marcas's face. When he sat opposite the table, his father's hand shot out to his, gripping his palm with a remarkable strength before dragging him into an embrace.

'My son,' Marcas breathed.

Forgiveness poured through him, and Kieran felt like a young lad once again, wanting so hard to please. 'I'm sorry.'

Marcas wept openly. 'Thank God you returned. I didn't want to lose both of you.'

'I blamed myself for losing Egan,' Kieran admitted. 'I was afraid to return.'

'But you did.' Marcas leaned against the table for support as he stood. 'The tribe has needed your strength these past few months. There is much to be done.'

'There is,' Kieran agreed. 'And it's time for a new beginning.'

Another moon waxed and waned, and Iseult's stomach grew rounded and fuller. The days were growing warmer now, and frost no longer coated the grasses each morn. Aidan was old enough to be fostered, but she could not bring herself to part with him. Not just yet. Often she would see Kieran swinging Aidan up on to his shoulders, speaking about fishing and the ringfort plans for Ennisleigh, as though the boy could understand every word.

He had only begun framing the palisade wall, and most of it was unfinished. Inside the fortress were six stone huts, one of them set aside for their own use until the *rath* was completed.

'Several of my kinsmen have promised to join us here,' he said. 'Perhaps one day we will have enough to become a clan of our own.'

'What of your father?'

'He prefers the old ways. Likes to argue, Marcas does. And he'll argue about a decision I've made.'

'And what is that?'

'I've taken another name for us. We will call ourselves after my brother's memory.'

'Your brother Egan who was killed?'

He nodded. 'We will be the sons of Egan, those my brother could never have. The MacEgan clan.'

Iseult embraced him, her hand touching the back of his neck. 'I think he would be pleased by it.'

Kieran led her inside the wooden fortress, its walls barely begun. 'Some day, this will be your home when it is finished.' One small area was sheltered, and he took her within its space.

To her surprise, Iseult found the dower chest that Kieran had carved. 'Where did you get this?'

'Davin sent it. As a gift.' He smiled, leaning down to kiss her. 'It has good memories for us, does it not?'

She touched the carvings. 'It does. You'll have to carve

another one in return for him. I've heard that he and Niamh are betrothed now.'

Lifting the lid, she found soft linen clothing, sewn for her unborn babe. 'Who made these?'

'Your mother.' Kieran closed the lid. 'She also sent clothing for the children and wedding gifts.'

Iseult ran her fingertips along the edge of the chest, her heart aching. The clothes were her mother's way of asking forgiveness for what she'd done.

Her heart bled as she traced the carvings upon the chest. Though her mother had hurt her in the deepest way possible, Caitleen was trying to make amends.

'I will ask her to come and visit, after the babe is born,' Iseult said at last.

Kieran's arms wrapped around her waist in silent understanding. 'I am getting too large to hold,' Iseult teased.

He ran his hands over her stomach, kissing her neck until she shivered. 'Never that, *a ghrá*.'

As he stood with his wife, Kieran watched the moon rise over their island. Beneath his palms lay their future, and in his arms, the woman he loved more than life itself.

* * * * *

Here is a sneak preview of
A STONE CREEK CHRISTMAS,
the latest in Linda Lael Miller's acclaimed
MCKETTRICK *series.*

A lonely horse brought vet Olivia O'Ballivan to
Tanner Quinn's farm, but it's the rancher's love
that might cause her to stay.

A STONE CREEK CHRISTMAS
Available December 2008
from Silhouette Special Edition

Tanner heard the rig roll in around sunset. Smiling, he wandered to the window. Watched as Olivia O'Ballivan climbed out of her Suburban, flung one defiant glance toward the house and started for the barn, the golden retriever trotting along behind her.

Taking his coat and hat down from the peg next to the back door, he put them on and went outside. He was used to being alone, even liked it, but keeping company with Doc O'Ballivan, bristly though she sometimes was, would provide a welcome diversion.

He gave her time to reach the horse Butterpie's stall, then walked into the barn.

The golden retriever came to greet him, all wagging tail and melting brown eyes, and he bent to stroke her soft, sturdy back. 'Hey, there, dog,' he said.

Sure enough, Olivia was in the stall, brushing Butterpie down and talking to her in a soft, soothing voice that touched something private inside Tanner and made him want to turn on one heel and beat it back to the house.

He'd be damned if he'd do it, though.

This was *his* ranch, *his* barn. Well-intentioned as she was, *Olivia* was the trespasser here, not him.

'She's still very upset,' Olivia told him, without turning to look at him or slowing down with the brush.

Shiloh, always an easy horse to get along with, stood contentedly in his own stall, munching away on the feed Tanner had given him earlier. Butterpie, he noted, hadn't touched her supper as far as he could tell.

'Do you know anything at all about horses, Mr. Quinn?' Olivia asked.

He leaned against the stall door, the way he had the day before, and grinned. He'd practically been raised on horseback; he and Tessa had grown up on their grandmother's farm in the Texas hill country, after their folks divorced and went their separate ways, both of them too busy to bother with a couple of kids. 'A few things,' he said. 'And I mean to call you Olivia, so you might as well return the favor and address me by my first name.'

He watched as she took that in, dealt with it, decided on an approach. He'd have to wait and see what that turned out to be, but he didn't mind. It was a pleasure just watching Olivia O'Ballivan grooming a horse.

'All right, *Tanner,*' she said. 'This barn is a disgrace. When are you going to have the roof fixed? If it snows again, the hay will get wet and probably mold…'

He chuckled, shifted a little. He'd have a crew out there the following Monday morning to replace the roof and shore up the walls—he'd made the arrangements over a week before—but he felt no particular compunction to explain that. He was enjoying her ire too much; it made her colour rise and her hair fly when she turned her head, and the faster breathing made her perfect breasts go up and down in an enticing rhythm. 'What makes you so sure I'm a greenhorn?' he asked mildly, still leaning on the gate.

At last she looked straight at him, but she didn't move from Butterpie's side. 'Your hat, your boots—that fancy red truck you drive. I'll bet it's customized.'

Tanner grinned. Adjusted his hat. 'Are you telling me real cowboys don't drive red trucks?'

'There are lots of trucks around here,' she said. 'Some of them are red, and some of them are new. And *all* of them are splattered with mud or manure or both.'

'Maybe I ought to put in a car wash, then,' he teased. 'Sounds like there's a market for one. Might be a good investment.'

She softened, though not significantly, and spared him a cautious half smile, full of questions she probably wouldn't ask. 'There's a good car wash in Indian Rock,' she informed him. 'People go there. It's only forty miles.'

'Oh,' he said with just a hint of mockery. '*Only* forty miles. Well, then. Guess I'd better dirty up my truck if I want to be taken seriously in these here parts. Scuff up my boots a bit, too, and maybe stomp on my hat a couple of times.'

Her cheeks went a fetching shade of pink. 'You are twisting what I said,' she told him, brushing Butterpie again, her touch gentle but sure. 'I meant…'

Tanner envied that little horse. Wished he had a furry hide, so he'd need brushing, too.

'You *meant* that I'm not a real cowboy,' he said. 'And you could be right. I've spent a lot of time on construction sites over the last few years, or in meetings where a hat and boots wouldn't be appropriate. Instead of digging out my old gear, once I decided to take this job, I just bought new.'

'I bet you don't even *have* any old gear,' she challenged, but she was smiling, albeit cautiously, as though she might withdraw into a disapproving frown at any second.

He took off his hat, extended it to her. 'Here,' he teased. 'Rub that around in the muck until it suits you.'

She laughed, and the sound—well, it caused a powerful and wholly unexpected shift inside him. Scared the hell out of him and, paradoxically, made him yearn to hear it again.

* * * * *

*Discover how this rugged rancher's
wanderlust is tamed
in time for a merry Christmas, in*

A STONE CREEK CHRISTMAS.

In stores December 2008.

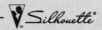
SPECIAL EDITION™

FROM *NEW YORK TIMES* BESTSELLING AUTHOR

LINDA LAEL MILLER

A STONE CREEK CHRISTMAS

Veterinarian Olivia O'Ballivan finds the animals
in Stone Creek playing Cupid between her and
Tanner Quinn. Even Tanner's daughter, Sophie,
is eager to play matchmaker. With everyone
conspiring against them and the holiday season
fast approaching, Tanner and Olivia may just get
everything they want for Christmas after all!

*Available December 2008
wherever books are sold.*

Visit Silhouette Books at www.eHarlequin.com LLMNYTBPA

MERLINE LOVELACE

THE DUKE'S NEW YEAR'S RESOLUTION

Sabrina Russo is touring southern Italy when
an accident places her in the arms of sexy
Dr. Marco Calvetti. The Italian duke and doctor
reluctantly invites her to his villa to heal…and
soon after, he is vowing to do whatever he
needs to keep her in Italy *and* in his bed….

Available December
wherever books are sold.

Always Powerful, Passionate and Provocative.

Visit Silhouette Books at www.eHarlequin.com SD76913

SPECIAL EDITION™

MISTLETOE AND MIRACLES

by *USA TODAY* bestselling author
MARIE FERRARELLA

Child psychologist Trent Marlowe couldn't
believe his eyes when Laurel Greer, the
woman he'd loved and lost, came to him for
help. Now a widow, with a troubled boy who
wouldn't speak, Laurel needed a miracle from
Trent...and a brief detour under the mistletoe
wouldn't hurt, either.

Available in December wherever books are sold.

Visit Silhouette Books at www.eHarlequin.com   SSE24941

REQUEST YOUR FREE BOOKS!

Harlequin® Historical
Historical Romantic Adventure!

2 FREE NOVELS PLUS 2 **FREE GIFTS!**

YES! Please send me 2 FREE Harlequin® Historical novels and my 2 FREE gifts (gifts are worth about $10). After receiving them, if I don't wish to receive any more books, I can return the shipping statement marked "cancel". If I don't cancel, I will receive 6 brand-new novels every month and be billed just $4.94 per book in the U.S. or $5.49 per book in Canada, plus 25¢ shipping and handling per book and applicable taxes, if any*. That's a savings of 20% off the cover price! I understand that accepting the 2 free books and gifts places me under no obligation to buy anything. I can always return a shipment and cancel at any time. Even if I never buy another book, the two free books and gifts are mine to keep forever.

246 HDN ERUM   349 HDN ERUA

Name	(PLEASE PRINT)	
Address		Apt. #
City	State/Prov.	Zip/Postal Code

Signature (if under 18, a parent or guardian must sign)

Mail to the **Harlequin Reader Service:**
IN U.S.A.: P.O. Box 1867, Buffalo, NY 14240-1867
IN CANADA: P.O. Box 609, Fort Erie, Ontario L2A 5X3

Not valid to current subscribers of Harlequin Historical books.

Want to try two free books from another line?
Call 1-800-873-8635 or visit www.morefreebooks.com.

* Terms and prices subject to change without notice. N.Y. residents add applicable sales tax. Canadian residents will be charged applicable provincial taxes and GST. Offer not valid in Quebec. This offer is limited to one order per household. All orders subject to approval. Credit or debit balances in a customer's account(s) may be offset by any other outstanding balance owed by or to the customer. Please allow 4 to 6 weeks for delivery. Offer available while quantities last.

Your Privacy: Harlequin Books is committed to protecting your privacy. Our Privacy Policy is available online at www.eHarlequin.com or upon request from the Reader Service. From time to time we make our lists of customers available to reputable third parties who may have a product or service of interest to you. If you would prefer we not share your name and address, please check here. ☐

HH08R

COMING NEXT MONTH FROM

HARLEQUIN®
HISTORICAL

- **HER MONTANA MAN**
by **Cheryl St. John**
(Western)
Protecting people runs through Jonas Black's blood, and
Eliza Jane Sutherland is one woman who needs his strong arms
about her. Despite blackmail and dangerous threats on their lives, the
attraction between Jonas and Eliza is undeniable—but Eliza bears
secrets that could change everything....

- **AN IMPROPER ARISTOCRAT**
by **Deb Marlowe**
(Regency)
The Earl of Treyford, scandalous son of a disgraced mother, has no time
for the pretty niceties of the Ton. He has come back to England to aid
a spinster facing an undefined danger. But Miss Latimer's thick lashes,
long ebony hair and her mix of knowledge and innocence arouse far
more than his protective instincts....

- **THE MISTLETOE WAGER**
by **Christine Merrill**
(Regency)
Christmas is the perfect season for Elise Pennyngton to put the sparkle
back into her marriage! Tired of what on the surface appears to be
the most amiable but boring husband in England, she attempts to stir
Harry Pennyngton's jealousy—little knowing that Harry is seething
at her games! His concealed passion will guarantee that Elise will fall
back into his arms—and the marriage bed—by the end of the festive
season....

- **VIKING WARRIOR, UNWILLING WIFE**
by **Michelle Styles**
(Medieval)
With the war drums echoing in her ears, Sela stands with trepidation on
the shoreline. The dragon ships full of warriors have come, ready for
battle and glory. But it isn't the threat of conquest that shakes
Sela to the core. It is the way her heart responds to the proud face of
Vikar Hrutson, leader of the invading force—and her ex-husband!

Harlequin® Historical
Historical Romantic Adventure!

THE MISTLETOE WAGER
Christine Merrill

Harry Pennyngton, Earl of Anneslea, is surprised when his estranged wife, Helena, arrives home for Christmas. Especially when she's intent on divorce! A festive house party is in full swing when the guests are snowed in, and Harry and Helena find they are together under the mistletoe....

Available December 2008 wherever books are sold.

www.eHarlequin.com

HH29525